I0536941

Deep Dark

By Amy Reece

Deep Dark

Copyright © 2017 by Amy Reece.
All rights reserved.
First Print Edition: September 2017

Limitless Publishing, LLC
Kailua, HI 96734
www.limitlesspublishing.com

Formatting: Limitless Publishing

ISBN-13: 978-1-64034-225-5
ISBN-10: 1-64034-225-7

No part of this book may be reproduced, scanned, or distributed in any printed or electronic form without permission. Please do not participate in or encourage piracy of copyrighted materials in violation of the author's rights. Thank you for respecting the hard work of this author.

This is a work of fiction. Names, characters, places, and incidents either are the product of the author's imagination or are used fictitiously, and any resemblance to locales, events, business establishments, or actual persons—living or dead—is entirely coincidental.

Dedication

For my mother. Thanks, Mom, for instilling a love of reading and writing in my life. I love you!

Chapter One

Izzy

"Why can't I go to the mall with you and Aunt Chrissy?" the small girl whined while her mother fastened her long, brown braid with a pink plastic ponytail holder.

Lord, give me patience! "For the fifth time, Janey, you can't go to the mall because I need to shop for your birthday presents." *And because I desperately need a short break from this adorable tyrant!* Janey's fifth birthday was less than two weeks away and Izzy hadn't purchased so much as a candle yet.

"But I could help you pick them out," Janey offered helpfully.

"I really don't think you want that, sweetheart. You love surprises. Besides, you get to spend the day with Hugh and Seamus. They're taking you to Chuck E. Cheese." Izzy would owe them both big time for this. She held back a grin at the thought of her two brothers dealing with the noise and general

1

chaos always present at the children's pizza parlor, especially on a Saturday. She would rather clean the bathroom than take Janey there.

Janey crossed her little arms and frowned. "Is Sloane gonna be there?"

"I doubt it." Izzy couldn't imagine Seamus's glamorous girlfriend wanting anything to do with screaming kids and greasy pizza.

"Good. I hate her. She's a total b-yotch!"

"Janelle Mackenzie! I will wash your mouth out with soap if I ever hear you say that again! Do you understand? Where did you learn that word?"

"That's what Aunt Cara calls her." Janey stuck her bottom lip out; she didn't appear remotely repentant. "It's true."

Lord, preserve me from my loving, yet profane family! "And do you even know what it means?"

Jane shrugged. "Not really, but she's awful and I don't like her."

Neither did Izzy. "Well, it's not a very nice word, and certainly not one I want my four-year-old daughter using."

"I'm almost five!" Jane was inordinately proud of her upcoming age advancement and was chomping at the bit to finally attend kindergarten in the fall. She could already read at a first grade level, and Izzy worried she would be bored when she started school; bored children tended to get into trouble.

"Yes, you are. But you won't have any birthday presents if you don't cooperate and let me go shopping today. Without you." Izzy gave her a pointed look that brooked no further crankiness.

"Fine," Janey mumbled. "I bet Gramma already got me presents."

"I'm sure she has. Your grandmother is retired and has more time to shop than I do." Izzy spoke around the hair clips clenched between her lips to restrain the baby-fine brown hairs at the nape of Janey's neck. The color was so similar to *his,* as were the piercing green eyes shared by father and daughter. They certainly stuck out in the sea of brown and blue eyes in the large DeLuca clan. She mentally chastised herself for bringing Janey's father to mind; she was usually better at keeping those thoughts at bay. Lately, though, he'd popped into her mind at the most unexpected moments. *Enough! It's ancient history and has absolutely no bearing on your present life. Leave it be!* She finished clipping Janey's hair as the doorbell rang.

"I'll get it!" Janey flung herself off the bathroom stool and ran for the front door. "Uncle Hugh! Hi, Aunt Chrissy! Where's Uncle Seamus?"

"Hey, squirt!"

Izzy entered the room in time to see her older brother grab his niece and scoop her into a bear hug that had the small girl squealing with laughter. His wife was more restrained and simply leaned over to kiss Janey on the cheek. Hugh was definitely a favorite with Janey, mainly because he made a point of spending large amounts of time with her. He had even turned one of his spare bedrooms into a playroom for her. Now that he was married, Izzy fully expected changes, especially once he and Chris decided to start their own family. She watched them exchange a private look and

3

experienced a pang of envy. Sometimes the whole single mother bit was hard to bear. *I'm just tired. That's why I'm thinking about him and what might have been. It's too late now, however. Snap the hell out of it, girl!* She shook her head to banish the silly thoughts that seemed to plague her more and more often lately. "Did Seamus weasel out of helping you with Janey?"

"No. We're going to pick him up on our way to the aquarium. You up for that, Janey-bear, before we go to Chester Cheese?"

Janey giggled. "It's *Chuck E.* Cheese, Uncle Hugh! *Chester* is the Cheetos cheetah! Chuck E. is a mouse!"

"Oh, that's right!" Hugh pretended to be confounded. "I can't keep them straight. Go get your coat, squirt." He set her on the ground and sent her off with a playful swat. "You okay, Iz? You look tired."

"Thanks a lot! I guess I should cover my dark circles better." She loved all four of her brothers equally, but she was closest to Hugh, due, in part, to their position as the oldest children in the DeLuca clan. The fact that they now owned the family business together and worked side-by-side on a daily basis merely cemented their bond. His recent marriage was keeping him busier than usual, but it hadn't affected their closeness; his wife, Chris, was wonderful, and fast becoming one of Izzy's best friends. She was incredibly happy for her brother, even as it caused a jolt of envy once in a while. He'd gone through a tough relationship a few years ago, although Izzy had thought for a long time he would marry Lauren. Their sudden breakup two years before had been a shock for everyone. A few weeks before his and Chris's wedding, he'd sat the entire family down and told them the true cause of the breakup with Lauren: she'd gotten pregnant and had an abortion without consulting Hugh. She knew how much something like that must have devastated her tenderhearted brother.

He put his arm around her and pulled her to his side, kissing the top of her head. "Now don't be cranky, sis. You're gorgeous, as usual. It's just my super-sensitive spidey sense picking up on your overall exhaustion. Let us keep Janey for the night. How long has it been since you had a night all to yourself?"

"About a hundred years. Thanks. If Chris is okay with dealing with my demon spawn all night, I'll gladly let you have her." She glanced at her sister-in-law, who nodded. Janey had plenty of clothes, pajamas, and a toothbrush at Hugh's house, so she wouldn't even have to pack her a bag.

"I'm ready!" Jane skipped back into the living room. "Let's go, Uncle Hugh!" She tugged on his hand and tried to budge his large frame toward the front door.

He chuckled and scooped her up again, then leaned over to kiss his wife. "Make sure you stop by Victoria's Secret for that item we talked about."

"I may vomit. Remember there's a child present," Izzy said. She waited until the door closed behind them to continue. "I'm not sure I can stomach helping you choose lingerie for my brother to take off of you."

Chris laughed delightedly. "Oh, don't be such a prude, Izzy. We're still newlyweds, so cut us some slack."

"Yeah, yeah. Whatever." She tried to laugh it off, but the thought invaded her brain: *I never had the fun of being a newlywed; I went straight to motherhood.* She mentally slapped herself for the micro pity-party and turned away from Chris. "Give me five minutes. I was so busy getting Janey ready, I haven't had a chance to finish my makeup. The coffee's still hot in the kitchen." Once in her bathroom, she stared at her reflection in the mirror. *God, I do look tired. Great.* She reached for her concealer stick and smudged a bit under her eyes. *Have I stopped trying? Maybe I should think about dating. Ugh. Maybe not.* The thought of having to meet someone new and go through all the rigmarole of starting a relationship was horrifying. And what about Janey? She knew it would be better for the little girl to have a father figure in her life, but what if she picked a loser? Her track record wasn't all that stellar, after all. Janey had her uncles—all four of them—and her grandfather. That would have to be enough, at least for now.

The mall was crowded, even for a Saturday. "I was hoping the after-Christmas rush would have died out by now," Chris said as they exited Victoria's Secret. Izzy had helped her choose some classy-yet-naughty teddies for her collection, saying she had been mostly kidding about vomiting. "This is horrible. When can we escape for lunch?"

"Soon. This makes me hate people and doubt the future of humanity. If I have to walk behind one more group of giggling teenage girls, I'm going to commit murder. Can't you wave your badge around or pull your gun?"

"Maybe the badge, but I don't carry my gun off-duty. But I might make an exception today. No!" She fairly exploded at the kiosk troll trying to sell her an over-priced hair straightener.

Izzy chuckled. "I just need to stop by Macy's for a new dress for Janey, then we can make our escape. God, this place is brutal!"

"Bella? Is that you?"

Izzy froze. The voice coming from behind them was a punch straight to her gut. *No. No way. Not possible.* She turned slowly, noticing Chris still walking, apparently unaware Izzy had stopped.

"It *is* you. Oh, my God!" The man stepped from the shadows in the side hallway leading to the mall's administrative offices. He looked to be around thirty-five or so with short brown hair, bright green eyes, and a muscular build. His infectious smile, complete with dimples in his cheeks, highlighted an extremely handsome face, one she hadn't seen for nearly six years, except in her dreams. He wore a gold law enforcement badge of some sort on a chain around his neck and had a black gun hanging from his belt.

Izzy swallowed audibly, and struggled to not pass out in the middle of the mall. "Mac?"

"Yeah. Hi! How have you been? God, I barely recognized you! You look...amazing." He grabbed her hands as he looked her up and down. "Hey, are you okay? You look kind of pale."

She snapped herself out of the mental fog and

attempted a smile. Chris had reappeared and was standing beside her, glancing between the two of them curiously. "I'm fine. It's, uh, great to see you, Mac. It's been a long time." *Oh God, oh God, oh God!*

"Almost six years, right? I wondered if you still lived here in Albuquerque. I just got transferred here last month."

"Wow, that's great." She could hear a faint buzzing in her ears. Were those spots raining down in her vision or was it snowing inside the mall?

"Hi. I'm Chris." Her sister-in-law stuck her hand out, forcing Mac to drop Izzy's.

"Oh." He recovered quickly and shook it. "I'm Mac. Bella and I are…well…we used to know each other."

A slightly hysterical hiccough escaped Izzy.

"Bella, huh?" Chris directed the words toward Izzy, then turned back to Mac. "Nice to meet you, Mac. What brings you to Albuquerque?" There was a slight edge to her question and Izzy could sense the protectiveness bristling.

"I work with Homeland Security." He turned back to Izzy. "God, it's good to see you."

She swallowed, trying to find her voice. "Yes, you too. How have you, um, been? You're not in the army anymore?"

He shook his head slowly. "Not for a couple years now. What about you? Are you, uh, married?"

"No!" The words exploded from her mouth, unbidden. She glanced quickly at Chris, who raised her eyebrows questioningly.

A slow smile spread across his handsome face.

"That's great. I mean, uh, we should catch up. Soon."

"Mac!" The man calling to him from farther down the hallway was dressed similarly, in crisp khakis and a long-sleeved denim shirt with the same kind of badge and gun. "Let's go! What are you—" He stopped speaking as he jogged to where they stood. "Oh, I see." He flashed his co-worker an amused look as he took in the sight of the two beautiful women. "I'm Darius Rogers. Mac and I work together." No introductions from the two women were forthcoming, so he rocked on his heels awkwardly.

"Well, I better get going." Mac took a small step toward Izzy, effectively blocking the other two. "Bella, can I call you?" He pulled his cell phone from his pocket. "What's your number?"

She rattled off a number; she hoped it was actually hers. Or maybe she didn't. She had no idea what she would say to him if he did call. She watched him wave and walk away with his co-worker. "Get me out of here, please."

"Sure." Chris took her arm and supported her as they walked away. "Don't you dare pass out on me."

"I won't." She spied the women's bathroom next to Kid's Gap and veered that way. "But I am going to throw up."

Chris, bless her, said nothing until Izzy emerged from the bathroom stall. She handed her a damp paper towel. "Are you okay?"

Izzy nodded. "I'm fine. Sorry about..." She gestured vaguely back toward the stalls.

"Not a problem. Why don't we get out of here? I'll bet you could do with a stiff drink."

"Or five. Yeah, that sounds good."

To her credit, Chris waited until they were seated at a nearby restaurant and the waiter had placed their drinks on the table—white wine for her and a single malt whiskey on the rocks for Izzy—to bring it up. "So, that's Janey's father." It wasn't a question.

Izzy took a large swallow of her whiskey. "I don't suppose it would do any good to deny it?"

"Those green eyes look awfully familiar. So," she said, and paused to sip her wine. "I'm all ears."

"Oh, God, Chris! I never thought I'd have to talk about this. Please." She shook her head, pleading to not have to explain.

"Sorry, sweetie." She laid her hand atop Izzy's on the table. "It's time, Iz. You've kept this secret long enough. Tell me."

Izzy reached for her drink, but nodded at her sister-in-law, realizing the time had finally come to tell her secret. "You're right. Okay, here goes." She took another large gulp of her whiskey, craving the momentary burn. She angrily wiped away the tears that she couldn't manage to stop. "Did you know I was engaged? Did Hugh ever tell you?"

"No."

"His name was Brent." She laughed, once. "I guess it still is. He's not dead. Nothing that romantic." She took another drink and signaled to the waiter to bring another. "We were engaged for three years. He would never set a date. He never even bought me a ring; he said he was saving up for a really good one. The sad part is I believed him. I believed him right up to the day I came home early and found him screwing his law partner in our bed."

"Oh, shit," Chris murmured.

"Yep." She flashed a watery smile at the waiter as he set her fresh drink on the table. "We're going to need a few minutes." He nodded and left them alone "So, I did what any self-respecting woman would do: I kicked him out. I cried for three days. Then I got dressed up and went to a bar to get drunk and get laid." She sipped her drink. "It seemed like a good idea at the time."

"I'm sure it did. And you met Mac?"

Izzy shook her head. "Not right away. Some other guy hit on me first, but he was kind of a creeper. I couldn't shake him. That's when I met Mac." She smiled crookedly as she remembered the bold young man who'd come to her rescue. "He told the creeper to get lost and then stuck to me like glue for the rest of the night."

"The whole night, huh?"

Izzy laughed, loving Chris's dark sense of humor.

"Yeah, well, we kind of hit it off. He was about to ship out for Iraq, and I'd just come home to find my fiancé having sex with another woman. We had way too much to drink and ended up in bed together. I woke up the next morning before him and left without saying goodbye. Nice, huh? I'm a real prize."

"I think we can cut you some slack this once."

"Thanks. Anyway, I discovered I was pregnant three weeks later. I didn't even know his full name.

11

I'm so embarrassed." She picked her drink up again.

"Well, that does explain it." Chris picked up her wine glass and sipped.

***

Mac

"So…she's pretty." Darius was clearly fishing.

"She's beautiful." Mac couldn't believe he'd run into her, in the mall of all places! Of course he'd been hoping, dreaming he'd meet her again. It was the main reason he'd accepted the transfer to Albuquerque with such alacrity. She looked different…not older, exactly, but more mature than he remembered. To be honest, he was a bit intimidated by her sleek glamour. The girl he remembered had long flowing hair, not the shining dark bob she now wore. And her face was more…determined, maybe…than he recalled. And she'd been shocked, obviously, to see him. It wasn't quite the reaction he'd been expecting. Or hoping for.

"And her name is?"

"Bella."

"Bella what?"

"I don't know." Mac grinned at his friend. They were more than co-workers; they had served together in Special Forces for nearly a decade. They had watched more than one of their fellow Green Berets torn apart by a roadside bomb, and Darius had been the one to pull Mac to safety when his career was ended by a sniper's bullet. When the opportunity had appeared to move closer to his best friend and the girl he'd never been able to forget, he'd grabbed it with both hands.

"Of course you don't." Darius shook his head and punched his friend on the upper arm. "She didn't look exactly thrilled to see you."

"Yeah. That was unexpected. Shit." The reunion he'd pictured in his head had gone down differently; there'd been a whole lot more hugging and, in some versions of the fantasy, even a little kissing. "At least I got her number. I can remind her what a great guy I am on our first date."

Darius laughed. "What I wouldn't give for a small dose of your cockiness. Just a small dose, mind you."

"I prefer to think of it as a healthy self-confidence. Hey, she went out with me once."

"That was a long time ago, wasn't it?"

Mac stopped walking, crossed his arms, and demanded, "What's your point?"

"Hey, don't be like that. I'm just saying, what if she's married or something?"

"She's not married. I asked."

"Well, what are the odds someone like her doesn't have a boyfriend? Women who look like that always have boyfriends."

"Shut up." Mac started walking again.

"Fine. I'm just sayin'." Darius jogged to catch up. "You should call her."

"I plan to. Now, let's get this threat assessment finished. I freakin' hate malls."

"God, that's for sure. If one more dude tries to sell me a cell phone, I'm gonna shove it down his throat."

"Get in line." They arrived at the glass doors leading to the mall's administrative offices. "Hello." Mac and Darius both flashed their badges. "We're with Homeland Security."

"Yes, we've been expecting you." The administrative assistant picked up the telephone receiver. "Have a seat, gentlemen. I'll call Mr. Aguilar."

It was nearly five o'clock before they were finished with the threat assessment at the mall and the accompanying paperwork back at their office. "Well, it's no Mall of America, that's for sure." Mac flipped through the pages of the report they'd spent the last three hours writing.

"Yeah, but it's definitely a soft target, with a crap-ton of ingress and egress points." Darius sighed as he stood to stretch.

"Is that a metric crap-ton?" Mac slipped the report into a manila folder and tucked it into a file drawer. He'd already emailed it to their boss, but they were required to keep hard copies.

"So, you gonna call her tonight?"

Mac grabbed his jacket and headed to the door. "Probably. Maybe."

"Don't be a chickenshit, Mac. Call her!" he yelled to his friend as the door closed.

Okay, yeah. He would call her. Definitely. But ten minutes later, he pulled his new SUV into the parking lot of his gym. *I really need to work out. My back will stiffen up like an iron vise if I don't.* He recognized the rationalization for what it was, but shoved it aside and changed into his workout clothes. After a punishing forty minutes, he showered, changed, and finally returned home to his new townhouse. He hadn't taken the time to unpack all his boxes yet, and had purchased only the most rudimentary of furniture: a recliner, a 50-inch flat screen, and a bed. His last apartment had been fully furnished and he'd sold his few crappy personal items before the move to New Mexico. He knew he should care about this place more, but he was rarely here. *Maybe I should get a dog. It might make coming home less depressing.* He grabbed a cold beer from the fridge and headed to his recliner. He pulled her number up on his phone and stared at it while he drank his beer. *Call her. What can it hurt?* It took three quarters of his beer, but he finally found the nerve to hit the call button. It went straight to voicemail, as if she'd turned her phone off. He left a short message, trying to sound upbeat, and clicked the end button. *Well, what did you expect? Nothing in your life has ever been easy, so did you really expect this to be any different?* He didn't. Not really, anyway. He'd met her a lifetime ago; they'd only had one night together, and he'd always known she'd almost certainly moved on and forgot all about him. But, for some reason, he hadn't been able to forget her. He reached into his wallet and removed the small scrap of pink paper he still carried.

Stay safe.
Love, Bella

Four words. But he'd kept them for nearly six

years. And he'd never been able to banish the memory of the beautiful girl he'd met in a downtown bar on his last night before shipping out for yet another tour of duty. He'd come to Albuquerque with Darius to visit his family before they both started their last overseas assignment in Iraq. Mac had already spent several days with his dad in Cleveland and was happy to spend a few with Darius's family, who treated him like a son. Darius had wanted to spend their last night with his girlfriend, so Mac had found his solitary way to a downtown bar, hoping for nothing more than a few drinks and maybe a game of pool. Meeting Bella had simply been a fortuitous accident. There had been other pretty girls before her and even a few since, but she remained, standing out for some reason. He knew next to nothing about her—not even her full name—but the memory of her smiling face and gorgeous blue eyes, dark hair spread across the pillow next to his, had lived strong all these years. And he had no idea why.

He downed the last swig of beer and heaved to his feet, his back protesting, causing him to suck in a quick breath. Some days were worse than others and standing around on the concrete floors of that damned mall all morning hadn't helped. His workout earlier had made inroads, but he knew walking would be the best thing in the long run. His stomach rumbled and he decided to walk to the grocery store for something to prepare for dinner. The mile round-trip hike, plus a few Aleve, would help insure a decent night's sleep.

Forty-five minutes later, he was staring at the

chicken breasts he'd purchased, wishing he'd gone for the sirloin. *Now what the hell do I do with them?* Years of army fare had nearly killed his palate and he'd never had much time to devote to learning to cook. He racked his brain, trying to remember what his mom had done with chicken in the distant past of his childhood. He rummaged through his meager pantry and came up with a solitary can of cream of mushroom soup. He shrugged, threw the chicken a baking dish, dumped the soup on top, and put the whole thing in the oven, praying it would be semi-edible in a half hour or so. He turned to the fridge for the salad fixings he'd also bought when his phone dinged with a text message.

Bella: I got your message.

His heart pounded as he texted back quickly.

Mac: Great! Listen, I'd like to see you again. Soon.

He waited impatiently for her reply, dying a little as he watched his stubbornly blank screen.

Bella: OK. When?

He grinned and decided to press his luck.

Tonight. Have you had dinner yet?

It seemed to take forever for her reply to appear.

Bella: *No. Where?*

Yes! Victory!

Mac: *I can pick you up. What's your address?*

This one came back quickly.

Bella: *Let's meet somewhere.*

Yeah, yeah. He knew about safe dating rules too, but it still pricked.

Mac: *Elephant Bar? In Uptown?*

It was nearby and had decent ambience without being too fussy.

Bella: *Sure. Half hour?*

Mac: *Perfect. See you there.*

He shoved his phone in his pocket, turned off the oven, and flew to his bedroom to shave and change. He barely remembered to cover the chicken with foil and shove it in the refrigerator before he left.

She was waiting in front of the restaurant when he arrived, pacing nervously, he thought. She smiled, though, when she caught sight of him, and he felt a tiny bit of renewed hope.

God, she's so beautiful! My memories didn't do her justice. "Bella. Thanks for meeting me. It's chilly out here. You should have waited inside."

"It's all right. I put our name on the list." She held up a small black pager. "It'll be about ten minutes."

"No problem." He opened the massive front door and ushered her inside. They chatted about inconsequentials until the pager lit up. They were shown to a booth in the far corner of the restaurant and he helped remove her coat before they sat down. "You look great, Bella." She wore a short dress in some sort of wine color and high heels, which brought the top of her head nearly even with his nose. Again, she was rather intimidating, but he was too happy she'd agreed to meet him to be bothered. He caught a whiff of perfume as she shrugged off her coat and was instantly transported back in time. It was all he could do to refrain from grabbing her then and there to see if her kiss was as amazing as he remembered. She'd probably slug him, though, so he simply smiled and took his seat.

"Sorry about earlier. I know I acted like a lunatic. I was just surprised to see you. I had no clue you lived here. I thought you were from the Midwest somewhere." She fiddled with her silverware and napkin as she spoke.

"Cleveland, yeah. After I got out of the army, I joined Homeland Security and worked out of Chicago for a while. When the transfer opportunity came up for New Mexico, I grabbed it. Darius was here—it's where he's from—and I was tired of snow."

She smiled and it lit up her whole face, sending a jolt straight to his heart. "My sister-in-law's from Chicago. She says she's glad to be away from the winters too."

"That's the one who was with you today at the mall?" He was eager to know everything about her.

She shook her head. "Chris is my sister-in-law, but I'm talking about Mel, my other sister-in-law."

"How many brothers do you have?"

"Four. And one sister. But Hugh and Finn are the only ones who are married yet. And I've got the only—" She cut off suddenly, a horrified look on her face. The waiter appeared at that moment and she turned her attention to ordering a drink.

He placed his own order. "Five siblings? Wow. That's, uh, intense. I'm an only. My dad still lives in Cleveland, but I'm trying to get him to move out here."

"I don't know what I'd do without my parents nearby. They've been a huge help with—over the last few years." She appeared to have said more than she planned again and took a rather large sip of the drink the waiter placed before her.

He wondered what she was keeping from him. They didn't actually know much about each other; their previous time together hadn't exactly focused on small talk. Well, he would honor her wish to hold back, at least for now. He'd waited this long to find her; he could be patient a bit longer. Maybe they could start with the easy stuff. "So, I realize I don't even know your last name. Or if you're seeing anyone." He was desperate to know if she was available.

"DeLuca. And I'm not." She smiled apologetically. "You really don't even know my first name. It's Isabelle, but everyone calls me

Izzy."

"Izzy? Okay. It's kind of cute. I can call you Izzy, if you prefer. Can I ask why you told me it was Bella?" He was rather taken aback that he'd thought of her all these years by the wrong name.

She shrugged, refusing to look at him directly. "I guess I was trying to be someone else that night, Mac. That is *your* name, isn't it? Is it short for something?"

"My full name is William MacNeil, but only my dad calls me Will. I've been Mac since middle school."

"Okay. It suits you." She fiddled with a piece of bread, crumbling it into small pieces.

"Izzy," he said, trying it out and liking it. "Can we both agree we weren't at our best that night six years ago and move on? I'd had way too much to drink and didn't act like much of a gentleman. I don't make a habit of one-night stands. I was about to ship out for a tour I was dreading. I didn't have much hope of returning, actually. I'm not trying to excuse my bad behavior, but, well…"

She smiled and reached her hand to touch his lightly, sending a jolt of heat up his arm. "I get it. I'm not judging, Mac. I was running away too, trying to be someone I'm not. That's why I told you my name was Bella. I was tired of being Izzy and thought I'd try something new. I don't make a habit of one-night stands, either."

He turned his hand over and clasped hers lightly. "Fair enough. We were both idiots once, a long time ago. I've never forgotten you, Izzy. I'd really like to get to know you. Maybe we could try a more conventional approach this time?"

She chuckled, but nodded. "I think I'd like that."

The waiter returned for their order and Mac waited until he had left to continue. "So, what do you do for a living?"

"I help my older brother run our family's construction company. I do the books and payroll; he works with clients and contractors. Not very exciting."

"I wouldn't say that. So, you're an accountant?" He didn't know what he'd pictured her doing all these years, but it wasn't anything business related.

"Yeah, basically. What do you do with Homeland Security? I guess I didn't realize we had it here in Albuquerque. I would have thought we were too small for something like that."

"I work with something called the Fusion Program. We help coordinate a multi-agency anti-terrorism task force here in New Mexico. There's a Fusion Program in every major urban center. Smaller states like New Mexico just have one for the whole state."

"Terrorism? Here in New Mexico?"

"You might be surprised." He turned the conversation in a lighter direction until their food arrived. He watched her throughout the meal, enchanted anew by her beauty, her dry sense of humor, her way of looking at him and really seeing him. She might look different and have a different name, but she was the same girl he'd foolishly fallen in love with during a one-night stand, nearly six years ago.

Chapter Two

Izzy

The chamomile tea was helping. Izzy sat on her sofa, wearing sweats and wrapped in a fluffy blanket, trying to process the events of the day. In the span of less than twelve hours, she had come face to face with a man she'd thought she would never see again, a man with whom she'd shared a stolen night six years before. A man with whom she shared a child. She remembered the first sight she'd had of him all those years ago, in a downtown bar.

"Is this guy bothering you, ma'am?" The new guy stood next to the pool table and gestured with his beer to the man she couldn't seem to shake. New guy was about a thousand times cuter and she was willing to bet he smelled better.

She'd only been at the bar for about thirty minutes and it already seemed like one of the worst ideas she'd ever had. She knew better than to bar hop alone, but a friend—or worse yet, a sister—

23

tagging along would defeat the purpose of tonight. She'd ordered a drink and wandered over to the pool tables. She'd found a game, but now she couldn't shake one of the guys. His name was Mark or Mike and he smelled like he hadn't bathed in a few days. He kept offering to buy her drinks and asking when they could get out of there. Um, 'no' and 'never.' If she were smart, she'd get out of this bar and go directly home—alone. But she was tired of being the smart, responsible one. She nodded slightly to the new guy, wanting the creeper gone, but not willing to cause a scene.

He took over, managing to firmly repel Mike/Mark without a scene. She couldn't hear what he said to him, but the unpleasant man left without another word. "I'm Mac, by the way."

His hand was warm and calloused as it clasped hers; it set her stomach to jumping. Her pulse hitched when he smiled, two adorable dimples appearing in his cheeks. He had bright green eyes that danced with humor and a sexy unshaven jaw. "I'm Iz—Bella. I'm Bella. Thanks for that." She waved her pool cue in the direction of the retreating Mike/Mark.

"No problem. I was watching you—hmm, that sounds kinda stalkerish. I happened to notice the most beautiful girl in the bar didn't seem to be enjoying the attentions of a certain guy, so I stepped in. I can step back out if you prefer. I don't want to be creepy."

She laughed and shook her head. "You want a game?"

He grinned, causing her stomach to flip. "Rack

'em up."

* * *

The early morning sun creeping through the crack in the curtains woke her. Her head pounded vengefully as she turned to look at the man next to her. She didn't have that Hollywood where-am-I moment; she knew exactly where she was and exactly what she'd done: she'd spent the night with a man she'd just met. She'd had a one-night stand. And it would definitely be one night only. Mac had told her he was in the army and shipping out for another overseas assignment the next day. They had played their game of pool, and then another. And another. They both drank freely, both seeming to crave the release of social constraints and responsibility as they continued. He was funny and nice and made her feel special. She hadn't felt special in a long time. The bar closed before they were ready to part and it had seemed natural to walk hand-in-hand across the street to the hotel. He'd paid for the room, while she stood in front of the tourist information stand, wondering if she had the nerve to go through with what they both wanted. He'd approached, placed a key card in her hand, and tipped her chin up, rubbing his thumb across her lips.

"No pressure, Bella. I'll call you a cab if you want."

She'd smiled up into those brilliant green eyes. "What do you want?"

He'd closed the gap between them and kissed her

25

softly. *"I want you."*

He was still sound asleep, on his back with one arm behind his head. His beard was coming in even heavier this morning and she remembered how wonderfully rough it had felt all over her body. The things he had made her feel! God! She wasn't terribly experienced, but knew instinctively they were extremely good together. It was supposed to have been simple, no-strings-attached sex, but sometime during the long night, she had realized they were making love. And it was beautiful. His chest was furred with light brown hair and there was a tattoo covering most of his left pectoral. She leaned closer and saw it was a skull and wings design of some sort. Her fingers reached for his dog tags, intent on discovering his full name, but she pulled back at the last moment. Better to simply let it be. They had stolen a wonderful night together, but real life was waiting for her outside this hotel room. It had been an amazing experience, but it would never be repeated. She wasn't this person; she knew that now. She had no idea what kind of person Mac was—not really—but he didn't deserve to be used like this, in a stupid attempt to get back at her cheating fiancé.

She slid from the bed and moved around the room quietly, picking up her clothes. Once dressed, she rummaged in her shoulder bag until she found a notepad. She grabbed the hotel pen and scrawled a few words on the light pink paper. She left it on the indentation in her pillow, along with the key card. Then she left.

Three weeks later, after a missed period and several mornings spent hunched over the toilet vomiting until her toes curled, she'd bought a pregnancy test. She knew it was Mac's; she and Brent hadn't had sex in well over two months, and she'd had her period right before she met Mac.

Izzy shook herself out of her self-indulgent reverie. *You really don't have time to obsess over the past, girl. The present has quite enough to keep you busy.* She knew she had to tell him. She'd been planning to tell him earlier in the evening, but she hadn't. Being with him again had brought it all back: how special he made her feel, what a nice guy he was. She'd convinced herself in the intervening years that she'd imagined most of it, that he couldn't possibly be as wonderful as she remembered. After all, any guy who would pick up a random girl in a bar and take her to a hotel for the night couldn't be all that great, could he? But he *was* nice. And smart. And he treated her with such respect. It had been such a long time since she'd had a date with a handsome man who listened more than talked. When they'd finished their shared dessert and he'd paid the bill, he insisted on walking her to her car.

"Can I call you again, Izzy? Please say yes." He'd looked so hopeful and vulnerable.

So she'd told him he could. Then he'd stepped closer and leaned down to brush his lips across hers quickly. He'd walked away, whistling, and she hadn't told him.

She finally dragged herself to bed and fell into a restless sleep. She indulged herself by sleeping in

27

Sunday morning, something she rarely got to do. She was due for dinner at her parents' house later, where she would pick up Janey, and decided to spend her rare free day lounging on the couch, reading a novel she'd bought and never had the chance to read. She read until lunch, then did something else she never got to do anymore: she took a nap. It was wonderful and refreshing to not have to speak to another soul for over six hours, and Izzy reveled in the quiet time. She loved her daughter and loved being a mother, but that didn't make it an easy gig.

By the time she let herself into her parents' spacious house that evening, she was feeling refreshed and better able to handle the crazy events in her life. She hugged her daughter, who had apparently arrived a few minutes earlier, and accepted the glass of wine from Chris.

"So?" Her sister-in-law steered her into the living room, away from the rest of the family.

"So what?" She sipped her wine and wished she could avoid this conversation, at least for a while.

Chris lowered her eyes and looked unimpressed. "Did he call?"

Izzy nodded reluctantly. "We had dinner together," she admitted.

"Great! How did he take the news?"

Izzy took another sip. "I didn't tell him."

"Izzy! You have to tell him. He has a child and deserves to know about it. You have to tell him!"

"I know! I know, okay?" She set her wine glass aside and began to pace. "I just need some time."

"How much time?"

"I don't know! But you can't tell Hugh! Please, Chris."

Chris crossed her arms and grunted. "He's my husband, Izzy. And he cares about you. Do you have any idea what this does to him, this whole situation with you and Janey? How much it hurts him?"

"It's none of his business!" She took in Chris's set jaw and furious stance. "Shit. Sorry. I just need some time, Chris. Please. I will tell Mac, but it didn't feel right last night."

"Don't put this off, Izzy. It won't get any easier, you know. And I won't tell Hugh."

"Thank you. I really—"

"Because *you* will."

***

"Izzy?" Hugh knocked quickly and entered her office.

Izzy started, slopping coffee on her desk. "Damn it. Sorry. What do you need?"

"Are you okay, Iz? You seem kind of jumpy. You were a little off last night too. Everything okay?"

"Yes, of course. I'm fine." Why did her brother have to be so perceptive? She'd promised Chris she would tell Hugh and the rest of the family soon, but insisted Mac deserved to be told first. She was having a difficult time, however, thinking how best to break the news to him that he had a nearly five-year-old daughter he never knew existed. Talk about your awkward conversations! "What do you need?" she repeated.

Hugh pulled out the chair in front of her desk and perched his large frame on the edge of the seat. "I need a favor. You know how I've been thinking about giving Lyon Millwork a contract?"

She nodded. "They're a well-respected finish carpentry and fine millwork firm. Sounds like a good idea to me."

Hugh frowned, a faraway look on his face. "Have you ever met George Lyon?"

"He's the owner, right? No, I've never met him."

"His father started the company back in the forties. I don't know, Iz. There's just something…off…about him. I can't put my finger on it, but something's off." He shook his head and smiled apologetically. "Anyway, I asked them to send over some of their most recent financials. I want to take a deeper look into the viability of their company before I sign a contract with them. We certainly don't want to get into a business relationship with them if they're on shaky financial footing. Would you mind putting some of your mad forensic accounting skills to work and look over the documents?"

She'd earned a master's degree in forensic accounting and had fully planned to work for the government, but their dad's retirement and Janey's birth had changed her plans. She'd always thought her dad would hand the construction business off solely to Hugh, who had worked with him part time through high school, college, grad school, and full time since. She herself had been doing the books for several years, at first helping their long-time bookkeeper, then fully taking over when the man had retired. She'd always thought it was simply something to do while she was in school. When she discovered she was pregnant, she found she was loath to pull up roots and move away from Albuquerque and her support system. Big Tony had shocked her—but obviously not Hugh, who had apparently been in on the plan—by naming her co-owner of DeLuca Construction along with Hugh. It turned out to be a good partnership: he took care of the clients and job sites while she handled the books and payroll. It wasn't a terribly exciting career, but it was solid and provided a good living. She was able to buy a nice house, a safe car, and all the things a growing child needed to thrive. It suited her. "I'll be happy to look over whatever files they send. It shouldn't take long."

"Great. I'll have them send over a few files."

"I'll keep a watch on my email for them."

***

She returned from lunch the following day to find a corner of the waiting area stacked with boxes. "What's all this, Malva?" she asked the receptionist. "We've already received the janitorial supplies for the month."

"I have no idea." The receptionist sounded slightly flustered. "They were delivered about half an hour ago from Lyon Millwork."

"What in the world?" she muttered as she pried the lid from one of the boxes. It was crammed full of manila file folders. "Where's Hugh?" she demanded.

"He said he'll be out all afternoon, checking job sites."

"I'm going to kill him."

***

Mac

"So, to review, what should you do if there's an active shooter in the mall?" He addressed the group of bored-looking mall employees. Hey, he got it: it was right after lunch and the room was overly warm. Plus, neither he nor Darius would ever win any prizes for their teaching ability. A woman in the front row was trying unsuccessfully to stifle a yawn, and he was pretty sure the redhead in the back row was playing *Words with Friends*. "Anyone?" *Bueller? Bueller? God, I hate my life right now.*

"Put our head between our legs and kiss our ass goodbye?" Muffled laughter greeted this comment.

He heard Darius snort from behind him. Mac chuckled and clicked to the last, boring slide. "Hopefully not. Get yourself to safety, outside the mall if possible and if it seems safe. Don't be a hero. Let law enforcement and security personnel do their job. Remember: *Run, Hide, Fight.* That's all. Thanks for listening."

Anemic applause preceded the speedy mass exit.

"God, that was brutal." Mac shut down the laptop.

"I never thought I'd prefer writing reports to field work, but I'm seriously reconsidering. We need to figure out a way to liven this training up, bro."

"It's fairly coma-inducing, that's for sure." He slid the laptop into his bag and checked his phone. No message from Izzy yet. He'd sent a text after their date Saturday—a loose interpretation of the word 'date' perhaps—but she hadn't replied. He'd thought it had gone fairly well and she'd said he could call again. So why the silent treatment?

"Texting is for pussies," Darius said. "Call her."

"Shut up. What makes you such a goddam expert?"

"I have a girlfriend. Last time I checked, you didn't."

"Yeah, well, I'm working on it." He figured his friend had a point, however. He opened his contacts app and pressed the button to call her. It rang several times then went to voicemail. *Damn. She's definitely avoiding me.* But he'd sensed her interest on Saturday and she hadn't freaked out when he brushed that quick kiss across her lips. "Hey, Izzy. It's Mac. You want to get together tonight? Um, give me call."

"Wow. No wonder you're still single."

"Screw you." He was happy to let Darius drive them back to their office. It left him free to ponder the reasons she might not want to see him again. He didn't think he was being overly vain or cocky about her reaction to him; he knew when a woman was into him or not, and Izzy had definitely been into him, even though he could tell she was holding something back. Well, that was fine. He was perfectly willing to take it slow and easy this time around. He hadn't been lying when he told her he didn't typically go for one-night stands. The one they shared had been his first and only and he was ninety-nine percent sure it was the same for her. Neither was the type. No, it had been an aberration for both of them, a product of his premonition of not returning from the imminent tour of duty and some unknown issue on her part. *'I was tired of being Izzy and thought I'd try something new.'* Well, he could understand that. Maybe he needed to ratchet up his wooing a notch or two. He knew her last name and she'd said she did the books for the family construction company. He pulled up the internet on his phone and did a quick search. "Hey, can you find a flower shop?

"A florist? Sure." Darius grinned and changed lanes. "I know a good one. Flowers are always a good idea."

They spent the rest of the afternoon in a monthly threat assessment briefing. Albuquerque and New Mexico in general might seem so far off the beaten path terrorists wouldn't bother with it, but the presence of two Department of Defense National Laboratories, two Air Force bases, and its proximity to the Mexican border made it much more of a viable target than most people would think. Mac was beginning to realize this assignment wouldn't be quite the relaxed gig he had envisioned, boring mall trainings aside. In addition to foreign threats, there were plenty of domestic issues to keep them busy, as well. He and Darius didn't work directly with the anti-drug task force, but drug trafficking was such a widespread problem they found themselves involved by virtue of other cases they were working on.

His cell buzzed in his pocket as he was shutting down his computer for the night. He glanced at the screen and his heart kicked up a notch. *Izzy.* "Hey. How are you?"

"I'm okay. Thanks for the flowers. They're beautiful."

He grinned and flashed a thumbs up across the cubicle to Darius. "You're very welcome. I was hoping you'd call. I had a great time Saturday night and was hoping you'd be free for dinner tonight. Maybe we could catch a movie too."

"Um." She was silent for several seconds, during which Mac died a little inside. "I could do dinner, I guess. I think I better take a rain check on the movie, though."

He'd take what he could get. "Great. What time should I pick you up?"

"Oh. Um, I can just meet you there."

"Are you sure? I don't mind picking you up." What was with her caginess? Did she not trust him or want him to know where she lived? They'd already slept together, for chrissake! He wasn't expecting to jump right back in bed with her, but was it too much to ask that she'd let him pick her up for their date? He was an ex-Green Beret and currently worked for Homeland Security, which meant he'd been through a rigorous security clearance. But she couldn't stand to be in the same car with him? Okay, fine. It stung a bit, but he was determined to power through. She was worth it.

"I think it's better if we meet there, Mac. I, uh, I

have to be somewhere later."

"Sure, no problem." He tried his best to sound casual, like it didn't matter in the slightest. "How do you feel about Asian fusion? There's a cool little place on Eubank and Montgomery."

"Sounds perfect. Is seven okay?"

He was able to get in a short workout before he rushed home to shower and shave again. He chose a burgundy shirt he'd been told looked good and slapped on some aftershave. He arrived before her this time and waited in front of the restaurant. He watched her pull in to a parking spot, eyes widening as he took in her vehicle, a dark blue Lexus 350 ES. He hadn't noticed the make and model when he'd walked her to her car on their last date. He mentally adjusted his assumptions of her family's construction company; if she could afford to drive a forty-thousand-dollar car, it must be more than the mom-and-pop operation he'd had in mind. The intimidation he'd been feeling since he'd first seen her in the mall reared its nasty head again.

"Hi. Sorry I'm late." She smiled and he forgot he'd ever been annoyed with her.

"No problem. I just got here." He held the door open for her, catching a whiff of her intoxicating scent as she walked past him. *God, if I could bottle that, I'd be a freakin' millionaire. How in the world is she still single? Maybe she's this skittish with all the guys she goes out with. Maybe that night six years ago was a fluke. Well, if it was, I'm the luckiest bastard in the whole world. Now I just need to figure out how to have a real relationship with her.*

He managed to get them a booth in the back of the restaurant, where it was dark and quiet. He helped her remove her coat, allowing his fingers to brush the soft skin of her arms. He wanted so badly to pull her back against him and slide his arms around her. He cleared his throat and handed her coat to her. The waitress came and he was surprised when Izzy ordered a Kirin. He asked for one too, and grinned across the table at her. "I wouldn't have guessed you like beer."

"I have four brothers. It's pretty much a requirement to like beer in order to hang out with them."

"So you all get along? All your brothers and your sister? Being an only child, I can't even imagine what that must be like." He was eager to get her talking about herself and her background; he felt like he knew next to nothing about her.

She shrugged. "We get along better now that we're all grown. We used to fight a lot. I don't know how my parents managed without selling us all to the gypsies." She looked thoughtful for a moment. "Hugh and I never fought much. We're the oldest, so I guess we were more inclined to keep the peace. Finn and Cara fought like cats and dogs, but they would defend each other to the death. Seamus would get into it with them from time to time, but Tony was the baby and hardly ever fought with anyone. I guess we do hang out fairly often now, especially compared to other people I know who never even talk to their siblings."

"So, I'm curious about the names. It sounds like an interesting international mix."

Izzy laughed, a tinkling, musical sound that caused a physical pang of yearning in his gut. "My mom is Irish and my dad's Italian. They took turns naming us and my mom went first, with Hugh. I'm Isabelle Marie, about as Italian as you can get."

"How many of them are married?" He thought she'd told him before, but he couldn't remember.

"Finn and Hugh. Seamus has a steady girlfriend, but if he marries her we're going to disown him. Cara was married, but it didn't work out. Tony's only twenty-three, so I hope he waits a while."

"And how old are you, Izzy? Or is it rude to ask?"

She smiled, crookedly this time. "Maybe, but it's okay. I don't mind telling you I'm thirty-two. What about you?"

"Thirty-five last month. So, do any of them have kids yet? Your parents must be eager for grandkids, huh?"

She choked on her beer and began coughing.

"Are you okay? God, Izzy. Here." He stood and came around the booth to pat her on the back.

"I'm fine." She held up her hand. "It's good, thanks. Um, no. Neither Hugh nor Finn has kids yet. Hugh just got married a few weeks ago and Finn has only been married for a few months. I think my parents are willing to wait for them to have kids."

"Well, that's good. My dad never loses an opportunity to ask when I'm going to settle down and provide him with grandkids."

Their waiter approached and he watched Izzy carefully while she ordered a sushi combo; she had freaked out a bit when he asked about the grandkids and he wondered if it was a sensitive subject for some reason. He ordered a fried rice dish and another round of Kirin.

"Can I ask what happened to your mother? You've only mentioned your father." Her soft expression told him she would understand if he chose not to answer her question.

"She died when I was fifteen. Cancer."

"I'm so sorry, Mac." She reached for his hand.

He squeezed her hand, loving how sincere she sounded. "Thanks. It totally sucked, but my dad is awesome and made sure it didn't wreck our lives."

"You said you'd like to talk him into moving closer?"

He'd been determined to get her talking about herself, but she'd turned the conversation to him again. "Yeah. I think I love the Southwest, and plan to see if I can stay around here long term. It'd be great to have my dad close. I'm going to get him to visit soon. Maybe he'll fall in love with it too."

"That would be nice for you. I hope it works out."

"Listen, Izzy. I have a dinner thing this Friday night. I'm one of the speakers—"

"Really? Wow."

He chuckled. "It's no big deal, believe me. But I said I'd do it, and I'd love it if you'd go with me. Will you?"

"Oh. Um, sure, I guess."

"Great." He refused to take her anemic agreement personally. "It's a black tie sort of thing. I hope that's okay."

She laughed lightly. "*Now* you tell me. I think I

can pull together something appropriate. What time?"

"It starts at six." He reached for her hand. "Is there any way I could talk you into allowing me to pick you up? I promise I'm trustworthy. I have a security clearance from the U.S. government that says so." He winked, trying to make a joke out of it.

"Oh. That's not—I mean—" She fumbled with her napkin, then sighed and finally looked straight at him. "That's not it. Yes, you can pick me up. I'll text you my address."

"Great. It's a date."

Chapter Three

Izzy

The giant stack of boxes had been moved to a corner of her office. Hugh had helpfully offered to do the grunt work after he initially expressed the same dismay she had, only with more profanity. A quick call to Lyon Millwork had revealed they had a temp working in the accounting department who'd had no idea what to send, and thus sent it all.

"I was expecting a few spreadsheets via email, you know." Izzy stood, hands on her hips, glaring at the boxes.

"I know. Sorry about this. You certainly don't have to look through it all, but I'm willing to bet you'll find out more from this mess than from whatever carefully chosen reports I was expecting them to send. This could actually turn out to be a good thing," Hugh said.

"Says the man who doesn't have to sift through it all. Yeah, fine. I'll take a look. I'll bet Mr. Lyon would have a fit if he knew his temp had sent so much of his company's financial history out of the office. Remind me never to use that temp agency."

Hugh chuckled and left her to it.

She opened the closest box and pulled out a stack of file folders. She set them on her desk and poured another cup of coffee to fortify herself for the job ahead. The files contained receipts and copies of contracts dating back well over two decades, plus expense and payroll sheets. Judging by the vastly different styles of accounting in the records, Izzy guessed Lyon Millwork had a hard time keeping a steady bookkeeper. When she saw the payroll records, she knew why. They seriously underpaid their employees, a classic sign of a company that had their priorities misaligned. It was definitely a red flag, at least in her book. Their gross receipts looked okay and the volume of work they produced matched what she and Hugh had heard about the company. Their expenditures seemed a bit haphazard, however, with various expenses she questioned, especially as to how they were legitimate to a millwork/finish carpentry business. The business seemed to make an inordinate number of charitable donations, particularly given their moderate size and volume of business. One that showed up repeatedly over the past ten years was to something called The Southwest Anti-Poverty League. She'd never heard of it and was surprised at the amount of money Lyon Millwork donated. It sounded great, but she wondered why it was singled out to receive such large sums. DeLuca Construction made a fair amount of charitable donations, of course, as did any company needing tax breaks, but they didn't begin to approach what Lyon Millwork apparently donated, especially to that particular organization.

"Sorry to interrupt." Chris's face appeared around her door. "You look completely engrossed in those dusty papers. Do you have a minute?"

Crap. I was really hoping to avoid her today. "Sure. Of course. Come on in." Izzy stood and stretched. "I've been hunched over these files long enough. "What's up?"

"Oh, Finn and I were in the neighborhood and decided to stop by and see if we could tempt you and Hugh out for a quick lunch."

"I don't know about Hugh, but I'm available."

"Finn's in his office right now, talking him into it." Chris walked into the room and closed the door. "So, did you talk to Mac again?"

Izzy sighed and wished she could bring herself to lie. "Yes, but I still haven't told him. I met him for dinner last night, but it just didn't seem right."

"Have you slept with him?"

"No, of course not! God, Chris! What kind of person do you think I am?" She realized the irony of her objection, of course. This whole situation, after all, was due to a one-night stand with Mac.

"But you have kissed him?"

"He kissed me!" Izzy narrowed her eyes at the other woman, recognizing too late the trap she'd fallen into. "You're using your cop questioning skills on me. That's not very nice."

Chris smirked. "Whatever it takes, sis. You need to tell the man he has a kid. It's not fair to get wrapped up in a romantic relationship before he knows, Izzy. It's manipulative."

"Please stop talking." She closed her eyes and rubbed her temples, attempting to massage away the headache she felt building. "I know all this, Chris, really I do. I will tell him. It's just really hard and it's going to change everything," she finished on a whisper.

"Hey." Chris came around the desk and put her arm around her sister-in-law. "Yes, it will change everything. But change isn't always bad. You've done this all by yourself for five years. Now you have a chance to share the burden—and the joy. If he's a decent guy, he'll step up and help out, at least with child support, and maybe more. Tell him."

Izzy nodded. "I know. I will. He's taking me to some sort of dinner event this Friday. He's making some sort of speech, but I'll tell him afterward."

"Good. Stop putting it off. Sorry to be such a bitch about it, but I don't like keeping secrets from Hugh. Now," she said with a quick hug, "let's get out of here. I'm starving."

***

She spent more time scouring her living room for any sign that a child lived there than on getting ready for the dinner. Her mother had greeted her request to watch Janey overnight—she had been asking quite often lately—with raised eyebrows, but quickly acquiesced when Izzy admitted she had a date. Then she had to endure the parental inquisition. She shuddered to think what her mother would have to say if she knew the date was with

Janey's father. She had every intention of telling him tonight, but it could wait until after his speech. It would be cruel to tell him something so earth shattering right before he was supposed to stand in front a crowd and speak. She would do it after the dinner, on the way home at the very latest. She glanced at the clock and cursed softly. With her hands full of the last of the toys, she raced to her bedroom for a quick shower. She blow-dried her hair, grateful it behaved itself, curling under in that one spot in the back that tended to flip outward, and applied her makeup, daring to go for a slightly more dramatic look for the evening. She spritzed on her favorite perfume and slipped the royal blue velvet evening gown over her head. She'd bought it last year for a fundraiser she attended with Hugh and had received quite a few compliments. It had spaghetti straps and a low V-neck in front with the straps crisscrossing in the back. The skirt was long and slim, with a slit that opened to her mid-thigh. It was gorgeous and made her feel sexy and confident. She figured she would need all the confidence she could muster for the evening. She was sliding her feet into strappy heels when the doorbell rang. She grabbed her wrap and hurried to answer the door.

He stared at her, eyes wide for several moments before she reached out to pull him inside. "Sorry. You look beyond beautiful, Izzy. Wow."

"Thank you. You look pretty great yourself." Did he ever. His black tux hugged his broad shoulders and narrowed to his trim waist. He wasn't as tall as any of her brothers, but he still towered over her five feet three inches, even in her heels.

She estimated he was around five foot ten or eleven, all of it hard-packed muscle. She sternly told herself to stop thinking about his body and closed the door.

"So…this is a really nice house." He stood in the middle of her living room, turning slowly. "The construction business must be better than I thought."

"We do all right." She certainly didn't want to take him on a tour; the rest of the house made it painfully obvious a child was in residence. "I'm ready if you are."

"Sure." He stepped over to help her with her coat. "I really appreciate you going with me tonight, Izzy."

She shivered as his calloused fingers brushed her bare shoulders. "Of course, Mac." She turned in his arms. "I'm happy to. I can hardly wait to hear your speech."

He rolled his eyes. "Oh, God. I'm still trying to figure out how I got roped into this. They must have been desperate." He leaned down and kissed her quickly. "Sorry, but I absolutely could not resist."

She smiled and gestured for him to precede her out the door as she set the alarm and locked up.

"So, you live here all alone? No roommates or anything? It's kind of a big house for a single woman."

She refused to look at him. "No roommates. It's an investment. Houses appreciate in value."

"Ah, that's the bookkeeper in you talking. I just bought a townhouse. How do they do on the re-sale market?" He opened the passenger door of his SUV and helped her in.

"No idea. So, where is this dinner?"

"It's at the Hotel Albuquerque in Old Town. You ever been there?"

"Yes. It's very nice." They chatted amiably for the rest of the short drive. He pulled into the valet parking lane in front of the hotel and jogged around to help her out, glaring at the valet when he put his hand out to assist her from the vehicle. He held her hand as they walked through the lobby to the ballroom. She had been expecting the event to have something to do with his job in Homeland Security and was surprised to see the signs announcing a fundraiser for the Wounded Warriors. She immediately felt better about the event and wondered if there would be an opportunity for her to make a donation sometime during the night. She hadn't known he was connected to the program, but it made sense, given his military background. It was just another thing that made him incredibly attractive to her.

The room was fairly full when they entered, with small groups of well-dressed people standing and chatting, while wait staff circulated with trays of hors d'oeuvres and glasses of wine. She accepted a glass of chardonnay and was selecting a shrimp kebab when Mac leaned in to whisper in her ear.

"I'm going to see if I can get a beer at the bar. I'll be right back."

She smiled and nodded as she began to nibble. She had skipped lunch in favor of a mani/pedi and was starving. While he was gone, she spied several people she knew and crossed the room to talk to them. Mac eventually found her, a bottle of Dos

Equis in hand, and she introduced him to the small group. He proved to be adept at small talk and they pleasantly passed the time until the meal. When the crowd began to move toward the tables at the far end of the room, she followed him to a reserved table in front of the stage. The food was decent, for hotel fare, and Izzy enjoyed the conversation with the people near them, including Mac's friend Darius and his girlfriend, Kendra. The program started as the waiters began distributing the dessert, a slice of rich cheesecake drizzled with caramel and sprinkled with sea salt.

Mac scooted his chair out and leaned over to kiss her cheek. "That's my cue. Snag me a piece of cheesecake if you can."

Izzy slid her own piece over to his place and turned toward the stage. The man who was speaking was in full military dress and was telling about the Wounded Warriors program. He then stepped back and someone else began to introduce the guest speaker.

"William MacNeil served in the U.S. Army Special Forces for over a decade..."

Izzy snapped to attention. *Special Forces? Oh, my God! I had no idea!* She searched her memory, but could only remember him saying he was in the army.

"He served two tours in Iraq and one in Afghanistan. He was in the middle of his fourth tour when a sniper's bullet ended his military career. Captain MacNeil was awarded the Purple Heart and the Silver Star and continues to serve his country today with his service in the Department of

Homeland Security. Ladies and gentlemen, please welcome Captain William MacNeil."

Thunderous applause erupted and Izzy found herself joining in mechanically. *A sniper's bullet ended his military career.* The words rang in her head and she missed the first part of Mac's speech. *He was wounded after he left me, seriously wounded. He's a Wounded Warrior. That's why he was asked to speak tonight.* She forced herself to push the thoughts into the back of her mind so she could listen to his speech. She wanted to be able to talk about it with him later, so she needed to pay attention.

He spoke well, with a self-deprecating style tempered by humor, which won over the crowd completely. She felt the pride bubbling up and at the same time was horrified by what he must have gone through in the wake of his injury. He glossed over his own experience, mentioning only a spinal injury and months of rehab, before highlighting other Wounded Warriors with missing limbs and severe head injuries. He finished with a call to action for everyone to donate generously to the program.

"And please don't forget to bid on a bunch of silent auction items. Thank you all!" He waved as he left the stage, and Izzy noticed, for the first time, a slight stiffness in his gait. He was stopped numerous times on the way back to their table, but finally arrived, slipping into his seat and reaching for his water goblet. "Ahh, you're the best, Izzy. Thanks." He stabbed his fork into the cheesecake.

"You did great, Mac. I had no idea you were a Green Beret."

He shrugged and forked another huge bite into his mouth. "It's not a big deal."

It was definitely a big deal. "And I didn't know you were injured." She placed her hand over his. "I'm so sorry." Suddenly, all the emotions of the past few days burst to the surface and she was unable to stop the tears from springing into her eyes and sliding down her cheeks.

"Izzy, hey." He reached toward her.

She ducked her head and stood. "I'm so sorry. Excuse me." She turned and made her way out of the ballroom as quickly as possible. She dashed into a nearby bathroom and shut herself in a stall, able to give her raging emotions free reign. It took a good ten minutes, but she finally pulled herself together, wiped her eyes and nose, then made her way to the elegant vanity mirror. She dug into her evening bag, glad she had tucked a few makeup essentials inside before leaving. She was able to repair most of the damage and ducked out of the bathroom, intent on returning to her date.

"Are you okay?" Mac leaned against the wall just outside the bathroom. He held out his hand and pulled her to stand in front of him. "What's going on? I thought you said my speech was good." He smiled crookedly, letting her know he was kidding.

She looked into his handsome face and melted. She stepped closer and put her arms around his neck. "It was really good. I started thinking about you getting shot and I guess I lost it."

"I guess so. I'm okay now. I promise. My back gives me some problems from time to time, but I'm fine."

"I'm really glad. And I'm really glad you're here, back in my life, Mac."

"Oh, Izzy, you have no idea. Are you sure you're okay?"

"I'm fine. Sorry to be such an emotional wreck."

"Not a problem. I really want to kiss you right now, so unless you don't want—" He was silenced as she stood on tiptoe and pressed her lips against his. He seemed shocked, but only for a moment; then he groaned, pulling her closer as he took over, sliding his warm tongue into her welcoming mouth, kissing her with a passion she hadn't felt since the last time he'd kissed her like this, nearly six years ago.

When he dropped her off several hours later, he walked her to the door and pulled her into his arms once again. And she went willingly, forgetting all about the awkward conversation she'd promised to have with him.

***

Mac

He was extremely pleased with the progress of their relationship, especially after last night. He'd worried when she ran off to the bathroom crying, but the way she kissed him afterward more than made up for it. Good God, the woman could kiss! And the way she felt in his arms was...perfect. He realized he was grinning like an idiot as he waited for his breakfast burrito and attempted to school his features into something a bit less giddy. He hadn't been able to resist pulling her into his arms again when he walked her to her door, this time allowing his hands to slide inside her coat and wander a bit over the soft velvet of her dress and her even softer skin. He had wanted nothing more than to suggest they continue inside her house and see where it led, but it was too soon. She was still a bit hesitant, as if she was holding back somehow. So he had reluctantly pulled away and waited until he heard her lock up. Then he'd returned to his own home for a nice cold shower. He was going to be certifiably crazy if he couldn't figure out a way to get her to open up soon. He was ready to go all in on a full-fledged relationship, but he knew she wasn't there yet. It might be premature, but he knew—deep in his soul—that Izzy was the one. He'd felt it all those years ago when they'd had one magical night together, and now that he'd found her again, he had no intention of ever letting go. He thought again about how she'd cried over him being shot and his heart ached inside his chest. God, that was sweet. He typically tried not to dwell on the shooting and, being a naturally upbeat kind of guy, was mostly successful. Yeah, it had been bad at the time—the bullet had nearly severed his spinal cord, after all. Four surgeries later and six months of rehab and learning to walk again had taken a toll. He'd had months of intensive therapy too, to help him deal with the damned PTSD, and still went occasionally when he felt it creeping back. But he was a hell of a lot luckier than many. He still had all his limbs and brain function. He knew of far too many soldiers who didn't.

The woman at the counter called his name and he went to pay for his breakfast burrito. He was planning to take it home and eat while he unpacked the rest of his boxes—finally. He'd quickly fallen in love with New Mexican food and ordered red and/or green chile whenever he could. He usually went out to breakfast on Saturday with Darius or other friends from work, but had decided today would be devoted to making his townhouse more like a home than simply the place he slept. He might even do a little furniture shopping later. He was hoping to invite Izzy over soon and wanted the place to look good. It wouldn't begin to hold a candle to her house, however. He'd been shocked at the size, especially for one woman. The inside, what he'd seen of it, looked like something he'd expect to see in a magazine or something. It made him realize they were from two different worlds. He was depressed about it for a moment, then his internal optimism fought its way back to the surface, gasping a bit for breath, and told him not to sweat it. She wasn't the type to look down on him simply because he made less money than her. A lot less. Oh, well. At least his military pension was decent.

As he walked down the sidewalk outside the restaurant toward the parking lot, he was preoccupied checking his bag to make sure they'd included salsa packets. He nearly ran straight into someone who was also not watching where they were going, stopping only at the very last second. "Izzy?" He reached to grab her arm so she wouldn't fall. "Hey."

"Mac!" She looked beyond surprised. "What are

you—"

"Momma, wait for me!" Mac glanced up to see a small girl break away from the older couple a few yards behind them and run to Izzy, throwing her arms around her waist. "Who's that?" The little girl pointed to Mac.

Izzy's face lost all color; she closed her eyes as she hugged the child.

"*Momma?* Izzy, do you have a..." His words faded into silence as the little girl tilted her chin up and looked at him, her vivid green eyes bright with curiosity. He stared at the small child, searching the little face, noting the shape of the nose, the chin, and the soft brown hair curling over her shoulders. His heart pounded as a gray haze descended in front of his eyes. *Holy shit.* "Izzy? What the hell? Is she—"

Izzy cut him off before he could finish the question. "Mom!" She called to the older woman behind her. "Take Janey, please. I need a few minutes. She looked back at Mac and whispered, "I'm so sorry." She handed the little girl off to her mother, waving away the questions she was clearly about to ask. "I'll meet you inside."

The older couple ushered the child inside the restaurant, all three of them glancing back curiously as they walked. He heard the little girl ask "Who's he?" repeatedly.

She waited until they were gone to address him, her face deathly pale. "Oh, God, Mac. I didn't want you to find out like this. I'm so sorry."

"I don't—I mean, I can't...what the fuck, Izzy?" He simply couldn't process what he'd seen and what she seemed to be telling him. "I need to sit." He stumbled as he turned, looking for a seat before he collapsed.

She took his arm and guided him to a nearby bench. "Here, sit." She took the crumpled paper bag from his clenched fingers and set it beside him. "Put your head down." She gently pushed it toward his lap. "It's a lot to take in, I know."

"Oh, my God." His words were muffled as he spoke into his lap. "How did this happen?"

"In the usual way. We were pretty drunk that night and I don't think we used a condom every time."

"She's mine? That little girl," he waved vaguely toward the restaurant, "is my daughter?"

"Yes. We can do a paternity test if you don't believe me."

He sat up and grabbed her upper arms, shaking her slightly. "Why the fuck am I just finding out?" He did believe her; he knew she wasn't a liar, and the green eyes he'd just seen were the same ones he saw in his mirror every morning.

Tears streaked down her cheeks. "I didn't even know your last name, Mac. I had no idea how to get in touch with you, or if I even should. It was a one-night stand! Why should you have to bear the responsibility for my carelessness?"

"Because it's my responsibility too! I should have known!" He stopped shaking her and apologized. "How old is she? What's her name? You called her Janey?"

"It's short for Janelle. Janelle MacKenzie. She'll be five next Sunday."

"MacKenzie?" He looked up, surprised.

Izzy nodded as she wiped away her tears. "Yeah. It was the best I could do only knowing 'Mac,' but I wanted her to have something from you. Besides your eyes, of course."

"And my nose and my hair color. God, Izzy. I don't know what to say or do right now. She's healthy?"

"As a horse."

"Why didn't you tell me earlier? It's been a week since I found you again and you've had time." He tried to tamp down the anger he was beginning to feel.

"I should have told you, I know. It was wrong. I just didn't know how. I was going to tell you last night; I'd promised myself I would, but—"

"But we got started kissing, and telling me I have a kid probably would have ruined the mood." He didn't know how he managed to drum up the humor, but it seemed to help both of them. He realized the impossibility of her situation and knew he couldn't blame her. She'd obviously done the best she could. But, Jesus Christ! He had a five year-old daughter he never knew about. Part of him wanted to run inside the restaurant and grab her, but the part that had almost passed out a few minutes before wanted to run far away. He settled for a middle ground. "I, uh, I need to go home and think about this for a while, okay? Can we talk later? I'll come by your place, if that's okay. I want to meet her."

"Sure, of course. I need to tell my family today."

"They don't know? You never told them who the

father of your child was?" He was incredulous. How could she possibly keep a secret like that for so long?

"I thought you should be the first to know. Now that you do...well, anyway. I'll see if I can get everyone together at my parents' house so I can tell them all at once. Why don't I call you when I'm finished and Janey and I are home?"

"We'll tell them together."

"What? No...no, you don't have to do that. You don't know my brothers—"

He crossed his arms and frowned. "It doesn't matter. I'm here now and we do this together. Why don't you make whatever calls you need to make? I'll wait."

"I thought you wanted to be by yourself for a while."

"This is more important. Make the calls, Izzy. I'm anxious to meet my daughter. I'd prefer to tell her afterward when we can spend some time together. You *were* planning to tell her, weren't you?"

"Of course. There's no reason not to. I'm not ashamed of it, Mac. I don't plan to use the phrase 'one-night stand' with my daughter, however. The rest of my family can think what they want. I don't need their approval." She lifted her chin, daring him to contradict her.

"Our daughter." He reached for her hand. "I won't lie, Izzy: this is a shock and I'm going to need some time to come to grips with it. But it doesn't change how I feel about you. There aren't any other deep dark secrets you're keeping from me, are there?"

She smiled slightly and shook her head. "I think this is enough. Mac." She reached her hand to cup his cheek. "I would have told you if I'd known how. After that night, I snuck away without even waiting for you to wake up. I'll always be sorry for that. It was a wonderful night, but it wasn't me. I was trying to be somebody I'm not and it backfired."

He leaned to kiss her quickly. "That's for sure. Come on." He stood and pulled her to her feet.

She left him in front of the restaurant while she went inside to speak to her parents. She returned a few minutes later and began making phone calls. Within short order, she had arranged for Chris to watch Janey while the rest of the family met at her parents' house. In the meantime, he drove them to her house and split his burrito with her. She didn't eat much. He knew she was nervous about the upcoming confrontation with her family. He didn't know them, but he certainly didn't plan to put up with any crap. He and Izzy were consenting adults, both now and at the time they'd conceived a child, and he was willing to take full responsibility.

"Izzy, why are you so worried? I thought you were tight with your family."

"I am, it's just...my brothers are really protective. I don't know how they're going to react."

"Yeah, well, so am I. Don't worry. It's going to be fine."

He insisted on driving them to her parents' house, and she spent the short trip gazing silently out the window. Multiple cars were parked in the driveway and at the curb. He parked behind a large truck and went around to open her door. He grabbed her hand as they walked up the path, determined to send a message—both to her and her family—that they were in this together.

She paused on the front step and took a deep breath. "Here goes." She opened the door and led him inside.

The large living room was filled with people. He recognized her parents from earlier that morning, but the rest were strangers. A beautiful woman, who strongly resembled Izzy, sat by herself in an armchair. A couple sat together on the love seat, holding hands, and looking at him curiously. Three other tall, muscular men stood together in front of the window, arms crossed, stern looks on their faces.

"What's this about, Izzy? Who is this?" the oldest-looking of the three by the window—Mac guessed it was Hugh—asked as he gestured at Mac.

"Holy shit!" the good-looking one on the couch exclaimed, narrowing his eyes at Mac.

"Finn!" It was the mother, admonishing her son.

"What? Look at him! Look at his eyes!"

"Oh, my God!" The one who looked most like his father said as he vaulted across the room, fists raised.

Mac didn't think; he simply reacted, pinning the young man's arms behind his back and taking him down to the floor. "You don't want to do that, kid."

"Let me up, goddammit! I'm gonna kick your ass, you bastard!"

"Tony! Stop it! Mac! Let him up! Everybody just

59

calm the hell down!" Izzy yelled.

"What the fuck is going on? Who is this guy?" The remaining man—Mac figured it had to be Seamus—came forward to help his brother off the floor.

"I'm Mac MacNeil and I'm Janey's father." It was time to get it out in the open. Dead silence followed his pronouncement for several long moments.

"Hot damn, Izzy!" The woman sitting by herself stood and hugged her sister. "He's gorgeous." She turned to him. "I'm Cara."

"Where the hell has he been all this time?" It was the oldest one again.

"You're Hugh, right?" Mac turned to face the angry man. "I've been in Iraq. I didn't know Izzy was pregnant."

"Someone better start talking right now," Izzy's father said, his voice gruff as he narrowed his eyes at Mac.

"If everyone will sit down, I'll explain." Izzy took Mac's hand and pulled him to sit with her on one of the sofas. The room was large enough to hold several sofas, a couple love seats, and multiple armchairs. The rest of her family, except Hugh, took their seats. He chose to remain standing, arms crossed, a furious expression on his face. Izzy proceeded to tell them how she had come home to find her fiancé—some loser named Brent—in bed with another woman. Mac made a silent vow to shove the man's teeth down his throat if they ever met. She told them how she had cried for a few days, then decided to get over him by getting out and meeting someone new. He noticed she glossed over the whole bar-hopping-by-herself aspect of the story and moved straight into the part where she and Mac met and hit it off right away, and ended up spending the night together. Her mother closed her eyes and shook her head. "Anyway, he had to ship out the next day, and we never actually exchanged last names. I found out I was pregnant a few weeks later. I ran into Mac last Saturday at the mall. He just moved here to Albuquerque. And like an idiot, I didn't tell him about Janey because I was scared. And he wasn't just in Iraq; he got shot and is a Wounded Warrior, and he's a Green Beret, so I wouldn't fucking mess with him!"

Mac's eyes widened as she continued to babble, clearly a bit hysterical. He couldn't blame her; she'd had a hell of a week. He put his arm around her as she let out a small sob.

"You're Special Forces?" The one who had helped the younger brother up—Seamus?—asked. "Shit, no wonder you were able to take Tony down so fast."

"I'm retired, but yes, I was Special Forces. Listen, everyone. I know this all sounds pretty sketchy, but I'm here now, and I will take responsibility for Janey—not that Izzy hasn't done a great job, but I will be helping out from now on." He'd felt her bristle when he talked about taking responsibility for Janey. She'd done a great job up to this point, of course, but she better get used to the idea of him being around, both for their daughter and for her.

"So let me see if I have this straight." Hugh

sounded dangerously calm. "You and my little sister had a one-night stand and she got knocked up. But you didn't bother to tell her your full name and took off to the Middle East and nearly got yourself killed. Did I miss any of the details? Does Chrissy know about this? Is that why she's not here?"

Izzy stood and walked to her brother, staring up into his face. "Yes, that's right, Hugh. You will *never* say the words 'one-night stand' in front of my daughter, though. You can judge me all you want, but Mac didn't know. And Chris has been nagging me all week to tell him because she didn't like keeping it from you, so don't blame her!"

They stared at each other, and Mac could see Hugh's jaw flexing. "Fine," he finally said and pulled his sister into his arms. "I've been so worried about you, Iz. Is this guy okay? I'll get rid of him if you want."

Mac rolled his eyes as he waited for her answer. These guys were unbelievable.

"Yeah, he's okay. He's a whole lot more than okay. I'm the one who screwed up."

That was enough. "Hey." Mac stood and crossed the room to gently pull her from Hugh's grasp. He turned her to face him, taking both her hands. "You did not screw up. We're in this together, Izzy." He addressed the rest of the family. "I look forward to getting to know you all, but right now I really want to meet my daughter."

Chapter Four

Izzy

She watched him carefully as he drove them back to her house. She knew he had to be stressed beyond belief by the events and the emotional rollercoaster of the day—and it wasn't even noon! Poor guy! She marveled at the way he'd handled himself so far, especially when he took Tony down to the ground, neutralizing him rather than engaging in the fist fight her brother clearly desired. She doubted she would have handled it so well. It did give a chilling glimpse into his past, however, and she realized the gentle man sitting next to her had most likely killed people during his career in the army. Maybe a lot of people.

He noticed her stare and reached for her hand. "Hell of a day, huh?"

"I've definitely had better. Are you going to be okay?"

He shrugged. "Eventually. When the shock wears off. Your brothers are…intense."

She chuckled a bit. "Yeah, you could say that. They actually handled it better than I expected. Especially Hugh."

"I don't blame them. If I had a sister, I'd probably act the same way." He squeezed her hand.

"Well, at least the worst part is over."

He glanced at her with a look that clearly said *'are you crazy?'*

"What? You're not worried about meeting Janey, are you?" she asked, incredulous.

"I'm scared to death! What if she doesn't like me? What if she cries? I don't know anything about kids, Izzy!"

"Do you like kids? Did you ever want to have any?" She felt horrible for him; he hadn't been given any choice in the matter, and now he was on his way to meet his daughter for the first time.

"Well, yeah. I always planned to have them someday. But I kind of thought they'd start small and we could get used to each other as they got bigger."

Izzy laughed softly. "Oh, Mac. Please try not to worry. Janey is sweet and pretty laid back for a four-year-old."

"I thought she was five?"

"Well, she will be next Saturday. She's very excited about her birthday. We're having a party at my parents' house."

"Shit. I need to get her a present. What does she like? I mean, if I'm invited. I didn't—" He reclaimed his hand and ran it distractedly through his hair, setting it on end.

"Of course you're invited. You're her father.

And I've got plenty of presents for her, so don't worry."

He pulled the SUV to the curb in front of her house and killed the engine. "Oh, my God. Okay." He wrenched the door open and met Izzy on the sidewalk.

She reached up to straighten his hair, then brushed a quick kiss across his lips. She had no idea whether or not he would still be interested in pursuing a relationship with her after all this, but she felt he needed it at this moment. "You've got this, Mac. I'll be right there next to you." She took his hand and led him up the walkway to her front door.

Chris and Janey were seated on the floor around the coffee table, coloring. Chris's tall frame looked uncomfortable, her long legs splayed at an awkward angle, but she was gamely filling in a page of *My Little Ponies* with bright colors. Janey looked up with a huge smile, but it faltered when she saw Mac standing beside her mother.

Izzy, recognizing the confusion, fear, and consternation on her daughter's face, dropped Mac's hand and went to kneel in front of the little girl. Janey leapt to her feet and hugged her mother, whispering in her ear, "Who is that?"

"I'll tell you in a minute, okay? I promise." She turned to Chris. "Thanks so much."

"No problem. How did it, um, go?"

"Fairly well. There was no bloodshed, at least."

"Good. I better get home. I'm sure Hugh will have a few things to get off his chest." She sighed and picked up her bag.

"I told him you were nagging me to tell, so he better not be mad at you," Izzy said.

"I never nag." She leaned down and kissed Janey. "Bye, sweetie. See you soon."

"Bye, Aunt Chrissy." Janey watched her aunt leave, then looked again at Mac. Then she hid her face in her mother's neck.

Oh, boy. Janey had never been super comfortable meeting strangers, a fact Izzy had decided not to share with Mac. He was nervous enough. Izzy stood and went to sit on the sofa, pulling Janey with her to sit on her lap. She nodded her head at Mac, telling him to sit across from them. "Janey, hon, I know you've been wondering who this is all morning."

"Nobody would tell me, and then you left, Momma." Her small voice was accusatory and her green eyes hinted at tears.

"I know. I'm sorry, sweetie, but Mac and I needed to talk. And then I had to talk to your aunts and uncles." She paused to take a deep breath. "Janey, this is Mac. He's your father."

Janey stared at Mac; he stared back, a small smile trying to find its place on his lips. Then she buried her face in Izzy's neck again.

"He's been wanting to meet you. He'd like to spend some time with you and get to know you."

"Is he gonna live here now?" The words were muffled against Izzy's neck, but she didn't feel any wetness from tears.

"No. He has his own house, but he might be spending some time here. Can you say hello to him, please?"

Janey peeked out, a frown marring her little

features, but Izzy recognized a nascent curiosity. "Hello. Can I see your house?"

Izzy was amused at the confusion on his face; leave it to Janey to latch on to something like that.

"Uh, sure, if you want."

"Do you have a bedroom for me there? I have a bedroom at Grandma and Grandpa's house, and I have one at Uncle Hugh and Aunt Chrissy's. Do you have a dog? My Uncle Hugh has Bob."

Mac swallowed, as if unsure quite how to process all this information. "Well, let's see. I have a spare room that we could certainly turn into a bedroom for you, if you like. I don't have a dog, but I've been thinking about getting one. Maybe you could help me pick one out."

Good job, Mac. Janey was animal-crazy, so offering to let her help him choose a dog was sure to win her over.

"Today?" Janey slid off Izzy's lap and walked around the coffee table to stand next to Mac. "Can we go today?"

Izzy smothered a smile and stepped in to rescue the poor man. "Not today, sweetie. Getting a dog is a big responsibility, and I'm sure Mac needs some time to prepare. And he said he's *thinking* about it. If he decides to really get one, maybe you can help him choose, okay?"

"Okay." Janey nodded seriously. "Momma won't let us get a dog 'cuz she says she doesn't wanna pick up poop all over the backyard. But she said *maybe* I could have a kitten when I'm five if I help clean the libber box."

"*Litter* box. And that's a big maybe," Izzy told

her manipulative offspring.

"Maybe if *you* ask her, she'll let me have one." Janey turned her big green eyes on him.

"Janey," Izzy warned, but saw Mac wink at her. *Oh, great. I might as well buy a damned 'libber box' already.*

"Do you want to see my bedroom?" Janey held her hand out to Mac.

He swallowed again and nodded, placing his hand in hers, dwarfing her tiny fingers. Izzy saw his eyes were distinctly shiny and her heart ached suddenly at the beauty of the moment.

"Why don't I make lunch while you show Mac around? How does grilled cheese and tomato soup sound?" She watched as Janey led Mac down the hall, then retreated to the kitchen to prepare a simple meal for them to share.

Izzy suggested a walk to the nearby park after lunch; she knew it would be better to have something for them all to do while Janey and Mac got acquainted. A bored child was a whiny child, after all, and she thought Mac didn't need to be exposed to that side of parenthood on his first day. The afternoon had turned pleasant and sunny, so they all donned jackets and headed out the door. Janey had apparently decided Mac was trustworthy, because she held his hand while they walked, leaving Izzy to bring up the rear. *So far, so good.* Izzy wanted Mac and Janey to start off well and be able to build a good relationship. She had no idea where they were headed as a couple and a family, but he deserved to have a chance with his daughter.

Once at the park, Mac pushed Janey on the

swing for quite a while, then spun her on the merry-go-round as she giggled wildly, her brown hair flying around her face as it escaped her ponytail. She finally found some girls her age to climb on the jungle gym with and Mac came to sit with Izzy on a nearby bench.

"She's amazing."

She reached for his hand. "I completely agree. You're doing great, by the way. Still scared?"

"Yeah, but I'm holding my own. She's sweet. And smart! I can't believe how well she reads already! She read me a book when we were in her room."

"She's exceptionally precocious. She's also a manipulative little minx, so be careful. You'll find yourself saddled with a dozen dogs before you know it."

He chuckled and dropped her hand, but it was only to put his arm around her and pull her close. "That's okay," he said as he kissed her hair. "You are going to let me buy her a kitten for her birthday, aren't you? I think that could seal the deal with her."

"Oh, probably." She leaned her head against his shoulder and sighed happily.

"I've missed so much, Izzy! God, I wish I'd been here for the last four years! How much did she weigh when she was born? Was it an easy birth? What did you look like when you were pregnant?"

She took her head off his shoulder and put a finger over his lips. "Shh. I've got a ton of photo albums at home and I can share all my digital photos with you. I wish you had been here too,

Mac. I'm sorry."

He smiled a bit sadly. "Yeah, well, I'm here now. I want to help support her, Izzy. I have no idea how to go about it, but I'll start paying child support."

"Why don't you just concentrate on getting to know her for now? I'm doing fine financially; I don't need child support. We can figure out all the legal stuff later, okay?"

He nodded. "I feel like I'm about to burst." He laughed shakily. "I don't know what to do with all these emotions. She's so beautiful. God, I have a daughter. My dad is going to freak."

"Janey will be thrilled to find out she has another grandpa. If you need to go home, Mac, it's okay. I know you wanted to be by yourself for a while."

"Did I? It doesn't seem to matter right now. I'd like to hang around, if you don't mind. Maybe we could take her out for dinner or something."

Izzy smiled and settled back with her head on his shoulder. "Why don't we order pizza and watch a movie together?"

"You don't mind? I don't want to make a nuisance of myself, but I'd like to spend more time with her. What do you do while you're at work? Who watches her?"

"She goes to a preschool daycare. It's a really good one. And you're not a nuisance. Not at all. I want you to be a part of her life, Mac."

"What about your life? This all took me by surprise, but where does it leave us?"

She sat up again and looked into his face. "I think that depends on you. Do you think you'll be able to forgive me for keeping Janey a secret from you?"

"Already forgiven. I get that it was hard to tell me this last week. I showed up out of the blue and pretty much hounded you into going out with me. I'm in awe of what you've had to do by yourself for the last six years, Izzy. You've taken such good care of our daughter, and I'm grateful. I want a relationship with you just as much as I want one with her. I'd like to think we could be in this together. Do I have any chance of that, Izzy?"

She smiled and pulled his head down for a kiss. She'd intended it to be quick, but he slid both his arms around her and slanted his mouth across hers, deepening the kiss. She tried to remember she had a child to watch, but it was difficult as she sank into the wonder of his lips.

"You're kissing." Janey stood directly in front of them, watching in fascination.

Way to state the obvious, darling. "Well, yes, we—"

Mac interrupted. "I hope it's okay to kiss your mom, Janey. I like her a lot."

"Are you her boyfriend?"

"Well, I guess that depends on your mom. I'd like to be her boyfriend, if she says it's okay. Is it all right with you?"

She appeared to think about it seriously for a moment. "Yeah, but you have to take her on a date. You have to bring her flowers. That's what they do on TV." She stood in front of them, hands on her little hips.

"A date. Flowers. Got it. Where do you think I

should take her? And what kind of flowers?"

Janey inserted herself between them on the bench, causing them to break apart, and turned to Mac. "She likes pink flowers. My Uncle Hugh took me to Red Lomster once. You should take Momma there."

Mac took his phone out and opened a notes app. "Red Lobster," he said as he typed. "Pink flowers. Anything else?"

"Always open the door for her. My Uncle Finn said it's important. He always opens the door for Aunt Mel." Mac added it to his notes while Janey craned her neck to see his screen.

Izzy watched, amused as the two of them strategized on the perfect date. Janey crawled into his lap as he scrolled through images of various flowers on his phone until she found one she approved of and looked up into her father's face with a smile. Izzy's heart swelled, and she wondered why she had been so afraid to tell this amazing man they shared a child. Right at this moment, she felt like the luckiest woman alive.

***

Mac

"So, how was your weekend?" Darius greeted Mac and set a paper cup on his desk. "I couldn't handle office coffee today."

"Thanks." Mac took a careful sip, relishing the hot dark roast. "My weekend was quite interesting, actually."

"Do tell." Darius raised his eyebrows up and down. "Did you spend it heating up the sheets with Izzy? Or did she dump you after the fundraiser?"

"I have a daughter." He figured it was easiest to throw it out there and cut straight to the chase.

Darius laughed and sipped his coffee. He glanced at Mac, obviously expecting him to join in the joke. After a long moment, he finally picked up on the fact that Mac wasn't kidding. "What? Holy shit! How? When? Who's the mother?"

"Izzy, of course. I apparently gave her more than fond memories that night six years ago. She got pregnant." He handed Darius his phone, open to his pictures. "Her name's Janey. Janelle Mackenzie. Izzy kinda named her after me."

Darius set his coffee on his desk and took Mac's phone, scrolling though the pictures. "Dude, she's beautiful. God, she looks like you. I was going to ask if you were sure it's yours, but it's pretty obvious. But...why? Why didn't she tell you?"

Mac took back the phone and cleared his throat. "She didn't know my name, either. All she knew was 'Mac.' She had no way to get in touch with me. Shit, Darius." He shook his head. "It was just supposed to be one night. Neither one of us thought it would ever go further."

"But you never forgot her, did you? And she obviously never forgot you." He picked up his coffee again and used it to gesture to Mac's phone. "So, what's she like? How old is she?"

Mac filled his friend in on all the details from the weekend and found he enjoyed talking about his little girl.

Darius shook his head in wonder. "Dude, you should see your face! You're glowing! And bragging! Oh, my God!"

"Shut up! She's amazing."

Darius laughed and clapped Mac on the back. "I'm sure she is. Calm down. When do I get to meet her?"

"I don't know. Soon, though. I'm a dad, Darius."

"You're a dad."

They stared at each other blankly for a moment, then Mac turned to grab his coffee. "Anyway, we better get to work. What's on our agenda today?"

"We have a 9:30 sit-down with the governor's chief-of-staff to go over her public appearances for the next few months. It takes about an hour, maybe more at this time of day, to drive to Santa Fe, so we need to get on the road." Darius began packing his laptop and various file folders into his bag. "So, are you and Izzy still on?"

Mac packed his own equipment as he answered. "I think so, but it's complicated now with Janey. We're going to give it a shot, though. I met her family Saturday."

"And?"

"I went with her when she told them about me. She's kept it a secret from them all these years and never told them who the father of her baby was."

"How'd they take it?" Darius led the way to the parking garage.

Mac chuckled. "Her youngest brother tried to punch me."

"He tried to punch an ex-Green Beret? What an idiot!"

74

"In his defense, he didn't know. They're a pretty fierce bunch, especially the oldest, Hugh. I don't think he likes me much." He shook his head. "You think we'll be done in time for lunch at Tomasita's?"

"Let's make sure we are. That sounds really good. I love their chile rellenos."

The drive to Santa Fe took closer to an hour and a half, due to a wreck on the south side of La Bajada hill, but they were able to expedite the meeting with the chief of staff. She gave them a run-down of all the governor's upcoming speeches and appearances through early spring; Darius and Mac were in charge of making sure a threat assessment was done for each location and giving recommendations to the governor's security detail.

"I will admit I'm a bit hesitant about the number of outdoor events the governor has planned. With the contentious political climate right now and her recent education reforms, I'm worried. But she doesn't listen to my concerns." The woman—Mac thought her name was Ellen or Helen—gave a sigh. Mac had read about the unpopular teacher evaluation changes in the newspaper and figured the governor's aide had plenty to worry about. The local teacher's union was out for blood.

"Ma'am, we understand and will make sure you and the governor have all the information you need to make an informed decision about each of these venues." He closed his laptop and stood to shake her hand. "We'll have our report to you in a few weeks."

"Thank you…Mac, wasn't it?" She held on to

his hand tightly.

"Yes, ma'am. Mac MacNeil." He actually had to pull his hand from her grasp. "You have a nice day now."

Darius chuckled as they walked to their car.

"What's so funny?"

"You. She was coming on to you and you were completely oblivious."

Mac looked back toward the building. "No, she wasn't. Besides, I'm not interested. I have a date with Izzy tonight."

"A date-date? A real one with no kidlet tagging along?" At Mac's nod, he continued. "Where are you taking her?"

Mac coughed and busied himself searching for his keys. "Uh, Red Lobster."

Darius stopped and stared at him, aghast. "Red Lobster? Dude! Is that the best you can do? Do you need to borrow some cash?"

Mac felt his face heating up, but laughed it off. "Shut up. No, I don't need a loan. That's Janey's idea of a fancy restaurant and the perfect place to take a date."

Darius burst out laughing. "You're taking dating advice from your five-year old kid? Good call, man. How does Izzy feel about it?"

"She thinks it's hilarious and said she's looking forward to Endless Shrimp."

Darius laughed again. "Izzy's a trooper. Can't you take her somewhere else and tell the munchkin you went to Red Lobster?"

Mac started the engine and shook his head. "Nah, I don't want to lie to her. Besides, I promised to bring her some of those cheesy biscuits. She loves them."

"Oh, man. Yeah, those are good. I can eat like a whole basket of them. Okay, now I'm starving. Let's head to Tomasita's."

As Mac drove, he thought about how excited Janey had been to help him plan the upcoming date. Izzy had given them free rein, seeming to enjoy their interaction. He thought he caught the slightest glimpse of how a person's priorities changed when one became a parent. Of course, Izzy had been doing it for nearly five years; he'd had less than 48 hours to get used to the idea.

They'd ended the evening Saturday with pizza and one of Janey's favorite movies, which turned out to feature talking animals. Izzy told him this was a strong theme running though all her cinematic preferences and he'd better get used to it. He didn't care and could barely pry his eyes away from the little girl long enough to catch what was happening on-screen anyway. He was enchanted by her giggles and the way she curled against him as they watched, making sure the popcorn bowl was within easy reach for him. Izzy had let him help her tuck Janey in her bed and let him read the bedtime story. He'd sat by her bedside until she fell asleep while Izzy returned to the living room to clean up and brew them some decaf.

"She's amazing. Thanks." He accepted the coffee and sipped.

"How are you doing with all this, Mac? You must be completely overwhelmed right about now." She sipped her own coffee and curled into a corner of the sofa.

He frowned slightly when he realized she was at the other end of the couch, entirely too far away. "I don't even know. It's all kind of a blur. What are my chances of talking you into sliding over here?" He patted the cushion beside him.

She smiled and set her mug on the coffee table before relocating to lean against him.

"That's better." He put his arm around her and kissed the top of her head. "We just put our daughter to bed together for the first time. I'm kind of in awe."

She tilted her face up and kissed his jaw lightly. "You are doing so great, Mac. I'm really proud of you."

He took the opportunity to lean down and kiss her properly. "We were interrupted before," he whispered against her lips, then stopped thinking as she opened her mouth under his. She tasted of coffee and buttery popcorn and it was all he could do not to devour her. His hand curved around her small waist and found the edge of her shirt. She didn't object, so he let his hand slide over her smooth warm skin, reacquainting himself with the feel of it. Her fingers slipped under his t-shirt and smoothed over his back, stopping suddenly as she felt the rough, raised flesh surrounding his lower spine.

"Oh, Mac," she whispered and threw her arms around his neck. "I know now is not the time, but I need to hear about it soon."

He knew she was right, but right now he was more interested in the taste of her neck, right where it met her shoulder. "Yeah. Another time."

Although he wanted nothing more than to scoop her into his arms and carry her back to her bedroom, he realized it was too soon. And then there was the presence of tiny eyes asleep down the hall. They'd rushed into bed six years ago; this time he could wait. This time was too important and he didn't want to push her.

So, he'd reluctantly pulled away from her intoxicating mouth and gone home.

He pushed the memories of the weekend aside as he pulled the SUV into the gravel parking lot of Tomasita's and searched for an empty spot.

* * *

"You ready for round three?" Mac gestured to her pile of shrimp tails. "These parmesan garlic ones are pretty kick-ass."

"I think I'm about done. I'm going to need to beach myself when we get home." She rubbed her hand over her stomach and groaned softly.

"You're letting the shrimp win, Izzy. I thought you were better than that. I'm not gonna lie, I've lost some respect for you." He grinned and flagged down the waiter to order another flavor for himself. "And can we get a few more of these biscuits, please?"

"More Cheddar Bay biscuits coming up." The waiter refilled their tea and left.

"What?" he said and shrugged. "I want to take some home for Janey."

Izzy shook her head ruefully. "It sure didn't take

her long to wrap you around her little finger. She's already spoiled rotten by her four uncles and my dad. I expect you to discipline her once in a while, you know."

"I'm sure I'll get around to it, but right now I can't imagine her ever needing it. She's about the sweetest thing I've ever seen."

"Just wait. She's on her best behavior right now because you're shiny and new. I warned you she's precocious; she can also throw the mother of all fits when she doesn't get her way. I've had to drag her kicking and screaming from the grocery store— leaving an entire cart of food, mind you—because I wouldn't buy her a *My Little Pony* lunchbox."

"Why wouldn't you buy her the lunchbox?" Surely she could afford it. What kind of mean person wouldn't buy their kid a lunchbox?

Izzy shook her head, a look of exasperation on her face. "I can see I have my work cut out for me. I wouldn't buy her a lunchbox, Mac, because I had already bought her one—Hello Kitty—at Target the day before. She needs to learn that she can't have everything, and sometimes one is enough. We stick with our decisions."

"Yes, ma'am." He stared down at his plate, trying to hide his smile. A shrimp tail hit his left ear and he looked up, eyebrows raised. "Don't start a food fight here, girl. I don't want to get kicked out before we get Janey her biscuits." He was enjoying himself hugely, getting to know the beautiful woman sitting across from him in an easy atmosphere. It turned out Janey had picked a great place for their date; they were able to dress casually and relax in each other's presence without having to worry about impressing the other. She looked great in jeans and a pink, flowing top made of some sort of soft material that made him think of cotton candy. He watched her tuck a strand of dark hair behind her ear as she smiled at him. He liked her. He'd suspected it years ago, but that night had been so fueled by alcohol and desperation, he hadn't had a chance to simply get to know her. She was fun and had a great sense of humor. She hadn't batted an eye when he'd told her the plans for the evening and she'd made a wonderful fuss over the flowers he'd brought—pink, and as much like the ones in the picture Janey had chosen as he could find. Janey had appeared thrilled at the way her suggestions had been implemented, and accepted being left home with her Aunt Cara with good grace. She did, however, beg them to be home in time for Mac to tuck her in.

When they finished dinner and Mac had paid the check, making sure he had a little bag of the biscuits to take home to Janey, he asked her what else she'd like to do. He wasn't ready to end their time alone together yet; he was enchanted with his new daughter and had fallen immediately and irrevocably in love with her, but he wasn't about to forget about Izzy and the relationship he hoped to have with her. He wanted it all and had painted a nice little picture of a future with the three of them together. Now he just needed to work on securing it.

"Hmm. I'm not ready to go home, either. It's nice to have some adult time for a change. I'd suggest a movie, but I'd rather do something where we could talk more." They'd reached his SUV and she turned to face him before he opened the door for her. "I think I like you, Captain MacNeil."

He smiled crookedly and stepped closer. "It's just plain, ol' Mr. MacNeil now. I'm retired." He leaned in to kiss her.

"I probably taste like shrimp. Sorry."

He chuckled. "Me too. What do you say we head over to Marble Brewery? They've got live jazz on Monday nights."

She was amenable, so they drove to the new brewery, which had opened just the previous summer, and enjoyed a few craft beers while the small jazz combo played. A few couples danced and he managed to convince her to give it a try.

They called it an early evening because of work the next day, and because he wanted to see his daughter before he left. Janey was fighting to keep her eyes open when they got back, and he carried her upstairs to bed while Izzy thanked her sister profusely for babysitting. Cara had already made sure Janey had taken her bath, brushed her teeth, and donned her footie pajamas, so he tucked her in bed and was three pages into a story when he noticed she was fast asleep. He closed the book and set it on her nightstand, content to sit and watch the little miracle in the bed next to him. *God, I don't how this happened, but I'm glad. I'm so glad.*

Izzy came in the room and put her hands on his shoulders, squeezing lightly. He looked up into her serene face and knew he was where he belonged.

Chapter Five

Izzy

The past two weeks had been the most amazing time in her life—with the exception of the day Janey was born—but it hadn't changed the size of the stack of boxes in her office. She'd ignored them in favor of more immediate items on her to-do list, such as payroll and paying bills. She would need to begin working on the company taxes in the next week or so; it was now or never for these damned boxes. She'd worn jeans and a hoodie today in honor of the occasion so she could spread the files out across the floor. She'd stopped for a venti soy mocha latte so she wouldn't even have to get off the floor for coffee refills—only bathroom breaks. She heaved a huge sigh and set to work.

"Did I miss the memo about casual Tuesday?" Hugh leaned against the frame of her office door.

Izzy chuckled but didn't get up. "Maybe it'll start a trend. I could get rid of all my dress slacks. I am determined to get through these boxes by the end of the day tomorrow at the latest. That's all the time I have to devote to this mess."

"Have I told you what an amazing sister you are lately?"

"Yeah, yeah." She waved her hand at him dismissively. "You are gonna owe me big time, Hugh."

"You are so right. I'm sure you'll figure out a way for me to pay you back. You always do." He pushed away from the door and settled his large frame on the floor across from her. "I'd offer to help, but—"

"Please don't. I won't stick my nose in your part of the business if you stay out of mine." It was the way their partnership worked best. She handled the financial side of the business while he dealt with clients and the actual construction issues.

"Agreed. So, what have you discovered so far?" He gestured to the scattered files.

"Not much beyond a rather extravagant number of donations to local charities. The number one recipient—by a long shot—is something called the Southwest Anti-Poverty League."

"Hmm. Never heard of them."

"Me neither, which is why I looked them up." She reached for her laptop and handed it to Hugh. "They look legit, but they certainly don't maintain their website; most of the links are broken. From what I can tell, they're dedicated to 'the eradication of poverty in the southwestern United States through education and direct assistance programs.' That's a direct quote from the website."

"Sounds okay. How much did Lyon give them

last year?"

Izzy handed him a notepad with a figure highlighted in yellow.

Hugh whistled and handed it back. "That's a lot of charitable donation. Seems a bit excessive."

"That's what I'm thinking. I wouldn't expect such a high level of giving from a business that size. There are other donations, as well. Lyon Millwork is hemorrhaging money, much of it going to charities around the country. I don't get it."

Hugh shook his head, clearly at a loss as well. "Anything else?"

"They underpay all their employees, except the fat cats at the top of the food chain, which doesn't impress me. If my vote counts for anything, we'll stay far away from Lyon Millwork."

"Of course your vote counts, and I'm inclined to agree with you. As far as I'm concerned, you can pack the rest of this crap and send it back. We'll find another finish carpentry firm to work with."

She stood and stretched. "You won't hear any arguments from me. Is it just me or did sitting cross-legged on the floor used to be more comfortable?" She rubbed her lower back and groaned. "There was one other thing I found, but…"

"But what? What is it?"

She shrugged but leaned down to pick up one of the files. "This note was attached to one of the check copies." She handed it to her brother.

"*AMCI: March,*" he read. "Any clue what this means? Is it some sort of accounting abbreviation?"

"Nope to both. I hate when I can't figure something out."

Hugh chuckled and handed back the file. "Don't lose any sleep over it. It doesn't matter now."

She slipped the file into one of the boxes and dusted off her hands. "Good. I have a million other things to do." She shoved a few boxes aside to make a path to her desk. "I've thought of how you can pay me back."

"That was quick." He stepped over files and made his way to her sofa. "Shoot."

She sat back in her chair and stared at her brother. "You can be nice to Mac tonight at dinner." Her mother had invited the family over so they could have a chance to get to know him. He had been present at Janey's birthday party on Saturday, but there hadn't been time for much conversation in the midst of all the party activities.

"I'm always nice."

"Ha! I mean it, Hugh. Mac is Janey's father and he's part of our lives now. I need my family to accept him."

"I'm having a hard time wrapping my mind around this, Izzy. You refuse to tell anyone who her father is for six years, then this guy shows up out of the blue, and bam! He's a part of your life suddenly and spending a lot of time with my niece, and we don't even know who he is!"

"Damn it, Hugh! He's the father of my child! That should be enough! You need to trust I would never let anyone come near Janey who isn't trustworthy." He was unbelievable! She'd had enough of his ridiculous overprotectiveness! "Why don't you call Finn and have him investigate Mac?" She watched her brother drop his eyes to his lap.

"Oh, my God. You already did, didn't you?"

"Of course I did. I won't apologize for doing what needs to be done to protect my family. And it turns out I didn't need to because Chrissy did it first, right after he ran into you at the mall. She called a friend in the FBI and got a full report on Mac."

She crossed her arms and stared at Hugh through narrowed eyes. She refused to grace his statement with a response; she didn't need to hear what he'd discovered.

"I can see you're not going to ask, so I'll tell you: Captain William MacNeil served his country with distinction in the Army Special Forces, earning the Silver Star and a Purple Heart when he was wounded in Iraq almost four years ago. Never married, no other children we know of. He's squeaky clean, at least on paper."

"Are you happy now? I could have told you all that. Mac is a good man, and you better get used to him."

"I'll reserve judgment until I know him better. He showed exceptionally poor judgment one night six years ago. I want to be sure he makes better choices now that he's spending time with my sister and niece."

"You're calling sleeping with me *'exceptionally poor judgment'*? Thanks a lot."

"Izzy, you know that's not what I mean! The man got drunk and had a one-night stand without making sure he used protection. That's what I call exceptionally poor judgment. Stop twisting my words. I'm on your side—yours and Janey's."

"So is Mac. He and I both showed questionable judgment that night. All I can say is there were extenuating circumstances for both of us. It's not who we are. Please, Hugh." She realized he had a point, but needed him to understand and give Mac a chance.

He sighed and stood. "Yeah, okay. I will play nice tonight. At the very least, I owe the man my gratitude for his service to our country. Hey." He crossed to stand next to her, then leaned down to kiss the top of her head. "I'm glad he's back in your life." At her disbelieving look, he said, "I am. You and Janey seem happy. I'm trying."

***

"You look great tonight. Thanks for doing this." Izzy reached up to smooth the lapels of Mac's jacket. He wore a dark gray casual suit with a navy shirt, open at the collar. They stood at the edge of her parents' porch, where she had stopped, needing to steal a moment with him before they went inside. Janey had run ahead and already let herself in.

"No problem. I'm hoping there will be more eating and less violence this time."

She laughed and stood on tiptoe to kiss him. He'd spent every evening of the last two weeks with them and most of the weekend between. He had begun coming over directly after work, stopping by his place only long enough to lock up his gun, but when Izzy found out he was skipping his workouts to hurry to her house, she'd scolded him, and insisted he take the time to care for his back. He still hadn't told her the details of what had happened to him, but she knew he would when the time was right. Right now he was concentrating on getting to know his daughter. He always stayed for dinner or took them out, then helped Izzy with the bath and bedtime routine. Their own routine had become sharing a couple glasses of wine while they sat on the sofa and talked, getting to know one another. Then he would kiss her goodnight and go home. She was glad he was willing to take their relationship slowly; it was overwhelming enough trying to help him establish a relationship with their daughter. Janey loved spending time with him and had taken to sitting by the window in the front room to wait for him in the evenings. Since Sunday, she'd been clutching the kitten Izzy had allowed him to adopt for her, refusing to be separated from the small ball of fuzz except at mealtime and bath time. Izzy hadn't loved the thought of her sleeping with the animal, but Mac had convinced her it was harmless. Janey hadn't wanted to leave it home tonight, and Izzy had needed to use her 'mom' voice to convince her otherwise.

"But Sophie will miss me! Please, Momma?"

Izzy steeled herself to resist the huge green eyes. "Janelle MacKenzie! I said no."

Janey's chin trembled with imminent tears, but Mac stepped in, scooping her into his strong arms. "Come on, Princess. Sophie will sleep the whole time. Don't worry about her. Cats know how to take care of themselves. I need you to introduce me to all your aunts and uncles. I'll never remember all their names without you. Do you think you can do that for me?"

She nodded and kissed his cheek for the first time.

Izzy smiled as she remembered the stunned expression on his face. "You ready for this?"

"Ready as I'll ever be." He pulled her against him and kissed her fully. "That will get me through the upcoming inquisition."

"Hey, you two!" Cara stood on the porch, an insufferable smirk on her face. "Are you gonna make out all night? It's freezing out here! Come on!"

Izzy smiled up at him and took his hand to lead him inside.

"Hey, Mac." Cara greeted him with a hug. "It's good to see you again."

The family, except for Izzy's mother, Moira, were gathered in the family room. Janey was in Hugh's arms, telling him all about her kitten, Sophie. When she saw Izzy and Mac enter the room, she squirmed to be let down. She ran to Mac, grabbed his hand, and towed him to stand in front of Hugh. "Uncle Hugh, this is Mac. He's my daddy and he bought me a kitten." She stared up at the two men, seemingly oblivious to the tension between them, yet frustrated by their lack of interaction. Each seemed to be waiting for the other to speak first. "Well?" Janey demanded, hands on her little hips.

Hugh looked down at his niece and sighed. "Good to see you again, Mac." He held his hand out.

Mac took it and the two shook briefly. "You too, Hugh."

Izzy still felt the animosity from her brother and the wariness from Mac, but at least they were civil. It was probably the most she could hope for at this point.

"Come on." Janey grabbed Mac's hand again and dragged him around to the rest of the family. Predictably, her brothers were hesitant, but at least Tony didn't try to hit him again. Mel was sweet and hugged him—something Izzy didn't think she would have done before becoming part of their exuberant family—then nudged Finn until he shook hands with him. Moira came through from the kitchen as Janey finished her circuit and greeted him with a hug. Thank God for the women in her family. This seemed to loosen the rest of them up enough for Seamus to offer Mac a beer and Finn to start talking about football teams.

Her mother had prepared one of her signature feasts, an interesting mix of northern Italian and Irish cuisine. The wine flowed freely and everyone's temper improved as the dinner progressed. Mac was the perfect guest, lavishly complimenting Moira's cooking and especially seeming to enjoy her Colcannon, a mashed potato dish with cabbage, bacon, and onions, which she always made for Janey, who tended to be a picky eater.

"So, Mac," her father began, "Izzy tells us you work for Homeland Security." It was clearly a prompt to continue.

Mac squeezed her hand under the table and winked at her. *And thus begins the inquisitorial segment of the evening.* "Yes, sir. I work with the Fusion Program here in Albuquerque. My team is responsible for threat assessments around the state. We also do quite a bit of training for various companies."

"What kind of training?" Seamus asked.

"Active shooter, bomb threats, that sort of thing. I can put an audience to sleep in under five minutes. I've mastered the art of a boring PowerPoint presentation." Everyone laughed with him.

"I could give you a few hints," Cara offered. "You can liven up a lecture and get your audience more engaged pretty easily. If you're interested."

"Absolutely. That would be great. Thanks." He scooted his chair back from the table as Janey climbed from her booster seat and asked to sit on his lap. Izzy knew she was getting sleepy and would most likely fall asleep during dessert. "Come here, Princess." He murmured the words and smoothed her hair away from her face as she snuggled into his arms. Izzy watched her brothers observe the closeness between the little girl and Mac and saw their frowns. Janey usually chose to sit with Hugh at the end of a family meal and Izzy wondered if he was feeling a bit bereft. His face gave nothing away, however, so she raised her eyebrows at him and nodded slightly toward Mac and Janey. He grimaced and rolled his eyes, but nodded a reluctant approval.

"Well, I have something to say and I guess I better do it before Miss Janey falls asleep, because I think she's going to want to know," Finn announced. "Mel and I are going to have a baby."

The stunned expressions around the table lasted only seconds before there was a general outcry of excitement and congratulations. Moira vaulted from her seat and nearly yanked Melanie from her chair to hug her, tears streaming down her face.

"Oh, my goodness! This is wonderful news! When?"

"Sometime in late September." Mel wiped her own eyes and laughed. "Sorry. I seem to cry at the drop of a hat these days."

"When she's not throwing up, that is," Finn added as he put his arm around his wife.

Izzy remembered those days. She'd been sick for three solid months with Janey, then it disappeared and she'd felt great for the rest of her pregnancy. But it had been lonely, and she was glad Mel had the love and support of a husband to help her through the next eight months. She felt an ache in her chest and sternly tamped down the jealous feelings trying to bubble up. *But I'll be thirty-three in a few months. I'm not getting any younger, and if I want more children it wouldn't be wise to wait too long.* She glanced at Mac cuddling their daughter in his lap and wondered if he would ever want more kids. *Whoa! Slow down, girl! Besides, that would require sex, which seems to have been taken off the table for now.* He looked up at that moment and smiled at her, causing an ache of an entirely different sort. She forced her attention back to the family and the good news. She couldn't help smiling at the expression on Finn's face as he accepted the hearty congratulations from his brothers. He's been through so much in the last year: nearly getting killed twice, first by a hit-and-run that left him in a coma for two weeks and a wheelchair for several months, then by a crazy stalker woman who had formed an obsession for him. He deserved every bit of the happiness he'd found with Mel.

The news seemed to set an easier tone for the rest of the evening, and Izzy had some hope her family would learn to accept and love Mac sooner, rather than later.

***

Mac

Janey was sound asleep when he took her from her car seat, so he carried her inside and told Izzy he'd put her to bed. Putting pajamas on her was like trying to dress a rag doll, but he managed, and tucked her under the covers with her kitten, who'd followed them down the hall to Janey's bedroom, seeming to accept her role as nighttime snuggler. He waited a few minutes to make sure she would stay asleep, then dimmed her light the rest of the way and returned to the living room.

"She's out. Thanks." He accepted the mug from Izzy.

"I figured we should stick to herbal tea tonight since there was so much wine at dinner. You don't have to rush off, do you?" She looked unexpectedly vulnerable as she sipped her tea.

"No, of course not. Come here." He took her tea, set it on the coffee table in front of them with his, and pulled her close. "I haven't kissed you in almost three hours."

She giggled softly, something he wasn't used to from the usually serious Izzy, and complied, lifting her face to his. "I think this evening went pretty well."

"Yeah, it was great," he murmured against her lips, not particularly caring to discuss it at the moment. Right now all he could think about were her lips and his need to taste them again. He sank into the kiss, pushing her down into the cushions and covering her body with his. God, she felt so good beneath him, and it was all he could do not to take this amazing kiss to its natural conclusion. But at the top of the list of Reasons Why He Shouldn't Make Love to Izzy Right Now was the fact that their five-year-old daughter was asleep down the hall. *Shit, how do married couples with kids manage sex?* If he could corral a few brain cells at the moment, he'd make a mental note to ask someone at work. There had to be way, though, right? Otherwise nobody would have brothers or sisters, would they? *I guess I could ask Izzy's parents. They certainly seemed to have figured it out.* He smiled against her mouth at the thought of asking her father about the finer points of sex after the first child, but then Izzy slid her hand down to rest on his rear end and all rational thought fled.

He was reaching for her bra clasp when a soft cough from the back of the house broke through his mental fog. "Sorry. I got a bit carried away." He sat up and pulled her shirt down. "Sit on that end of the couch, woman." He reached for his rapidly cooling tea and took a large gulp. "God, Izzy. What you do to me." He shook his head.

She ran her hand through her hair and reached for own tea, an adorably flustered look on her face. "Right back at you, Mac."

"Why don't you tell me about your day at work? That seems like a safe topic."

"Um, okay." She shook her head, as if to clear it. "Sure. I've been looking through some boxes of financial records for a millwork company to see if we want to extend a contract to them. Boring enough for you?"

"Not at all. What are you looking for?" He didn't think he could ever be bored listening to her.

"Nothing specific, but we wanted to make sure the company is as strong as they claim before we put our name alongside theirs. We asked for a few recent bank and payroll statements, but they had a temp that day and she sent over at least a dozen boxes. I found all sorts of interesting stuff."

"Such as?" He listened as she told him about the extravagant donations and the low wages they paid their employees. Her face lit up as she talked about it and he realized she loved her job. "So, you majored in accounting in college?"

"Forensic accounting. I got a master's degree in it. I planned to work for the government, but then Dad retired and asked Hugh and I to take over. It's not exactly what I was planning, but I like it."

"I'm sure it pays better than government work too. I don't think many government accountants could afford a house like this." He gestured around the room. *Not to mention that luxury car she drives.*

"This is a DeLuca Home, you know. I got a very good price."

"An employee discount, huh?"

"Something like that. My daddy didn't give it to me." She bristled and crossed her arms.

"Hey." He grabbed her feet and put them in his lap. He stripped off her socks and began massaging her feet. "I wasn't implying anything. Don't be cranky, sweetheart." He rubbed for a moment, concentrating on her arches. Even her feet were sexy. "The Southwest Anti-Poverty League? Let me take a look tomorrow. It's ringing a bell, and that's not a good thing, given what I do for a living."

***

"Hey, Dar." Mac looked up from his screen as his partner entered their cubicle. "Does the Southwest Anti-Poverty League sound familiar? I swear I remember running across the name, but now I can't find it."

Darius removed his jacket and set it on the back of his chair. "Yeah, it does. Give me a few minutes. I'm sure I can find it."

It took quite a bit longer, but by lunchtime Darius had found it. "Got it! They're on a watch list that was sent out last week. They're low priority, but...ugh. They're pretty icky."

"Icky? Let me see." Mac stood and peered over his shoulder. "Hmm, I see what you mean. Icky is right. Can you print that out for me?"

"Sure." He clicked the print command, then handed him the sheet of paper. "Where are you off to?"

Mac finished putting on his jacket. "I think I'll see if Izzy can do lunch. Shut up," he muttered as Darius gave him a knowing look and laughed, saying he wouldn't expect him back anytime soon.

He'd never been to her office before, but it wasn't hard to find, especially given he had the resources of the U.S. Government at his disposal. He parked his SUV and admired the modern edifice with *DeLuca Construction* in large silver letters across the front.

"May I help you?" The receptionist was middle-aged and short, with dark, graying hair.

"Yeah, hi. I'd like to see Izzy if she's here."

"Hmm." She frowned at him over her reading glasses. "Have a seat. I'll see if Ms. DeLuca is available."

He sighed and resigned himself to waiting while the receptionist/watchdog picked up her phone and spoke quietly into it. A moment later, he heard a door open down the hall beyond the reception desk and then Izzy was rushing into the outer office and into his arms. He enjoyed the surprised look on the receptionist's face over Izzy's shoulder as he hugged her. He decided to have some fun by pulling back and then laying a searing kiss on Izzy's lips. "Hey, beautiful."

"Hey." She looked dazed for a moment, then, prompted by the 'ahem' behind them, she turned in his arms. "Malva, this is Mac MacNeil. He's, well, he's…"

"I'm a friend of Izzy's," he said, stepping forward to shake the woman's hand.

"A very good friend, apparently." Malva shook his hand briefly and sniffed.

Izzy laughed delightedly. "Oh, Malva, don't be like that! Mac is Janey's father. And my boyfriend." She raised her eyebrows, daring him to contradict her.

She was crazy if she thought he'd do that. He wrapped an arm around her waist and greeted the receptionist. "Hi. Malva. It's really nice to meet you."

Malva relented and shook his hand before Izzy pulled him back to her office. She shut the door and pushed him onto her couch, following him down, then proceeded to kiss him thoroughly. Long moments later, he reluctantly set her away.

"I hope you don't greet all your visitors this way." He cleared his throat and chuckled.

She laughed and stood, straightening her blouse. "Only the cute ones. I see you found my office. Any particular reason?"

"Beyond the obvious?" He stood and kissed her on the nose. "Actually, I do have a reason. I found some information on the Southwest Anti-Poverty League."

"Really? Let me get Hugh."

Within a few minutes, Hugh and Izzy were seated together on the sofa while Mac disclosed the background information he'd discovered. They watched him, disgust dawning on their faces, as he explained.

"Eugenics? The poverty gene? What the literal

fuck?" Izzy exclaimed.

"The league vows to support the eradication of poverty through the destruction of communities with a high concentration of people they feel possess this 'poverty gene.' In Albuquerque, that means poor Hispanic families," Mac explained. "They're on a domestic terror watch list."

"That's the kind of charity Lyon Millwork is supporting?" asked Hugh. "Do you know how many people that could include in this city? We're majority-minority here, you know."

"More than supporting. From what we've seen, Lyon Millwork is an integral part of the organization. They're laundering money through the carpentry business. And yes, we have exact figures on how many people that may include in Albuquerque." He pulled his cell phone from his pocket. "Have you sent the boxes of financial documents back yet, Izzy?"

"No. They're packed and ready to go, but I'm still waiting on the courier service."

"Call and cancel them. I need a couple hours with those boxes." He pointed to his cell phone. "I'll call a federal judge and get a subpoena. It shouldn't take too long. Maybe we could go to lunch and pick it up on the way back?"

Izzy nodded and grabbed her jacket.

"Don't you need a warrant?" asked Hugh.

Mac shook his head and smiled. "The police would, but Homeland Security operates under the USA Freedom Act, and this is an issue of national security. A subpoena will do, and will be easy to get for something like this."

He was right. The subpoena was waiting at the federal courthouse by the time they were finished with lunch, so he was able to get started as soon as they returned to Izzy's office. He spent the next few hours photographing the relevant documents from Lyon Millwork. He would have had little idea what was relevant and what was not, but Izzy worked alongside him, keeping notes on a legal pad of what he'd photographed and why it was important. Hugh brought them coffee a couple hours in, then left them alone for the rest of the afternoon.

"Oh, shoot!" Izzy glanced up at the clock and grimaced.

"What?"

"I'm supposed to meet Cara for drinks in a little while." She stood and dusted off her slacks.

"So go. I can finish up here." He barely looked up from the documents.

"I have to pick up Janey from daycare and take her to my mom. Maybe I can call Cara and reschedule." She started toward her desk.

He stood and grabbed her hand. "Hey. Don't reschedule. I'll pick up Janey and take her to your place. Go have fun with Cara."

She stared up at him, clearly trying to decide if what he was suggesting was remotely plausible.

"Come on, Izzy. I'm her father. I need to start figuring all this stuff out. We'll be fine." He had no actual confidence in his words, but he didn't want her to miss out on her plans with her sister. He knew being a single mom had to be tough, leaving little time for herself, and he wanted to help.

"Well, I guess I could call the daycare and let

them know. I'll need to put her car seat in your SUV too."

"All right, then. Sounds like a plan to me." He flashed her a grin and leaned down to kiss her. "Let's do this."

He called Darius and told him he wouldn't be back that afternoon, then headed to the daycare to pick up Janey. He was pleased when the daycare director asked to see his photo identification before she released her into his custody, even though his daughter had greeted him excitedly, telling her teacher he was her daddy. She seemed to love to say the word, but had yet to refer to him directly by the moniker. The fact that he had a badge around his neck and handcuffs, a gun, and a knife on his belt also helped establish his credibility with the daycare workers. He managed to get Janey in her car seat without too much trouble—she did most of the work—and then suggested they go out to dinner before he took her home. She didn't seem bothered that her mother wasn't there once she had ascertained that she was with her Aunt Cara and would be home later. All in all, he was feeling good about his ability to tackle this parenting thing, at least for one evening.

"I need to stop by my place to put away my badge and gun, Princess, but then we can eat. Where should we go?"

"Can we go to Red Robin?"

"Of course." He was relieved she hadn't chosen McDonald's or some totally kid-themed place. He felt a little out of his depth as he examined the menu, trying to find something appropriate for

Janey to eat, but she knew exactly what she wanted—something called Cluck-a-Doodles—and ordered it herself in a self-possessed manner that reminded him strongly of Izzy. She colored on her kid's placemat while she chattered, telling Mac all about her day.

"And we got to walk to the park after lunch while the little kids were taking their naps 'cuz it was sunny. And I got to pick the book for story time and I picked *Skippyjon Jones* and everyone liked it."

Mac would not have had a clue what she was talking about a month ago; now he felt like he was on a first name basis with Skippyjon, since he'd read the whole series about the adventurous and imaginative Siamese kitten to his daughter multiple times. She was an enjoyable and adorable dinner companion, and he found himself especially enjoying this time together, just the two of them. They shared a dessert, then headed home so he could get Janey bathed and ready for bed. Izzy had given him a spare set of keys a few days before and her alarm code, a mark of trust that humbled him a bit.

He'd barely begun to draw Janey's bath when his cell phone buzzed in his pocket. He pulled it out and recognized Izzy's number. "Hey, sweetheart. Everything is going fine here, so don't worry. Are you and your sister having fun?"

"Mac? This is Cara. Don't freak out, but we're at the emergency room—"

"What?" he exploded and turned off the bath water. "Tell me."

"We were leaving the restaurant and she was ahead of me. This car came out of nowhere! I was too far away to grab her. She saw it at the last second and jumped out of the way, but she fell and hit her head and cut her leg. She's going to be okay, but she wanted me to call and let you know we'll be late getting back. I'm sorry I'm rambling, Mac. I'm a little shaky." Cara finished with a slight hiccough.

"Which hospital?"

"Downtown Presbyterian, but she said—"

"I'll be there in a few minutes. Can you call your mom and let her know I'm going to drop Janey off?" He hung up as she was still talking and strode to his daughter's room. "Janey, honey, I need to go in to work for a little while, so I'm going to drop you off at your grandma's house."

She'd been playing with her kitten on the rug and looked up at him with those huge green eyes. "Okay. Why do you have to leave?"

He didn't want to worry her, so he repeated the fib about work. "But I'll see you tomorrow, okay? You're going to sleep at your grandparent's house tonight."

"What about Momma? When will she be home?" Janey was frowning, as if she was starting to see through the quick fabrication.

He scooped her into his arms and hugged her. "I'm not sure, but I promise we'll both come get you tomorrow morning, okay? But right now I need you to grab your coat."

Janey seemed to sense the urgency and nodded, then ran to get her coat. Mac didn't like the quiet fear in her eyes as he buckled her into her car seat, but was afraid his own eyes held the same expression.

Chapter Six

Izzy

Well, at least my leg doesn't hurt anymore. The lidocaine had done its job and she could no longer feel the pain from where the bumper of the car had glanced off her calf, ripping her slacks and creating a two-inch gash in her leg. There had been a lot of blood, but the emergency room doctor had assured her it would heal well with minimal scarring. The shots before the stitches had hurt almost worse than the cut, and she'd probably permanently damaged her sister's hand by squeezing it so tightly. The more concerning injury was the concussion she'd suffered when her skull cracked against the pavement with impressive force.

"We're sending you up for a CT scan," the ER doctor said as he checked her pupils again. "You seem to be doing well, but we need to be sure. How's the pain level on a scale of one to ten, with ten being completely unbearable?"

"Um, maybe a four or five? It's mainly

throbbing, so much I can't think straight. Sorry." She rubbed her forehead and frowned.

"You don't have to apologize." He pocketed his penlight and smiled. "Let's see what's going on with this CT scan, and then I'll get you something for the pain. Relax for a few minutes while I get the techs in here to move you." He patted her shoulder and left.

"Did you reach Mac?" she asked as Cara re-entered the room.

"Yeah. He's on his way."

"What? I told you to tell him to stay there with Janey. God, Cara! I don't want him to see me like this. There's no need." She rubbed her head harder, willing the ache away. She was having a hard time holding on to her thoughts.

"I barely got a chance to talk! He shouted a few questions and then hung up. He's kind of scary."

"No, he's not. Intense, yeah, I'll give you that, but never scary." She brushed her hair away from her face. "How bad do I look?"

"Pretty damn good, considering you got hit by a car." Cara crossed the room to the sink and wet a paper towel so she could wipe some of the blood from Izzy's arms. "So, it's getting serious with you two, huh?"

"More serious than sharing a child? I don't know. I think so, but..."

"But?" Cara prompted.

"But I'm not sure how he feels about me."

"Oh, you mean rushing over here to the hospital doesn't give you a hint?" Cara rolled her eyes at her sister. "Seriously, Iz. The man's completely in love

107

with you."

"He hasn't said that."

"Yet. Give him some time. This whole thing must be kind of overwhelming for the guy, you know. How do you feel about him?" She handed Izzy a tube of lip gloss.

"I'm not sure. I think…I mean…I think I'm in love with him, but is it just me?"

"What are you talking about?"

"What if it's just me and the fact that I'm lonely and desperate and being a single mother is really hard?" She swallowed against the lump in her throat.

Cara laughed and hugged her gently. "Oh, sweetie! You're so full of shit! But I love you anyway. Listen, I get that it's hard sometimes, but if you love Mac, it has nothing to do with being lonely or desperate. Stop trying to talk yourself out of it and just enjoy being in love." She cocked her head to the side. "Ah, are those his dulcet tones I hear?"

"If you don't let me see her, I swear to God I'll arrest you! Goddammit! Izzy?" His shouts could be heard all over the emergency room.

"I'd better go get him before they throw him out." Cara disappeared and returned a few seconds later with Mac in tow.

He crossed the room in two steps. "Are you okay? Where are you hurt?"

She looked up into his handsome, wonderful face and knew. "I love you, Mac," she blurted.

He stared at her for a moment then turned to Cara. "What kind of meds do they have her on?"

"None yet. Well, three's a crowd, so I'm going

to go find the cafeteria and see if I can get a cup of coffee. I'll bring you one, Mac. They should be by to take her for a CT scan soon. Bye." She wiggled her fingers in their direction then left.

Izzy wished she could disappear in the wake of her embarrassing revelation, but she was stuck in this damned bed. "Sorry about that. I hit my head. I'm not responsible for what I say."

"First, tell me where you're hurt and then we'll get back to what you said, okay?" He smiled gently at her.

"We can pretend I never spoke. Really. I cut my leg. Well, technically a car did." She pulled back the sheet to show him the bandage on her calf. "And I hit my head on the pavement. They think I have a concussion."

"That's all? How many stitches?" He ran his fingers gently over the skin above her bandage.

"I'm not sure. Ten maybe. You'll have to ask Cara. I forgot." She rubbed her forehead again. "I'm having a hard time keeping thoughts in my head right now."

"What about your head? Any stitches there?"

She shook her head, then winced at the pain.

He placed his hand on her cheek. "Shh. Be still. Would it be okay if I kissed you? I'll be very gentle." He smiled hopefully at her.

"Please." She raised her lips to his as they descended.

He brushed his lips across hers softly. "I love you too, Izzy. Of course I do. Hopefully you'll still want to say it to me after you recover."

"Probably." She smiled and pulled him down for

another kiss. "Where's Janey?"

"I dropped her at your parents' house before I broke every speed limit to get over here."

"You didn't tell her—"

"Of course not. I said I had to go into work."

The techs showed up at that moment to take her for a CT scan. Mac was not allowed to follow, so he told her he'd call her mother and then find Cara.

He and Cara were both waiting in her room, sipping coffee from Styrofoam cups, when she returned. The smell hit her as the orderly wheeled her across the threshold and she nearly vomited. She didn't want to say anything, though, because they'd both feel compelled to throw their cups away and she didn't want to cause a fuss. Her head ached worse than ever and she wished the doctor would hurry with the pain medication. She closed her eyes and listened as Mac and Cara chatted in subdued voices, actually drifting off to sleep for a few minutes as their voices droned on.

"All right, Ms. DeLuca." The doctor breezed into the room. "Your CT scan was clear—no subdural hematoma or swelling that I could see. I've ordered some pain meds for you that should help you get rid of that headache. Do you live alone?"

"Um, no." It was hard to force the words out with her brain feeling so foggy. "I live with my daughter. She's five."

"Well, you're going to need to stay with someone for a few days while you recover. Is that possible?" He asked the question while he shone the penlight in her eyes again.

"I'll be with her," Mac said. "She won't be

alone."

"Good. She needs lots of rest for the next few days." He turned back to Izzy. "I want you to go home and sleep. No television, music, computer, cell phone, or anything else. You need physical and cognitive rest for the next twelve hours. Then you can take it slow for a couple of days. Don't go back to work until Monday." He put the flashlight away. "I'll send the nurse in with your pain medication and an antibiotic for your leg. We'll get some paperwork signed and you should be out of here soon." He shook hands with Cara and Mac, patted Izzy on the foot, then left.

The nurse entered a few minutes later and Izzy greedily swallowed the high-octane ibuprofen, then lay back with her eyes closed again. She hoped Mac was listening to all the instructions the nurse was delivering. She wasn't sure how much time had passed before another nurse or tech was back, insisting she get out of the bed. She groaned and tried to roll over and ignore her.

"Come on, Izzy, love." Mac was there on her other side, urging her to wake so she could get into a wheelchair. "I'm going to take you home and you can sleep in your own bed."

She simply couldn't keep her eyes open as she was rolled through the hospital corridor and out to Mac's SUV, waiting at the curb. When had he left to move it? He helped her into the front passenger seat and buckled her seatbelt, reclining the seat as far as it would go. It seemed like hours later when he stopped the car and turned off the motor.

"Let's get you inside." He helped her out of her

seat, then lifted her into his arms to carry her into the house.

"I can walk," she murmured against his shoulder.

"No need, hon." He set her down to unlock the door and punch the code on the alarm, but then scooped her up again and carried her to her bedroom.

She felt the bed against her thighs and sank down gratefully. "Would you take my shoes off, please?"

"Sure." He lifted her dangling legs onto the bed and gently removed her shoes. He continued, unbuttoning her ruined slacks and pushing them down her legs, being extra-careful around her bandage. Then he reached to unbutton her blouse, pulling her to sit up slightly so he could remove it.

"I wish I was less sleepy so I could enjoy you undressing me more," she murmured.

He grinned and kissed her nose. "Soon. I promise to give you a turn next time." He left on her bra and panties and managed to pull down the covers without making her stand. He pulled them up to her shoulders and leaned down to kiss her again. "Get some rest, sweetheart. I'll be here when you wake up."

She pulled her hand from under the covers and found his. "Sleep with me. Please?"

He brushed her hair away from her face and smiled crookedly. "Sure. Let me lock up and turn off all the lights."

She fought to stay awake until he returned, wanting to make sure he came back. She heard him clicking off lights and checking all the doors. Then he returned to the bedroom. He went around to the other side of the bed and she watched through half-open eyes as he toed off his shoes and pulled his shirt over his head. He unhooked his belt and unsnapped his jeans, pushing them past his narrow hips and off his legs. Clad only in a pair of boxers, he lifted the covers and slid in next to her. He scooted over and put his arms around her, gently cradling her against his warm body. "Where's Janey?" She remembered asking earlier, but couldn't seem to recall what he'd told her.

"She's with your mom. You'll see her tomorrow, love."

"Thank you, Mac. I like your body." She'd meant to add 'next to mine,' but it didn't happen.

He chuckled lightly. "Go to sleep, Izzy. I'm here." He kissed her hair.

She fell asleep surrounded by his warmth.

***

Mac

God, she's so beautiful. She didn't seem to have moved since she fell asleep the night before, still curled on her side and tucked against him. *This is how I want to wake up every morning, with this gorgeous woman in my bed.* Technically, it was her bed, but whatever. He wanted to be in it with her. He hated what had brought him here the night before, but he was realistic enough to know he would have been there soon enough, given the way things were going between them. *And soon enough there will be more than sleeping going on in whatever bed we find ourselves.* But not today. She'd been hit by a car and needed rest. His blood boiled when he thought about what he'd like to do to the asshole who'd done it and driven off. She could have been killed; the thought made him dizzy. She was still sound asleep, so he carefully edged away from her warmth and slid out of bed. He pulled on his clothes and headed to the kitchen, leaving the bedroom door open slightly so he could hear if she called.

He put some coffee on, then made a quick call to Darius, letting him know what had happened to Izzy and that he wouldn't be in today. "Hey, can you get a copy of the police report and email it to me?"

"Sure. What are you looking for?"

"I don't know. I'm not sure I'm buying a random hit and run, though." He'd thoroughly questioned Cara the night before while Izzy was having her CT scan. The police had questioned both women, plus a few other witnesses, at the scene, but nobody had managed to get even a partial license plate number. All Cara could remember of the vehicle was 'big, black car.' "I want to see the report. Do you think you could check into security cameras in the immediate area? I would love to get a look at the car."

"Yeah, me too. I'll make some calls. How's Izzy?" Darius asked.

"Still asleep." He ran a hand over his unshaven jaw. "She has a concussion and a nasty cut on her leg. God, Darius, it could have been so much worse. If I ever get my hands on the fucker who hit her—"

"I'll do what I can to make that happen, man. Do you need anything?"

"I don't think so. Thanks. Talk to you later." He hung up and poured a cup of coffee. He took it with him out to the driveway to pick up the newspaper. Izzy was still sleeping when he checked on her a few minutes later, so he rooted around in her kitchen until he found what he needed to fix breakfast. He was turning the bacon when he felt slim arms slip around his waist from behind. He turned the heat down under the pan and turned to embrace her. "How are you feeling today?"

"About a thousand percent better than last night. That smells amazing. I'm starving."

"That's a good sign." He tipped her chin up and searched her face, noting she did, indeed, look better this morning. He leaned down to kiss her, then turned her toward the table. "Sit. I'll get you some coffee. Breakfast is about ten minutes out."

She was quiet while he finished cooking breakfast. It was one of the many things he appreciated about her: she never felt the need to fill the silence with chatter. In short order, he set a plate with scrambled eggs, bacon, and toast in front of her.

"This looks great, Mac. I didn't know you could cook so well." She took a bite of the bacon, groaning in appreciation.

"Breakfast is about my limit, so don't get too excited." He watched as she stood and went to the refrigerator, returning with a small bottle of something reddish, which she sprinkled over her eggs. "What's that?"

"Cholula. It's hot sauce. Here." She handed the bottle across the table to him.

He twisted the top off of the bottle, smelled it, and put the cap back on. "No thanks."

She grinned and dug into her eggs. "Aren't you going to be late for work?"

"I called in. I'm staying with you today."

She gave him an exasperated look. "I don't need a babysitter."

"Doesn't matter. I'm staying." He was prevented from saying more by the sudden pounding on the front door. "I guess the news has spread to your brothers. Wonder which one it is." He stood, gesturing for Izzy to say seated and continue eating.

"A hundred bucks says it's Hugh. I'm glad I threw some clothes on." She had dressed in yoga pants and a hoodie before coming into the kitchen.

Mac opened the door to find both Hugh and Finn, with Chris standing behind them. "She's okay. She's in the kitchen eating breakfast." He stood aside and allowed the three inside. He swallowed his annoyance at the intrusion and offered them coffee, enjoying the way Hugh's eyes narrowed as he realized Mac had obviously spent the night.

"Cara called this morning," Hugh explained. "I would have liked to know about this last night."

"Oh, Hugh," Izzy said. "I told Cara not to call you. There was no point."

Mac watched Hugh's jaw flex as he struggled not to reprimand his sister. "I called Finn and Chrissy at the precinct as soon as I heard."

"I pulled the police report before I left," Chris added, handing a copy to Mac. "I'd like to hear your story again, Izzy."

"Sure," she said with a sigh. "I'll tell you what I remember, which isn't much. Cara and I were coming out of the restaurant. We went to a new sushi place on Central." She frowned as she spoke. "Cara's strap slipped on her shoes and she stopped to fix it. I was ahead of her. I guess I'd already stepped off the curb when I looked back. I heard something—it must have been the car—and I turned around. I didn't really see much—it was more an impression and a reaction, I guess. I jumped back, but something hit my leg. Then I was falling and I hit my head, I guess on the curb. I blacked out for a couple seconds."

"It was nearly five minutes, from what Cara said," Mac added.

"I must have scared the living shit out of her," Izzy muttered.

"Pretty much." Finn spoke for the first time. "She said there was a lot of blood from your leg."

"Yeah, but the doctor said it would be fine. How many stitches did he put in?" She turned to Mac.

"Twelve. It's a nasty cut, but it should heal pretty well." He turned to the others. "She's got antibiotics, which she should take with food." He pushed away from the counter and went to find the prescriptions he'd brought home the night before. "Here you go. I'll bet you're ready for some pain pills too, huh?"

She nodded and accepted the pills he put into her palm. "That's all I remember. I woke up and barfed all over the sidewalk. There were paramedics. They made me ride in an ambulance. I'm glad I didn't have to stay overnight in the hospital."

"Her CT scan came back clear, so the ER doc said she could go home as long as someone stayed with her. She needs to stay home from work until Monday." He addressed these last words to Hugh.

"No problem. Mac, thank you for taking care of her. Cara said you took Janey to Mom and Dad's too."

"Of course. They're my family." And Hugh and the rest of them had better get used to it.

Hugh simply nodded and turned back to his sister. "You scared the hell out of us, Iz."

"Sorry. I certainly didn't mean to." She looked up at Mac. "When is Janey coming home?"

He was glad she didn't ask where she was again. It had freaked him out a bit the night before when she couldn't seem to remember. "Your mom took her to daycare so you could get some sleep today. She'll drop her off here later this afternoon, okay?"

She smiled. "Okay. I miss her. You'll stay, won't you? After Janey gets back, I mean."

"Of course." He turned to grab the coffee pot to refill her mug.

Finn stood and carried his mug to the sink. "We'll let you get back to your rest, Izzy. Glad you're okay, sis." He kissed the top of her head and looked at the other two expectantly. Chris and Hugh each hugged her, then walked with Finn to the front door.

Mac winked at Izzy, then followed the others out of the kitchen. "I've asked my partner to locate any security camera footage in the area that might have captured the car. It's a long shot, but—"

"It's worth a try. Good call, Mac," said Finn.

"Do you think this could possibly have anything to do with what we found in those boxes?"

"It seems like awfully coincidental timing." Hugh frowned at Mac as he asked. "Is it possible this wasn't random?"

"I don't know, but I think it's worth looking into." He filled in the details for Finn and Chris, who looked confused.

"Shit. Okay, we'll see what we can find out from our end. Chris, can you call Jared and see if the FBI knows anything about this Poverty League?" Finn reached for the small notebook in his shirt pocket and jotted a few notes as he spoke.

When Mac returned to the kitchen, Izzy was stacking their dishes in the dishwasher. "Hey." He took the plate from her hands and steered her back to the table. "I'll clean up. You are on strict orders to rest, young lady."

"Fine. Thanks for breakfast." She sipped her coffee silently while he finished stacking the dishes in the dishwasher. "You guys think it might not have been an accident, don't you?"

He sighed and tossed the rag he'd been using to wipe the counter in the sink. "Maybe. We're looking into it. I wish you wouldn't worry about it, at least not today."

"Hmm. I could probably be distracted fairly easily." She let her eyes drift up and down his body.

He laughed and held his hand out to her. "I'll have to take a raincheck on that, love, at least for a few days." He tipped her chin up and kissed her, long and deep, stroking his tongue against hers

119

lazily. She tasted of coffee and bacon, and he wished he could scoop her into his arms and take her back to bed, but he knew he needed to wait until she was fully recovered. He groaned and reluctantly pulled away. "You are a temptress, woman." He rubbed his thumb across her full lips. "Sex is definitely on the list of forbidden activities for you today."

"What about tomorrow?" she asked, a pouty expression on her face.

"A guy can dream." He tweaked her nose. "Why don't you show me some of Janey's baby pictures?"

Her face lit up, as it did any time her daughter was mentioned. "Sure. Do you want to see some of her videos too?"

"I want to see all of them."

Two hours later, he'd worked his way through several photo albums and birthday videos from age one through four. He couldn't get enough; his hunger for the time he missed in Janey's life was unquenchable. "What's that one?" He pointed to a DVD still in the basket she'd set on the coffee table.

"Oh, that's her birth video. You don't want to see that. It's not for the faint of heart, trust me." She laughed and reached for another photo album.

But he barely heard her. He closed the album on his lap and reached for the DVD. "Of course I want to see it. I've done two and a half tours in Iraq and one in Afghanistan, Izzy. I think I can handle it."

Nearly an hour later, he had to rethink his brash statement. He rested his head against the back of the sofa, his arm slung over his face. "That was brutal. Oh, my God."

She patted his leg. "Be glad it was only the highlights. You want some water?"

He shook his head and sat up. "I'm fine. God, Izzy! I can't believe you had to go through that." He took her face in his hands. "Did you ever think of not doing it?"

"What do you mean?"

"When you found out you were pregnant and alone, did you ever think about having an abortion? You could have just gone back to your normal life. Nobody ever would have known."

She leaned in and kissed him softly. "Not even for a second."

He sighed and pulled her close. "Thank you. Thank you for giving my daughter an amazing life. I love you, Izzy."

"I love you too, Mac. Sorry for blurting it out at the hospital last night. I'd blame it on the drugs they gave me, but I don't think I'd had any yet."

"Well, you had hit your head pretty hard. And you can blurt out that you love me any time you want. How's the head today?"

"Still aches some." She rubbed her forehead. "Where did you put my pain meds?"

"I'll get them." He turned off the television and pushed himself off the sofa. He tried not to be concerned that she'd seen him set the meds on the table earlier. She was still obviously confused. He gave her two pills and a glass of water and made sure she took them. "What would it take to convince you to lie down for a nap?"

"Hmm, let me think." As she spoke, she crawled across the couch toward him.

He let her push him back until she was positioned on top of him. He was perfectly happy to let her take control of the encounter and enjoyed a few minutes of the finest kissing he'd ever experienced. Hands down, Izzy was the best kisser he'd ever known. She seemed content to keep things fairly innocent, though, and he realized she must be exhausted. He slowed it down and sat up. "I could do this all day, sweetheart, but you need to rest. Come on." He pulled her off the couch and into her bedroom. He helped her settle on top of the comforter, tucked a blanket around her, and kissed her head. She was already asleep before he closed the door.

He took the opportunity while she slept to call Darius. "Did you find anything?"

"Yeah. Would it be okay if I came over? I actually found quite a bit, but I'd rather talk to you in person."

"Sure. I'll text you the address, but don't knock or ring the bell, okay? Izzy's asleep."

Darius arrived within fifteen minutes; they soon had files and notepads spread over the kitchen table. "It's going to be a few days before we have the security feed from the businesses around the restaurant, but I had our accountants go over the files you sent from Izzy's office and they found some interesting patterns. The amount of the donations from Lyon Millwork to various entities ebbs and flows."

"Why is that interesting?"

"Because the upswings over the past decade always precede some sort of protest or public spectacle by whatever group they've donated to. Lyon has a predilection for supporting racist groups of one sort or another, at least according to his donation history. The part that really concerns us is the recent spike in donations to this Southwest Anti-Poverty League, a known domestic terror organization."

"Do they have a history of violence?" Mac reached for the file Darius had brought on the organization and began flipping through the papers.

"Not here in Albuquerque, but they've tried to cause some trouble in Phoenix and Denver. There were some nasty incidents at pro-Hispanic rallies, the kinds of things we don't want to see here."

"Well, shit. Okay, what kind of things do we have coming up in the next few months that might entice this group to action?"

"No idea. We'll get our people on it, though." Darius smiled suddenly and looked past Mac. "Hey, Izzy. Lookin' good."

Mac turned and saw a sleepy-looking Izzy smile and push her messy hair out of her face.

"Hi, Darius. What's all this?" She entered the kitchen and gestured to the cluttered table.

"Just some work files. I'll clear it up and get out of your hair." Darius started gathering the papers.

"Is it the Lyon Millwork case?" She sat at the table and glanced at the open file in front of her. "Did you figure out what AMCI stands for?"

"What? What are you talking about?" Mac and Darius spoke at the same time.

"Didn't I tell you?" she asked Mac. "It was a little slip of paper stapled to one of the donation receipts, along with a canceled check. It was one of things you photographed, Mac. I know it was." She began rifling through the files, agitated.

"Sweetheart, it's okay." Mac didn't want her getting upset, but he didn't remember her telling him anything about a slip of paper. Added to her confusion and general mental fogginess following her concussion, it was worrisome.

"Listen, Izzy." Darius caught Mac's look and gently took the files from her. "I'll look through all these back at the office. I'm sure I'll find it."

She looked like she was going to argue for a moment, but then frowned and stood to get a drink of water. "Yeah. Okay. Thanks, Darius."

Mac saw his partner to the door, then returned to find Izzy pacing the kitchen.

She turned as he entered. "Mac, where's Janey?"

Chapter Seven

Izzy

Her whole body ached, with the pounding headache acting as the cherry on top of the pain sundae. She didn't want to complain about it to Mac, though. He was already worried enough about her confusion and memory loss. Yes, she'd seen his reaction when she kept asking about Janey, and when she freaked out about the handwritten memo she thought she remembered seeing in the files from Lyon Millwork. Now she was doubting herself and wondering if she had imagined it. Mac was so sweet about it all. He hugged her and reminded her what the doctor had said about short term memory loss over the next few weeks until her brain had a chance to heal.

"Sweetheart, give yourself some time. Listen, why don't I see if your mom can bring Janey home a little early? I think you'll rest easier once you see her."

She nodded and sniffed, determined not to get

weepy yet again. "Yes. I need her here."

She was still exhausted after her nap, but she didn't want to go back to bed. Mac fixed sandwiches and canned soup, but she had little appetite and threw most of it away. He talked her into sitting with him on the couch while they watched one of her all-time favorite movies, *While You Were Sleeping.* She knew he must have hated every minute of it, but he never complained. Instead, he dimmed the lights and made sure she was comfortable, with her feet in his lap and a soft afghan covering her. Janey's kitten, Sophie, leapt onto the couch and settled into a fold of the blanket, purring softly. Izzy drifted in and out during the movie, but felt relaxed and fairly calm, knowing her baby would be home soon. She had a moment of panic at the end of the movie when she looked around and didn't see Janey; she almost asked where she was, but Mac must have noticed.

"Your mom is on her way with Janey, love. They should be here soon."

Moira arrived shortly with Janey and several bags of groceries. "I put together a few casseroles, as well. Would you mind fetching them from the trunk, Mac?"

Janey followed her grandmother in quietly, obviously warned that her mother had been hurt. She sat next to Izzy on the sofa, not touching her, and frowned. "Are you okay, Momma?"

Izzy pulled her into her arms, inhaling the smell of her shampoo and the warm scent of her little girl. "I'm fine, baby. I promise. I had a little accident, but Mac and Aunt Cara took care of me."

Janey pulled back and looked at her mother seriously. "Grandma said you had to go to the hospital."

"I did, but only for a little while."

Janey glared across the room at Mac as he came in, carrying a cardboard box laden with casserole dishes. "You lied, Mac. You told me you had to go to work."

He set the box on the floor and came to kneel in front of her. "I'm sorry, Janey. That wasn't cool. I should have been honest with you. I know that now. I was scared and I didn't want you to know. I promise I'll never lie to you again."

She crossed her arms and continued to glare. "You better not. Are you gonna stay with us and help take care of Momma?"

"I am."

She was silent for a long, excruciating moment. "Okay," she said finally. "I'm not allowed to touch the stove, so you have to cook dinner. Grandma made chicken spaghetti and lasagna." Janey scooped her kitten into her arms and kissed the furry head.

Mac looked visibly relieved at Janey's easy forgiveness. "They smell great too. Which one should we have tonight?"

"Chicken spaghetti. It's Momma's favorite. I can set the table if you reach the plates for me. Here, Momma. You can hold Sophie." She deposited the cat into Izzy's lap and skipped off to the kitchen.

"Whew," he said as he hefted the box of casseroles. "That was close."

Izzy stroked the kitten's head as she listened to

127

her mother and Janey boss Mac around in the kitchen, amused by the conversation and relieved to have her daughter home. She finally felt calm and less worried about her concussion.

"Izzy, dear, let me have a look at you." Moira bustled in, drying her hands on a dishtowel. She took her daughter's face in her hands and examined it carefully. She made Izzy show her the bump on the back of her head and the stitches while she told her what the doctor had said.

"I'm having trouble remembering some things, Mom. I think I freaked poor Mac out. He's been amazing, though."

"That he has. You're a lucky girl, Isabelle Marie. Don't let him slip away this time. He's a keeper. How bad is your headache?"

Izzy shrugged. "It's there, but nothing I can't handle."

"Well, you're a strong woman, of course. We all know that, but don't be a martyr, dear. Take the medicine the doctor gave you and get lots of sleep. That's the best thing, you know."

She smiled at her mother's fussing, delivered in her soft brogue, a leftover from her youth in Ireland. Izzy allowed herself to be coddled and tucked under the blanket again as she sipped the chamomile tea laced liberally with honey her mother brought to her.

"Now, Melanie is going to come and stay with you tomorrow so Mac can go in to work. He'll drop Janey off at preschool in the morning, but I'll bring her home after lunch. I know you'll rest better with your wee chick close to the nest." She winked and kissed her daughter's forehead. "I need to get home to your father, but call if you need anything at all."

Seamus and Tony stopped by after dinner, bearing flowers and a box of her favorite French chocolate mints. "We needed to see you with our own eyes, Iz," Tony said as he scooped Janey into his arms and tickled her. "We wanted to come earlier, but your watchdog here made us wait until now."

Mac merely sipped his beer, without comment, and continued to watch television.

"Thanks, guys." She ate a chocolate to please them, but her stomach was still a bit queasy. She'd managed a small amount at dinner, but it wasn't settling well.

They waited until Janey was in her bath to ask about the accident. "Did Finn find the person who hit you?"

"Not yet," Mac said. "Both agencies are looking into it. We're hoping one of the security cameras in the area managed to get a shot of the car. A license plate would be helpful."

"I hope you find the son-of-a-bitch and nail his balls to the wall," Seamus said with a growl. "This was way too close a call, Izzy."

"I agree. It could have been a woman, you know." Something clicked in her mind as she said it, but she couldn't pin it down. She frowned as she concentrated.

"What's your point?"

"About what?" She couldn't remember what they'd been discussing. At the concerned looks on the three men's faces, she shook her head, then smiled and turned to her youngest brother. "How's your semester so far?"

Tony took a swig of beer and grimaced. "Slow. I'm so ready to graduate and be done with college. Speaking of, I have a paper to write, so I need to get out of here." He and Seamus finished their beers and left, wishing Izzy a speedy recovery. She noticed the non-verbal communication going on between the three, however, as they were obviously worried about her.

She sighed as Mac returned from seeing them out and sat next to her. "What did I forget? You all looked worried."

He put his arm around her and explained. "Do you think it was a woman you saw driving the car, hon?" he asked as he finished.

She rubbed her forehead and tried to concentrate. "I don't know. Maybe. Ugh! This is so frustrating, Mac!"

"Hey." He pulled her aching head against his chest. "Don't force it. It won't help you remember any faster."

Janey came into the room, carrying a stack of books. "I can read to you, Momma. Pick which one you want."

Izzy smiled and chose, content to lean against Mac while Janey sat on his other side and read, stopping to show the pictures on each page. Then she listened as Janey told her about her day at preschool, and the afternoon helping her grandmother make the casseroles they'd brought home.

Later, curled against Mac's warm body in her

bed, she tried to remember what it was that had made her think it might have been a woman driving the car. "How long did the doctor say this memory loss would last?" She laughed softly as she finished speaking.

"What's so funny?" he murmured against her hair.

"Oh, I just think it's kind of ironic that I can't remember what the doctor said about my memory."

"Well, at least you still have your sense of humor." He rolled her over gently and kissed her. "He said it could last a few days or a few weeks. Head injuries are anybody's guess, hon. I wish you wouldn't worry."

She raised her eyebrows at him, but realized the expression was lost in the dark. "You're one to talk, mister. Don't think I haven't noticed how worried you've been all day. You didn't bank on a crazy girlfriend, did you?"

"Shh. You're not crazy, sweetheart. Of course I'm worried. I love you and I'll be worried any time you're not at a hundred percent. I know you would feel the same if it was me."

"Speaking of which, now would be a great time to tell me about your injury." She reached around to smooth her hands over the scars on his lower back.

He sighed. "Yeah, I guess I should, but I need you to not freak out, okay?"

She nodded and reached for his hand, bringing it to her lips.

"We were on a mission—it's still classified, so I can't tell you what or why—near Mosul. That's in northern Iraq, in case you're not up on your Middle

131

Eastern geography. We were on a sweep through the town when we came under sniper fire. One of my team was hit and went down as we were crossing an open space. I couldn't leave him there, so I sent the rest of team to find cover while I went back for Ben. I managed to get him back to the team, but I took two bullets in the back before I got under cover. Darius dragged me into the building before they could finish me off."

"What about Ben? Did he live?"

He shook his head. "He'd been hit in the head."

She shuddered as she realized Mac had risked his life for a dead man. She suspected that was why he'd been awarded the Silver Star. "What about you? What happened?"

He sighed again. "I had to be evac'd out, but it took almost six hours to get the helicopter in there because of all the sniper fire. Longest six hours of my life. They sent me to Landstuhl—that's the military hospital in Germany. I was there for eight months, then stateside for another surgery and a year of rehab."

"And you didn't want to go back into the army when you got better?"

"It wasn't an option. I had to learn to walk again and—"

"What?" She sat up and reached to switch on the bedside lamp. "You couldn't walk?" She'd had no idea his injury had been so serious.

He remained flat on his back, but reached his hand up to push her hair behind her ear. "One of the bullets damn near severed my spinal cord. I was lucky. Hey, don't cry."

She stared through her tears at this amazing man who had been through so much. "What about now? How is your back now?"

He reached over to the nightstand for a tissue. "Here. I'm okay, for the most part. It gets pretty stiff if I don't keep up with my exercises. I don't do a lot of heavy lifting anymore."

"You shouldn't have carried me last night!"

"It's fine, Izzy. I wouldn't consider carrying you 'heavy lifting.'"

"William David MacNeil, you are not to carry me ever again! I would never forgive myself if I hurt you."

He laughed, causing the whole bed to shake. "Did you just middle-name-scold me? God, Izzy, you're priceless!" He stopped laughing when he saw she was still crying. "Ah, sweetheart. It's okay, I promise."

She nodded and sniffed again. "I wish I'd looked at your dog tags that morning."

"What?"

"That morning after, well, after our night together. You were still asleep and I wanted to look, but I didn't. I just left. I left a stupid note with a fake name. I'll always regret it."

"I still have that note. It helped me get through some dark times. Listen, Izzy. We both have a lot of shit we could regret about that night. I'll always wish I hadn't missed your pregnancy and Janey's first four years. But I don't regret meeting you. And I can't seem to find it in me to regret making love to you all night all those years ago. It was the single best night of my entire life." He grinned at her.

"Tonight's pretty awesome, though. Anytime I find myself in a bed with you, I call it a win. What if we try to forget about the stuff we should have done six years ago and focus on what we're going to do for the rest of our lives?"

"Mac." She leaned down and kissed him. "I love you so much. I know it's crazy because we've only known each other for a couple of weeks, but I do."

"Sweetheart, we've known each other for six years. It's not our fault most of it was spent apart. I love you too. And I love Janey. God, three weeks ago I didn't even know I had a kid and now...I can't imagine life without either one of you." He pulled her down the rest of the way to lie in the crook of his arm with her head on his chest. "Go to sleep, Izzy. Janey and I need you to get well."

***

Mac

"Here. Special delivery." Mac set the small plate covered with plastic wrap in front of Darius.

His partner carefully lifted a corner of the wrap. "A cinnamon roll? It's still warm." He lifted the sticky confection and took a huge bite. "Oh, my God! This is amazing! Did Izzy make it? You need to marry her ASAP, dude."

Mac laughed as he turned on his computer. "Izzy sent it, but Mel made it. She brought a whole pan over this morning."

"Who's Mel? Can I marry her?"

"How do you know Mel's a she?"

"Doesn't matter," Darius said around another mouthful. "I'll still marry him. It's legal in New Mexico."

"Kendra would probably have something to say about that. Mel is a woman and is married to Izzy's brother. Sorry. She's staying with Izzy today so I could come in to work."

"Man, all the good ones are already taken. Did you bring anymore?" Darius craned his neck toward Mac's desk.

"Sorry, no. You better hope I never repeat your comments to your girlfriend. They could slip out at any time, you know, so you better be nice to me."

"I'm not worried. Kendra's a terrible cook and she knows it. She'd probably be thrilled if I brought home someone who would cook and clean. Too bad polygamy's illegal." Darius and Kendra had recently moved in together, but neither was much of a housekeeper. "How's Izzy doing today?"

Mac sighed as he pulled up his department email. "Better. She's less agitated with Janey home."

"Good. She's great, Mac. I really like her. Be sure to tell her and Mel thanks for the cinnamon roll." He turned back to his desk.

They worked in companionable silence for an hour. Mac's cell phone buzzed as he was returning from the break room with fresh coffee. "This is Mac."

"Hey, Mac. It's Finn. We got the security video from the area if you want to swing by sometime today and take a look. We've officially handed it off to Albuquerque Police because it's their jurisdiction, but I thought you might want to see."

"Definitely. Thanks, man. My partner and I will swing by after lunch, if that works for you."

At noon, Mac told Darius he'd be back in an hour, then drove to Izzy's house to check on her.

"She's in the shower, Mac," Mel said as he let himself in. "But lunch will be ready in a few minutes. Why don't you go check on her?"

He found Izzy sitting on the edge of her bed, wrapped in a silky robe, her wet hair clinging to her neck as she concentrated on removing the bandage from her calf. "Here, let me do that." He knelt in front of her and finished the job she had begun.

"Thanks." She ruffled his hair. "It's an odd angle and it hurts my head to twist it around like that. The instructions the doctor gave you said I could take a shower today and remove the bandage so it can get some air. Hmm, doesn't look as bad as I expected."

Mac ran his hands over her leg appreciatively. "Yeah, looks great."

She laughed. "I meant the stitches."

"Those too." The doctor had done a good job, placing the neat stitches close together. The scar would be minimal. He bent down and placed a kiss above the wound, inhaling her warm scent.

"Don't start something you're not willing to finish, Mr. MacNeil." She groaned and ran her hands through his hair.

He grinned against her silky skin. "Oh, I'm perfectly willing." He levered himself up and kissed her, pushing her gently back onto the bed. He lay beside her and cupped her head, indulging them both in a wickedly deep kiss. "But perhaps not right this minute," he whispered against her lips. He stood and pulled her up with him. "Come on. Mel has lunch ready."

"You're a tease, Mac."

***

He and Darius arrived at the state police precinct shortly before 2:00 PM. Chris and Finn led them to a small room with several large computer monitors and told them to sit.

"Okay, the first video is from the restaurant and shows the accident pretty well." Chris pressed play and they watched the black and white video. The camera was obviously mounted above the front door, for they saw people entering and exiting the restaurant. About ten seconds in, Mac saw Izzy and Cara exit. Izzy was in front and stepped off the curb as she turned back to say something to her sister, who was leaning down, doing something with her shoe. There was no sound but the picture was surprisingly decent quality. A dark sedan appeared in the corner of the frame, heading straight toward Izzy. He saw her head jerk around as she jumped out of the way. He was grateful there was no sound; listening to her scream would have been intolerable. It was bad enough watching as the car's bumper caught her lower leg and her head hit the curb; she collapsed, unconscious, her leg bleeding all over the sidewalk. The next few minutes were much as Cara had described in her statement: Izzy remained unconscious for nearly five minutes, coming around as the paramedics arrived. She sat up and vomited into the gutter, then one of the paramedics ripped her trousers to the knee while the other started an IV. Within minutes they had her loaded into an ambulance and away to the hospital.

"Shit," he muttered and cleared his throat. "Okay. Can you back it up and freeze on the car?"

But the driver wasn't visible from the angle of the restaurant camera; it only captured the front, right side of the vehicle. New Mexico did not require front license plates, so there was nothing to go on.

"The only other video we have is from the ATM across the street. It's crappy quality, but it shows the car a lot better." Finn pulled up the video. It was the typical quality of an ATM: jumpy and exceptionally grainy. But it showed the entire vehicle, a dark 4-door Chrysler 200. Finn froze it on the image of the car as it sped away. "We got a partial plate number."

"And?" Mac demanded.

"And APD is running it. Top priority, I promise. She's my sister, Mac." Finn frowned, eyes narrowed at him.

"Yeah, I know. I just…"

"Knock it off, you two," Chris said. "We don't need a pissing contest to see who cares more about Izzy. APD is on the hit-and-run; it's outside our jurisdiction. What we need is to figure out how we're going to bring that son-of-a-bitch Lyon down, because I have a hunch Hugh is right about the timing being a bit too convenient. I think we can get a warrant to search the business based on the records they sent Izzy and Hugh. State police can handle that. Finn and I can talk to a judge this afternoon. "

"Homeland Security is working on a warrant to raid the headquarters of the Southwest Anti-Poverty League," Darius added. "If all goes well, it will be waiting when we get back to our office. Can your precinct lend a support team on short notice?"

"How short?" asked Finn.

"This afternoon, if the warrant is ready. We don't want to give them time to clean up."

"We'll make it happen." Chris stood and led the way to the door. "Let's keep in touch."

***

The warrant was delivered shortly after they arrived back at their office. They made the necessary calls and met up with the state police support team a block away from the home that had been identified as the headquarters of the group in the southeast part of town. Mac placed his laptop on the trunk of one of the police cars and showed the other team leaders the plan.

"We'll wait until you and Finn are positioned at the back door. Are you clear on the positions for the rest of your team?"

Chris nodded absently as she studied the screen.

"Good. Darius and I will go in the front. Let's go." He stowed his laptop in the trunk of his car and grabbed a black flak jacket, handing one to Darius. They both donned the body armor and checked their sidearms. The plan was for them to approach the residence from the front and simply knock on the door. He had high hopes this would go down without the need for weapons. He waited until Chris radioed in to say she and Finn were in place, then checked in with the rest of the team. They got the green light, so he and Darius made the short walk to the residence in question, a small, unkempt adobe flat-roofed house. He noted the closed shades and curtains at all the visible windows, but didn't feel the accompanying dread this type of situation would normally cause. There was an empty, abandoned feel to the property that boded ill for this raid. He drew his weapon and rang the doorbell. No answer. He opened the screen and knocked. Nothing.

"Police! Answer the door!" Darius shouted, but there was no answer or sound from inside.

Mac reached to check the doorknob and found it unlocked. He pushed it open and stepped to the side as Darius did the same. When nothing rushed out to shoot/greet them, they carefully peeked inside. The house was empty.

"Shit. They were tipped off." Mac radioed Chris and led the way inside. A quick search indicated the occupants had left in a hurry, leaving folding chairs, stray papers, and trash all over the floor. The other police officers executed a quick search of the rest of the rooms, but only found more of the same. "Gather up all the papers and bag anything else you find. Let's get a forensic team in here to dust for prints. Fuck!" He kicked a pile of trash at his feet.

There was nothing else to do. He and Darius walked with Chris and Finn back to where they'd parked their cars. Chris's phone rang and she stepped away, returning a moment later.

"That was APD. They have a suspect in custody for Izzy's hit-and-run. I'll head downtown and check it out."

"Is that your way of saying it's my turn to file the report for this shit-fest?" Finn grumbled.

"Damn straight. I did it last time. See you back at the precinct." She laughed and walked away.

"I hate paperwork. See you guys later. Call us if you find out where these fuckers are now." Finn waved and walked away.

"How did this happen?" Mac demanded.

Darius shrugged. "We'll keep looking. They're sure to surface soon. In the meantime, maybe we should focus on the upcoming events in the area they might be tempted to disrupt. We can start looking into that angle tomorrow. Go home to Izzy and your daughter."

***

He decided to stop by his townhouse and pack a bag to take to Izzy's. He wasn't sure what Izzy was expecting since she was feeling better, but he thought it might be wise to be prepared. He wasn't totally comfortable leaving her and Janey on their own yet, but he'd leave it up to her. He firmly shut down the hopeful part of his brain that wondered if she would feel up to more than just sleeping next to him tonight. *Don't be a dick! She was in a serious accident two nights ago. Plus, your daughter sleeps right across the hall from Izzy's bedroom.* He left his bag in the SUV.

Janey was watching a cartoon when he let

himself in. "Mac!" She jumped off the floor, where she'd set up a blanket with about a dozen stuffed animal companions, and ran to him.

He lifted her up and was thrilled to feel the little arms hug his neck. She smelled like the outdoors and candy, and he loved it.

"Hi, Daddy."

He melted. *Oh, God! Izzy's going to have to clean up a big puddle of what used to be me, right here on her living room carpet.* "Hi, Princess. Did you have fun at preschool?"

"No. Jeremy pulled my ponytail and called me a baby. I hate boys."

Mac felt a sudden and intense desire to have five minutes alone with this Jeremy character. "That's okay, sweetie. You can hate boys as long as you don't hate me."

She giggled and put her small hands on his cheeks. "You're not a boy! Your cheeks are cold."

"It's pretty cold outside. And I used to be a boy. Where's your mom?"

"In the kitchen with Auntie Mel."

He left Janey watching her show and went to find Izzy. She was seated at the kitchen table, sipping a mug of something while Melanie stood at the counter, chopping vegetables.

"Hey, Mac." Mel turned from her cutting board with a smile. "Hope you like vegetable beef soup."

"Sounds great." He leaned down to kiss Izzy's upturned lips. "Hey, beautiful."

"Hey yourself. How was the afternoon? Did the warrant come through?"

He'd told them both about the planned raid when

he was home for lunch. "It did, and we executed the raid as planned. The house was empty. They'd already moved on. Either they were tipped off, or they habitually change locations."

Izzy reached her hand to cover his. "That must be really frustrating."

He squeezed her fingers lightly. "You have no idea."

"Everyone's safe, though, right?" Mel had stopped chopping. She and Izzy had known it was to be a joint operation with Finn and Chris and their team.

"Yeah, of course." He realized he was witnessing a small cop's wife moment. "Finn's absolutely fine."

"Good." She turned back to her cooking.

Izzy stood and crossed to the refrigerator to get a beer. She opened it and placed it in front of Mac with a quick kiss, then turned to her sister-in-law. "Go home, Mel. I'll finish up the soup. You've been here all day and I know you must be dead on your feet. I remember what early pregnancy was like."

Mel tipped the vegetables she'd finished chopping in the stockpot and stirred it briefly. "It's done. Let it simmer for about an hour and it should be good to go. Are you sure you don't want me to come tomorrow?"

Izzy stood and hugged her. "Positive. I'm fine. Let's get together for lunch next week, okay?"

Mel smiled and slipped on her coat. "Sounds fun. Call if you need anything."

Izzy waited until she had said goodbye to Janey and closed the front door behind her. She led Mac back to the kitchen and pushed him into a chair. "I thought she'd never leave." She sat sideways on his lap and pulled his head down for a kiss, slipping her tongue between his lips and stroking. She slipped her hand under his shirt and over his ribs to stroke his chest.

He opened his mouth, welcoming her inside with a groan. He felt like he could devour her right there in the kitchen. He slid his hand around to her wonderfully rounded rear end and pulled her closer, delighted at the feel of her squirming against him, trying to get closer. "Izzy, love." He rested his forehead against hers, panting slightly. "Janey's in the other room."

She smiled and hugged him. "Yeah, I know. Tonight, Mac. You're all mine tonight. If you can't handle that, then you better not stay here. If you sleep with me tonight, we're not just going to sleep. Fair warning."

He gulped and nodded. "But what about Janey?"

"What about her?" she asked with a frown.

"We can't...I mean with her in the house, how do..." He shook his head, unable to form his flailing thoughts into actual sentences.

She smiled, clearly amused. "We lock the bedroom door, hon. She's a sound sleeper. Don't worry."

Chapter Eight

Izzy

He was nervous. She was amused, but did feel a bit sorry for him throughout the evening as they joined Janey in the living room to watch *My Little Pony* for half an hour while the soup simmered on the stove. She prepared a quesadilla for Janey, who would undoubtedly complain about the soup, and offered to make one for Mac. He refused, and tried to object to her standing at the stove, but she shushed him with a kiss and directed him to set the table. She also insisted on cleaning up the dishes after dinner while he helped Janey get her bath and into her pajamas.

"Mac, I'm fine and I need to do something. I've done nothing but sit on my ass for two days. Stop worrying about me."

He nodded a bit mechanically, and scooped Janey up and over his shoulder.

She was relieved to be busy and found the mundane chore soothing. If she were perfectly honest with herself, she had to admit to some nervousness as well. It had been a long time since she'd been with him—or anyone—and childbearing had changed her body. It was nerve-wracking to think about him seeing her naked in a few hours. And exciting. She hummed as she filled the sink with soapy water so she could wash the stockpot.

By the time she had the kitchen clean, Mac and Janey were back in the living room, setting up a board game on the coffee table.

"And if you land on the black ring, you have to wear it until someone else lands on it and you can't pick up any of your color stuff until you don't have it no more."

"Any more," Izzy corrected as she took her place next to Mac. She looked up at him, an unholy grin on her face. "She talked you into *Pretty, Pretty Princess*, huh? I'm going to enjoy this. Let me grab my cell phone. I may need a picture." She made to get up.

He reached out, lightning fast, and pulled her back. "Don't even think about it. I didn't know I was going to have to *wear* the jewelry. Please tell me there's no makeup involved."

She bit her lip and contemplated teasing him longer. "No makeup." She leaned in to whisper in his ear. "I'll make it up to you later."

He gulped and she could swear he blushed a little.

"What color do you want to be, Daddy?"

Izzy hadn't heard Janey call him that yet and it made her chest ache. She squeezed his hand and suggested he might want to be blue or green, as they were slightly more masculine.

He rolled his eyes and chose blue. He was a good sport and she would never forget the sight of him wearing a pair of blue plastic earrings and a sparkly ring on the tip of his pinky finger, since it wouldn't fit any higher. He 'accidentally' dropped the dice when he was within range of landing on the final tiara, making sure he didn't win, and she fell even deeper in love with him.

When the game was over, she helped Janey put it away, then sent her to brush her teeth. Once she was tucked in, she took Mac's hand and led him back to sit on the sofa with her and flipped on the television, not caring what they watched. "We need to give her a little while to fall asleep."

He nodded, but said nothing.

She curled against him, willing herself to be patient. It was one thing to fall drunkenly into bed with a guy; it was another thing entirely to coldly plan it and then have to wait several hours to implement it. Some interminable medical drama finally ended and the late news began. "I couldn't care less about what's happening in the world right now. Let's go to bed, Mac."

He nodded, then chuckled. "I've never been so nervous in my entire life. This is ridiculous."

"Especially considering we've already done it, huh? I'm nervous too. It's been a while for me."

"Me too. How long has it been for you?" He turned to face her.

"Um, nearly six years, actually. You?"

"Same."

"You're kidding! There hasn't been anyone since

we…"

"In my defense, I was in Iraq for two years, then in the hospital and rehab for a long time. I dated a few times in the past couple years, but nothing serious. What about you? I can't believe you haven't dated in six years."

"In my defense," she smiled as she parroted him. "I spent nine months of it pregnant and have been raising a child and trying to build a career since then."

"And doing a fabulous job of both. I'm really proud of you." He tipped her face up and kissed her. "To bed, then. Neither of us has any reason to be nervous." He stood and pulled her with him.

Once in her bedroom, she locked the door and dimmed the lights. She held out her hand to him. "It's finally our time, Mac. Let's not wait any longer."

He took her in his arms and kissed her deeply as his hands stroked, reacquainting himself with her curves. "Izzy, love, I'm not sure how long I'm going to last this first time. I'm out of practice and you feel incredible."

She took his hand and led him to the bed. "I'm about to explode, Mac. Make love to me, please. Hurry. We have all night to take it slow."

Clothing became superfluous and hit the floor as they undressed each other and fell to the mattress. After what he'd said, she expected the first time to be quick, but he kissed and tasted every inch of her body before returning to her mouth. She tried to return the favor, but he laughed shakily and shook his head. "Next time. I can't wait any longer." He took a moment to roll on a condom, then settled between her thighs and entered her in one smooth stroke. "I love you, Izzy," he whispered. Then he began to move.

***

"That was intense." She was sprawled across his bare chest, still panting from her exertions of the last hour.

"I'm not sure I can speak yet."

She laughed and propped herself on her forearms so she could look into his handsome face. "I don't remember this tattoo from last time." She traced the design on the right side of his chest, which she could barely make out in the dim light: a rifle, helmet, and initials.

"I didn't have it then. It's a memorial for Ben, the one who was shot the same day I was."

"Oh." She continued to trace it for a moment. "You've been through so much, Mac, things I can't even begin to understand."

He brushed her hair back from her face. "I was thinking the same thing about you." He looked thoughtful for a moment. "Is this okay, Izzy? Me being here with you like this while Janey sleeps across the hall?"

"Well, it needs to be, because I have no intention of giving it up now that we've started." She leaned down to kiss him. "I don't know what the protocol is, Mac. I know I would never bring a random boyfriend home to sleep with me while my daughter is here, but I think this is a little different. You're her father."

"Yeah, but…I don't know, either. I just don't want to do anything that might hurt you or Janey." He pulled her face down for a lengthy kiss. "I can leave if you think it would be better."

She shook her head and kissed him quickly. "You've been here the past two mornings. I think she'd be more upset if she woke up and you weren't here. But I do need to unlock the door in case she needs something in the middle of the night or has a bad dream, so we need to put on some pajamas." She started to move away.

He wrapped his arms around her, imprisoning her against his hard chest. "In a little while. As long as I'm staying, I might as well make love to you again. This time will be nice and slow. I feel like I kind of rushed last time."

She grinned and kissed his chest. "Well, since you're already here." She moved lower. "Besides, it's my turn to explore."

Slower was a relative term; the long, slow lovemaking Mac promised would have to come later. It had simply been too long for both of them. Nevertheless, it was after midnight before they'd recovered enough for Izzy to don a silky nightgown and Mac to find his boxers. They checked on Janey and found her still sound asleep. Izzy tucked the comforter around her shoulders and then led Mac back to their bed.

***

Mac's phone alarm woke them at seven. Izzy

groaned and rolled over, intent on returning to sleep. She felt a strong arm snake around her waist and pull her against his strong body.

"Morning, love." He kissed her bare shoulder. "Don't get up. I'll make sure Janey gets breakfast and I'll take her to preschool on my way to work."

She rolled over in his arms and snuggled closer. "I hate mornings."

He chuckled and let her burrow against his chest. "Duly noted." He kissed the top of her head and slid out of bed. "I'm going to make some coffee. Go back to sleep, hon."

She was sorely tempted to remain under the covers and do exactly as he suggested; she was still on the doctor's orders to stay home from work for one more day before the weekend, after all, and Mac had offered to take care of Janey. *This must be what it's like to co-parent: shared responsibility and the rare opportunity to sleep in.* She heard Mac in the bathroom, relieving himself, and the mundane sound of the flushing toilet made her smile. She dozed off and woke again to the intoxicating aroma of coffee brewing and something else that smelled delicious. Her stomach growled and she realized she was hungry for the first time since the accident. She crawled from the warmth of the bed and found a pair of sweatpants and a hoodie to wear to the kitchen in place of the silky nightie. "Something smells amazing."

"Momma!" Janey greeted her with a hug. "We were trying to be quiet. Mac's making pancakes."

"You were very quiet, sweetie, but the coffee and pancakes smelled so good I couldn't stay in bed any longer. I'm starving!"

"That's good to hear, hon." Mac handed her a steaming mug of coffee and kissed her on the lips, which made Janey giggle. "Have a seat. Pancakes will up in five."

This was definitely worth getting up for. She sipped her coffee and watched Mac and Janey at the stove. He had pulled a stool in front of it and was teaching her to flip the pancakes.

"See the bubbles popping on the surface? That's how you know they're ready to turn. That's it! Good job, Janey!"

Izzy could see the batter dripping off the edge of the griddle from where Janey's first effort had landed and was glad she had a ceramic stove top; it would clean up easier than the gourmet gas range she'd lusted after when she'd bought the house. She loved how patient Mac was with their daughter, not seeming to mind that everything took longer when Janey helped.

"Are you ready to taste the first batch, sweetie?" he asked the little girl.

"No." She concentrated as she carried the plate to the table. "These are for Momma." She waited beside her mother while Izzy slathered them with butter and poured maple syrup on top.

"Delicious!" she pronounced around a mouthful. "Best pancakes I've ever had." She hugged Janey and winked at Mac over her shoulder.

She insisted on cleaning up the kitchen while he showered and got Janey ready for school, and in short order found herself alone in the house, something she rarely experienced any more. She made the bed and started a load of laundry, then wandered aimlessly from room to room, wondering what to do. *I'm always bemoaning the lack of alone-time in my life, but now that I have a whole day of it, I have no clue what to do. I seriously need to get a hobby.* She thought about cleaning, but she had a weekly cleaning woman who was due Monday, and felt it would be silly to do her job for her. When she found herself seriously considering reorganizing her Tupperware cabinet, she took herself firmly in hand and settled in front of the television to binge watch something—anything—on Netflix. Two episodes into the latest drama everyone was raving about, she was bored. Then the doorbell rang, startling her. She was about to answer the door when she had a flash of memory from the night of the accident. *You don't know who's out there! What if it's the person who tried to run you over, come back to finish the job?* Heart pounding and hands shaking, she tiptoed to the door and carefully peered through the peephole. No one was there. *Oh God! What if they're trying the windows or the back door?* She raced around the house to make sure everything was shut and locked, then crept to the front window and peeked through a slit at the side of the curtain. Nothing. She returned to the front door and quietly unlocked and pulled it open a fraction of an inch. When nothing jumped out at her, she slowly pulled it open the rest of the way. She opened the screen and found it partially blocked by the package resting on the doormat, the familiar Amazon logo staring up at her. *Well, it's official: I've gone off the deep end. I'm crazy. I've been terrified of a bathmat for the last fifteen minutes.* She took the package to the kitchen and slit it open with a knife. *At least it's a nice bathmat.* She placed it in front of the shower in her bathroom and returned to the boring television program.

When her father called a few minutes later to invite her to lunch, she accepted with alacrity and clicked the television off. She rushed back to her bedroom to change into real clothes and apply a little makeup.

Her dad arrived twenty minutes later. "Let me look at you." Big Tony pulled back from his giant bear hug and framed her face in his large palms. "You're still pale."

"I feel fine, Dad, really. I'm glad to get out of the house for a little while, though. Thanks for springing me. Cabin fever was starting to set in."

He drove them to Le Peep, one of her favorite lunch spots. He waited until the waitress had delivered their drinks. "How are things with Mac?"

She choked on her tea slightly. *Great, Dad. Really great. We made love half the night.* "Good." She couldn't quite meet his gaze. "He's been amazing through all this."

He nodded. "I'm impressed with him, Izzy. He seems like a good man."

"He is, Dad. He's so patient with Janey." She sipped her tea for a long moment. "I'm so sorry about all of this. I know you and Mom must be so disappointed in me."

He stood and pulled her from her seat into his arms. "Not even a little bit, sweetheart. Don't ever think that. Your mother and I are extremely proud of you and the life you've made for Janey. You've given us the best granddaughter in the whole world, you know."

She wiped her suddenly wet eyes as she returned to her seat. "Thanks." She wasn't sure she totally believed him, though. How could they not have been disappointed when she'd told them she was pregnant, unwed, and refused to divulge the identity of the baby's father?

As if he'd read her mind, he continued. "Your mother and I never worried about you, Izzy. Not really. You were so matter-of-fact when you announced your pregnancy, at a family dinner, no less." He chuckled as he remembered. "Sure, we were a bit shocked, but never disappointed. I was surprised to find out Brent wasn't the father; I figured he had refused to step up and take responsibility and you were covering for him."

She laughed softly and shook her head. "Hugh wouldn't shut up about it, so I finally agreed to have a paternity test done. He forced Brent to do it."

"Hugh's always been so protective of you. Well, Mac doesn't need a paternity test; Janey looks so much like him it's scary." He was silent as the waitress placed their food in front of them. "I'm glad he's been staying with you, Izzy. Is there any chance the arrangement might become more permanent?"

She shrugged. "It's awfully soon to be thinking about that yet. Who knows? Once the shiny newness wears off, he might get sick of the whole fatherhood bit. I don't want him to end up feeling trapped or anything."

Tony took a bite of his sandwich and chewed thoughtfully. "Hmm. I thought you were a smart woman, Isabelle, but now I'm not so sure."

Uh oh. He only called her Isabelle when she was in trouble. "I'm sorry? Why—"

"If you could see what I see, you wouldn't worry about him feeling trapped. I've never seen a man so happy with his circumstances as Mac. The way he looks at you and Janey—well, it's special. And it doesn't come along every day, so I highly recommend telling your self-doubt or whatever it is to go straight to hell. Then grab on to what's right in front of your face and never let go." He patted her hand on the table top. "But that's just my opinion."

***

Mac

He was afraid Darius would take one look at him and burst out laughing, then flash him a thumb's up. He could feel the silly, self-satisfied grin on his face, but couldn't seem to stop it as he thought about the previous night. *God, it was amazing. She was amazing.* It had been even better than the last time they'd made love—sobriety was surely a large part of that. But he knew it was mainly due to the fact that he knew and loved the woman in bed with him. Yes, it was the end of a long, celibate period in his life—thank God—but he was finding love made sex even better. And he could hardly wait to see if it kept getting better.

"What are you smiling about—ohhhh." Darius

laughed and punched Mac on the arm. "You dog! Good for you!"

Shit. I've got to work on my poker face. "Shut up. I'm not saying anything."

"You don't have to."

"Never mind. Hey, have you heard from Chris or Finn yet about the suspect APD picked up yesterday?" He figured his best bet was to change the subject.

"Not a thing. Why don't you give her a call?" Darius stood, mug in hand. "I'm gonna get a refill."

Mac dialed the number Chris had given him the day before.

"Mac, we've got a problem," she said in greeting. "The suspect, a Donald Maldonado, was found dead this morning at the Bernalillo County Detention Center. He didn't return to his cell after breakfast and was later found dead in a bathroom stall, his throat cut."

"Well, fuck. Did they get anything out of him during the initial interview yesterday?"

"Not a thing. He lawyered up almost immediately. Listen, we got the warrant to arrest Lyon and search the premises. It's going to happen in about an hour. Do you and Darius want to be in on it?"

"Definitely. We'll meet you at your precinct."

***

They followed Chris and Finn to the office of Lyon Millwork. They'd brought a small team of state police officers with them to execute the search warrant while they arrested Lyon.

"I don't expect any excitement today, but we appreciate you lending us the support of Homeland Security," Chris said as she fastened her body armor.

"No problem. I wanted to be in on this," Mac said.

"And I go where he goes," Darius added.

Finn checked his sidearm and holstered it. "Let's do this."

They all entered the building together, then Chris sent her team to stand watch in the stairwell until she radioed them. The whole building belonged to Lyon Millwork, with the second floor devoted to offices and the first floor a spacious workshop area that smelled of sawdust. The loud buzz of machinery drowned out any possibility of last minute instructions, but once upstairs with the door closed, it was much quieter. They paused to collect themselves and prep their weapons, then entered the office. The receptionist glanced up and did a double-take as she saw four police officers with body armor enter.

"Good afternoon. I'm Lieutenant DeLuca and this is Lieutenant Hart. We're with the state police and we need to talk to George Lyon," Finn stated. They'd called ahead to make sure he was there.

"O-of course," the receptionist stammered as she picked up the receiver of her desk phone. "May I ask what this is about?"

"Just tell him the police need to speak with him," Chris said with a tight smile.

Within thirty seconds, George Lyon appeared

from his office. He was a large man, casually dressed in jeans and a western-style shirt. He had obviously been muscular and fit in his youth, but now his gut was straining against his buttons and overhanging a large belt buckle. "What's this about?"

"George Lyon? We have a warrant for your arrest. We also have a warrant to search the premises." Chris showed him the warrants while Finn recited his Miranda rights.

"What the fuck is this about?" He wadded the warrants into a ball and dropped them. "I want a lawyer! Do you hear me? I demand to call my lawyer! What are the charges?"

"Oh, we'll get into all of that down at the precinct, Mr. Lyon. You're welcome to have your lawyer meet us there. I'm sure your secretary can call for you," Finn said as Chris handcuffed the man.

"Goddammit! Call my lawyer, Gina."

Mac could still hear him hollering as Chris escorted him out the door and down the hall. He turned to the receptionist with an apologetic smile. "Sorry about all this. You can have Mr. Lyon's attorney meet him at the state police precinct on Copper Avenue."

She met his gaze with a sardonic smile. "I'll be sure to tell him. When I get around to calling him."

Mac raised his eyebrows, surprised, then nodded as he ushered the rest of the state police team inside the office. He gestured to the warrant Chris had set on the woman's desk. "You can read over everything in that warrant they're allowed to search.

You don't have to help them, but please stay out of their way."

She smiled as she stood. "Well, I don't work here anymore, Officer...?"

"MacNeil, ma'am."

She retrieved her bag from a desk drawer and walked to the door. "Under the circumstances, Officer MacNeil, I don't think I need to give two weeks' notice." She tossed him a set of keys. "Lock up when you're finished. Or not. I really don't care." She turned back with her hand on the knob. "George Lyon is a bigoted asshole. I have no idea what he did, but I hope you put him away for a long time."

Darius whistled as she sauntered away. "That is one pissed-off secretary."

Mac chuckled. "I kinda like her. Let's see what goodies we can find in Lyon's files." They had told Chris and Finn they would oversee the search and meet them back at the precinct to catch up on what, if anything, Lyon said. Two hours later, the uniformed officers had finished and loaded at least ten boxes into their van. Mac locked the office with the keys Gina had given him and followed Darius downstairs to the workshop area to find the mill supervisor.

Back at the precinct, Mac and Darius watched through the one-way mirror into the interview room as Chris and Finn questioned Lyon. Darius reached to press the speaker button so they could hear.

"Nothing, Mr. Lyon? Your company has donated over two hundred thousand dollars this year alone to a known domestic terror organization and you have nothing to say?" Chris asked.

"Those were tax deductible donations made to a 403b charitable organization. I think you'll find my company was well within the law, Detective." He had replaced his earlier anger and bluster with a cool, calculated expression, complete with an irritating smirk.

"Homeland Security disagrees, Mr. Lyon," Finn added. "They seem to think you're supporting terrorism here in New Mexico."

"Well, I think I'll wait until my lawyer arrives to say anything else." He crossed his arms and smiled coldly at the detectives.

Finn and Chris asked a few more questions, but Lyon remained silent, so they had him taken to a cell while they stepped out of the interview room.

"He's not talking," Finn said.

"We noticed. Hopefully you'll get enough evidence from the boxes we brought back from his office to charge him. You guys will check to see if there's any evidence he hired the driver of the car that hit Izzy, won't you?" Mac asked.

"Of course." Chris smiled sympathetically and led them to the break room. "How's she feeling today?"

"I heard she's feeling really good," Darius said with a chuckle.

Mac punched him—hard—on the upper arm as Finn narrowed his eyes at both of them.

"That's my sister you're talking about. I gotta tell you, MacNeil, I'm not crazy about the thought of you bragging to your partner about sleeping with her." Finn stepped close to Mac, threat oozing out of every pore.

"I didn't—"

"Whoa! Dial it down!" Darius slid between the two angry men. "My fault! Sorry! I was way out of line. Mac didn't brag or say anything."

"Then how'd you know? What was with your stupid-ass comment about her 'feeling really good'?" Finn's jaw flexed as he stared Darius down.

"Uh, well, he just had a…well, kind of a shit-eating grin when he came to work this morning…" His words faded as he realized he wasn't making it any better.

Finn rounded again on Mac. "She has a concussion, you ass!"

Mac scrubbed his hands over his face, unsure how to deal with an angry brother.

Chris pulled her partner away. "Calm down! Jesus, Finn! Izzy is a grown woman and can sleep with her boyfriend if she wants. She certainly wouldn't appreciate your interference."

He ignored her and pushed his way back to Mac. "If you hurt her—or Janey—I will bury you, MacNeil."

"I wouldn't expect anything less," Mac said. "I'm in love with your sister, and Janey is my daughter. I would never knowingly hurt either one of them. You have my word on it."

Finn crossed his arms and frowned. "And?"

"And what?"

"Are you going to stick around this time? Are you going to marry her?"

"Finn!" Chris exploded. "That's none of your

business!"

"Yes, it is." Finn didn't take his eyes off Mac.

"If she'll have me. But I haven't asked her yet, so I'd appreciate if you kept this to yourself. For now, at least. The one thing I can tell you is: I'm staying."

Finn stared for a long moment before finally nodding. "Good. Don't wait too long."

"I won't."

He and Darius took their leave, correctly judging that the former easy camaraderie with the detectives was at an end, at least for the time being.

Darius waited until they were seated in their car. "Dude, I'm really sorry. That was a shitty thing to say. I was way out of line."

Mac sighed and started the engine. "It was and you were. We've known each other a long time, Dar, so don't take this the wrong way, but if you ever say anything like that about Izzy again, I'll have to kick your ass."

Darius simply nodded. "Man, your future brother-in-law is pretty intense. Holy shit!"

"He's actually the easy-going one. Wait 'til you meet Hugh."

"Is he the one who tried to punch you?"

"No. That was Tony, her little brother."

Darius shook his head. "Better you than me, bro. Kendra's an only, thank God."

They drove in silence, Darius no doubt relieved he'd gotten off so easy and Mac contemplating what he'd told Finn he intended to do with regard to Izzy and Janey. *I'm going to marry her, if she'll have me. Then we'll be a family: Izzy, me, and Janey.* Of course, he needed to run these ideas past Izzy and, oh, yeah, actually propose to her at some point. It was probably way too soon in their relationship to be thinking about marriage, but he thought this might count as extenuating circumstances. He wondered if he should be operating a motor vehicle with the crazy swirl of thoughts running through his head. Mac's phone buzzed as he pulled into a parking spot at their office building. The name and picture on the screen brought a smile to his face. "Hey, Dad. What's up?"

"Well, I know I said I couldn't come for a visit right now because of this contract I've been working on, but there's been a delay. Long story short, I packed a bag and managed to luck into a stand-by flight. I'll be landing in Albuquerque around five this evening."

Uh...Mac's brain had a hard time processing what his father was saying. "That's, um, that's great, Dad. I'll, uh, I'll take off a few minutes early and be there to pick you up." He was thrilled at the thought of a visit from his dad, but the timing was...not ideal.

"No need for that. I'll rent a car and meet you at your place. Text me the address."

"Sure." He gave himself a mental shake. "Dad, this is great. I can hardly wait to see you. I'll send you my address as soon as I hang up. I'm really glad you're coming." He'd called him within hours of finding out about Janey and his dad was every bit as excited as Mac thought he'd be, but was in the middle of a contract job and couldn't get away for a few weeks.

"Will I be able to meet her tonight?"

Mac smiled. "Yeah, of course. I'll call Izzy and let her know. Ah, Dad, you're going to love Janey; Izzy too. I can't wait for you to meet them."

"Me, neither. Listen, I've got to run or I'll miss my plane. See you soon, son."

Chapter Nine

Izzy

She took a short nap after her dad dropped her off and woke feeling refreshed and almost back to normal. The headache was finally gone and she decided to head to the grocery store, then swing by the daycare to pick Janey up. Her phone rang as she was about to lock up.

"Hey, hon. How are you feeling?"

She smiled as he spoke, realizing the sound of his voice made her happy. "Great. I went to lunch with my dad and took a nap. My headache is gone, so I'm going to make a quick trip to the grocery store, and then I'm going to pick Janey up so you can just come straight home. Anything specific that sounds good for dinner?"

"Listen, Izzy, I'm glad you're able to pick her up because my dad is flying in this afternoon. I'm supposed to meet him at my place."

"Oh. Wow, Mac. That's great. I didn't know he was coming."

Mac laughed. "Yeah, me neither. I invited him when I first learned about Janey, but he couldn't come right then. He called a few minutes ago and said he was unexpectedly available and found a last-minute stand-by flight. Listen, I know the timing's not great, but he really wants to meet Janey. Tonight, if possible."

"Of course. I can hardly wait to meet him. Bring him for dinner. Is there anything he's allergic to or hates?" She fished in her purse for the list she'd created earlier.

"Why don't I take everyone out for dinner? I don't want you to have to cook."

"I don't mind. Besides, I think it would be nice to be relaxed at home when Janey meets her grandfather for the first time. You've seen how shy she gets around new people."

He was silent on the other end for a moment. "Are you sure, sweetheart? I don't want this to be a giant pain in the ass for you."

"Mac," she said with an exasperated sigh. "Stop worrying. I'm fine, and I am happy to fix dinner for your father. Are you happy he's coming for a visit?"

"Yeah, of course. I'm dying for him to meet our daughter and you, but, well, I guess it means I can't stay with you tonight and that kind of bums me out."

She thrilled to hear him call her 'our daughter' but was less than thrilled at the rest of his news. "Well, that sucks. I just lured you into my bed and you've already found a way to escape?"

He laughed and she could imagine he was running his hand through his short brown locks.

"Believe me, hon, escape from your bed is the last thing on my mind, but I can't exactly hand Dad a house key and tell him I'll see him in the morning."

"No, I suppose that would be tacky. How tacky would it be to ask how long he's staying?"

He chuckled. "Not tacky at all, but he didn't say." He spoke to someone on the other end, his voice muffled as if he'd put his hand over the microphone. "Listen, hon, I gotta go. At least let me pick up dessert, okay? I hate the thought of you slaving over a hot stove all afternoon."

"I'm going to shove my mom's lasagna in the oven and make a salad. There will be very little slaving involved. I love you, and I'll see you tonight."

Janey was confused when Izzy told her about their dinner guest. "But I already have a grandpa." She frowned as Izzy buckled her into her car seat.

Izzy had never believed in shielding Janey from the truth of their situation: she was a single mother and had never been married. She wasn't ashamed of it and certainly didn't want Janey to feel there was anything wrong with the way she was being raised. Izzy had four brothers and a father to help make sure the little girl had plenty of male influence in her life. But Janey's father was back, and things were different now. "Poppa Tony is my father, so he's your grandfather. But Mac also has a father and he's your other grandfather."

Janey thought about this for several minutes as Izzy backed out of the parking spot and turned onto the street. "Does Mac have a momma? Is she my other grammy?"

"Mac's mother died a long time ago, sweetie."

"That's sad, Momma. Did Mac cry?"

Izzy bit her lip as she watched Janey in the rearview mirror. Her daughter had such a tender little heart, often crying over small injustices the rest of the world seemed to callously brush off. "Oh, Janey. I'm sure he did, but it was twenty years ago, baby."

"That's a long time."

Two hours later, the house smelled like an Italian bistro and Janey was setting the table, adding a specially chosen *My Little Pony* beside each plate. "Mac gets Big Macintosh 'cuz it sounds like his name. My new grandpa gets Prince Shining Armor. Momma, do you want Rarity or Fluttershy?"

"Hmm, tough choice. I think I'll go with Rarity tonight." Izzy set the salad on the table and checked the clock. Mac was due any minute and she was slightly nervous about meeting his father. What would he think of her, a woman who'd gotten pregnant after having a one-night stand with his son? She'd spent an inordinate amount of time choosing the perfect outfit and making sure her makeup was fresh, but still subtle. At that moment she heard a key in the front door and rushed to the living room. Mac entered, followed by an older man who was slightly taller than Mac with gray-brown hair and hazel eyes. He looked fit and was exceptionally handsome, a trait he'd clearly passed on to his son.

"Hey, beautiful." Mac held a brown bakery box in one hand, but encircled her waist with the other and pulled her close for a kiss.

"Daddy!" Janey ran to him, throwing her arms around his legs.

He smiled at Izzy and handed her the box before bending down to hug Janey. "There's someone I'd like you to meet, Princess." He picked her up and turned to his father. "Janey, this is my dad. Dad, this is my daughter, Janey. She's your granddaughter."

Izzy wasn't surprised when Janey hid her face against Mac's neck, but she noticed her peeking out at her grandfather.

Mac let it go for the moment and reached a hand to Izzy. "Dad, this is Isabelle. She's Janey's mother. Izzy, this is my dad, David MacNeil."

His father stepped forward and shook her hand. "It's wonderful to meet you, Isabelle."

"Please call me Izzy." She shut the door and gestured for them to follow her to the dining room. "Would you like a glass of wine?" At his nod of assent, she poured them each a glass of the merlot she'd bought earlier.

"What's that?" Janey, still in Mac's arms, pointed to the brightly wrapped package David had set on the table.

David smiled. "Oh, it's a present I brought for my new granddaughter." He shrugged casually and sipped his wine.

"That's me." She squirmed in Mac's arms.

He set her down and winked at Izzy.

"You know, I think you're right. This present must be for you." David sat and handed her the gift.

She looked to her mother for permission, then took the box from his hand. It contained a small stuffed dog, a chocolate lab puppy. Janey adored it, judging by the hug and kiss she bestowed upon it. She stepped closer to her grandfather. "Thank you."

"You're very welcome."

"My other grandpa is Poppa Tony. What's your name?" She took another step closer.

David frowned, as if thinking. "Well, I'm not sure. How does Grandpa Dave sound?" It was abundantly clear he'd put some thought into it beforehand.

"Okay. Do you want to come see my kitten, Grandpa Dave? My daddy gave her to me for my birthday and her name is Sophie." She held her hand out for him, the stuffed dog tucked under her other arm.

Izzy was sure she saw his eyes mist as he took his granddaughter's hand and followed her to find Sophie. "Come help me in the kitchen for a minute, Mac." She tugged his hand and pulled him into the kitchen.

"Sure. What do you need—" He was stopped by Izzy's mouth pressed against his.

"I need you, but I'll settle for a kiss," she murmured against his lips, then kissed him again. She opened her mouth under his and welcomed his warm tongue against her own. She moaned and stepped closer. "Are you sure you can't stay tonight?"

"I wish, but it wouldn't be very nice to hand my dad the keys and send him back to my townhouse alone." He wrapped his arms around her waist and pulled her close as he kissed her again deeply. "All right." He set her slightly away. "We'd better focus on dinner for now or I'm going to end up dragging you into your bedroom so I can have my wicked way with you."

She laughed. "That would be awkward with your dad and Janey here wondering what happened to us. If you'll get the lasagna out of the oven while I slice the bread, we'll be good to go."

"Man, this smells great." He found the oven mitts and lifted the casserole from the oven. "Janey did really well meeting my dad. I was worried."

"The present helped. She's shy around new people, but usually gets over it fairly quickly. Your dad is very handsome. Now I see where you get it."

"Flattery will get you everywhere, sweetheart." He winked at her and carried the lasagna to the dining room.

Dinner was lively; David was a fun guest and included Janey in the conversation throughout the meal, asking her about her preschool, her favorite foods, and her family. He seemed fascinated by the vast amount of aunts and uncles in her life.

"You are so lucky to have such a big family, Janey! I was an only child and so is your dad, so he doesn't have any aunts or uncles or cousins," David said.

"I'm gonna have a cousin soon. My Auntie Mel is having a baby. My Uncle Finn said it would be my cousin."

"That will be nice for you."

Janey slipped out of her seat and sidled next to David. "Can I sit on your lap?"

Izzy smiled wryly as she watched her small daughter wrap her newly discovered grandfather around her little finger. "Who's ready for dessert?"

Mac had brought a small berries and cream cake from Whole Foods. He sliced and served it while Izzy poured decaf for the adults and milk for Janey, who decided it was the best cake she'd ever had. Mac volunteered to help Izzy clear the table and stack the dishes in the dishwasher while David followed Janey to the living room.

"Do you want to play *CandyLand*, Grandpa Dave?"

"I would love to."

Mac tried to get Izzy to sit while he did all the work, but she was having none of it. She felt almost back to her old self and needed to be busy.

"I love your dad."

"Me too." He closed the dishwasher and took the empty lasagna pan from her.

"Just let that soak in the sink." She put the last of the leftovers in the refrigerator. "So, are you going to show your dad around Albuquerque tomorrow? It's Saturday, so you don't have to work, right?" She knew he typically had weekends off, but he'd said he sometimes had to go in if there was a pressing case.

"Um, yeah. I guess that would be a good idea. Where should I take him? You're the lifelong Albuquerque resident."

"Well, Old Town is always good. It's kind of cold to take him up the tram; you might want to save that for a spring visit. Is he a *Breaking Bad* fan?"

"Yeah. We both are."

"You could take him on a tour. There are official ones but you can also look up locations online and just drive around."

He grabbed her hand as she passed and pulled her down to sit on his lap on a kitchen chair. He pushed her hair behind her ear and began to nibble her neck. "Let's meet for breakfast and spend the day together, as a family."

She shivered as his lips found an especially sensitive spot. "That sounds wonderful. We have a family dinner on Sunday to celebrate Seamus's birthday. It would be great time to introduce your dad to the rest of my family."

His hand slid under her sweater and up to caress her breast over her silky bra. "Good plan." He found her earlobe and gently bit it, then soothed it with his tongue. "I love the taste of you. It's my favorite flavor in the entire world."

She wriggled closer, thrilled to feel his reaction against her thigh. "Mac," she sighed. "Tonight will be endless."

He nodded then retrieved his hand from under her top. "All right, witch. Enough of your seduction." He swatted her lightly on her bottom. "Let's go see if our daughter has found her way through the Molasses Swamp yet." He'd been a frequent competitor in all of Janey's favorite games over the past few weeks.

Since it was a Friday night, Janey was allowed to stay up later than usual. After her bath, she trooped back to the living room, wearing pink footie pajamas and cuddling her kitten. She curled up between Mac and David while they all watched the movie she'd requested, the latest animated animal hit which her Uncle Hugh had bought for her a few days previously. With all the excitement of the evening, she didn't last forty-five minutes before she fell asleep. Mac scooped her into his arms and carried her down the hall to her bedroom.

David was looking weary, as well, after a full day of traveling and meeting his granddaughter, so he and Mac took their leave. Izzy locked up behind them and went through the house turning out lights and straightening up—anything to avoid going to bed alone. *Oh, for heaven's sake! You've only slept together three nights! You shouldn't be missing him this much already!* But her heart had different ideas, and when she finally slipped under her comforter, it was only to toss and turn for hours. His pillow still smelled like him, so she pulled it closer and finally fell asleep.

***

Mac

He couldn't recall seeing his dad this happy in a long, long time. He and Janey had totally hit it off and she had insisted on walking beside him, holding his hand, as they strolled through Old Town, looking at the unique southwest architecture and the silver and turquoise jewelry sold by Native Americans sitting on blankets in front of the shops. They'd met for breakfast at Weck's, one of Mac's favorite places, and he'd introduced his dad to the amazing world of huevos rancheros: eggs, beans, and hash browns on a corn tortilla, smothered in red chile and cheese. When Janey got tired of walking,

Mac and David took turns lifting her up to their shoulders. They had lunch at La Posada, an iconic restaurant in Old Town with a tree growing in the middle of the dining room, which fascinated Janey. After lunch they walked across the street to the Natural History Museum, Janey's all-time favorite. When she got a bit cranky, Izzy suggested it would be a great time to make the hour-long drive to Santa Fe, so Janey could nap on the way and hopefully wake up in a sweeter mood.

It worked, for the most part. She claimed she was tired of walking around and looking at stuff and couldn't they get a drink? Mac could see Izzy was starting to lose patience with their daughter, so he offered to take her to find some hot chocolate while Izzy and David explored the Palace of the Governors, the oldest continually occupied government building in the United States.

"We'll meet you there in about an hour, okay?" He took Janey's hand and led her across the street to a coffee shop. He was happy to take her; his back was stiff today and the slow pace of museum walking wasn't helping. He hadn't rested well the night before, tossing and turning for hours before finally falling into a restless sleep around three in the morning. He was thrilled his dad was there— he'd been trying to get him to come for a visit since he'd moved to Albuquerque—but he longed to hold Izzy in his arms. And he missed getting up to check on Janey in the middle of the night. He sternly told himself to man up and get a grip.

He and Janey enjoyed a mug of hot chocolate apiece and shared a slice of frosted gingerbread.

She seemed to perk up and kept up a running chatter while they ate.

"Why didn't you stay last night, Daddy? Sophie and me missed you." She had an adorable chocolate/whipped cream mustache.

He contemplated correcting her grammar—Izzy surely would—but decided to let it go. "Well, Princess, I needed to be with my dad at my house. I didn't want to leave him alone on his first night in town."

"He can stay at our house too!"

Mac chuckled. "Maybe next time. Hey, your mom said tomorrow is your Uncle Seamus's birthday, so why don't we pick out a present for him after we finish here?"

Janey was amenable, so they looked in the shops nearby until Janey found a fireman action figure she thought looked just like her uncle and said he would love. They had it gift wrapped and Janey proudly carried the bag as they went to find David and Izzy.

It was nearly nine o'clock by the time he and his dad pulled into his garage at the townhouse. Both were weary as they set their various packages of souvenirs they'd found on the kitchen table.

"You want a beer, Dad?" Mac opened the refrigerator and offered one to his father.

"Sure. I was wondering if I could also get a spare key to the house? If you don't mind."

"Of course." He shut the fridge and went to rummage through his junk drawer for the set he remembered stashing there. "It will keep you from being housebound when I'm at work Monday."

"I was actually thinking it would enable you to

go back to Izzy's house tonight." He watched his son over the top of his beer.

Mac could feel the heat creeping up his neck, much like when his dad had found a box of condoms under his bed when he was seventeen. "Oh, um, no, Dad. That's not necessary."

"Will, I'm not judging." David smiled. "The cat's already out of the bag that you've slept with her, you know. A five-year-old daughter is a dead giveaway. I just had no idea how close you are now. I was too busy meeting Janey to notice yesterday, but I'm awake today and aware. I could hear you tossing and turning all night. Go be with your family, son. They need you."

"Are you sure?" He wanted to, of course, and was barely able to keep himself from grabbing his car keys and flying out the door.

"Positive. If you're smart, Will, and I think you are, you'll marry that girl as soon as possible. She's a keeper."

Mac grinned as he shrugged back into his jacket. "She sure is. Good night, Dad. Why don't you come over to Izzy's for breakfast tomorrow?"

The best feeling in the world was letting himself into Izzy's house ten minutes later and stepping into her arms. Janey was already asleep, but they walked to her bedroom hand-in-hand to check on her before retiring to Izzy's bedroom. He locked the door and then took his time stripping off her clothes, kissing and tasting each square inch of skin as it was bared to him. He took it slow and made sure she found her pleasure twice before reaching for a condom. When he was finally inside her, he rolled them so she was on top and in control, letting her set the pace of their loving.

"Have I told you how beautiful you are today, love?" He smoothed his hands over her warm skin.

"I don't think you mentioned it." She leaned down and took his mouth in a deep kiss. "Shh," she whispered against his lips. "No more talking." Then she began to move and he forgot how to think.

***

Sunday was wonderful, starting with breakfast at Izzy's—he taught Janey how to make French toast—and ending with the birthday celebration at the DeLucas'. The family seemed much more relaxed about him, although Finn did give him the evil eye when he first walked in, holding Izzy's hand. Mac simply ignored him; the whole DeLuca clan had better get used to the idea of him being around from now on. If they didn't like it, they could just go...whatever. He knew he needed to find a way to be charitable toward his future in-laws.

"This is quite a family, Will." His dad spoke quietly as they stood together at the rear of the group watching Seamus open his gifts. "It's good to know Izzy and Janey had such a good support system these past few years."

Mac closed his eyes as he nodded, acknowledging the hit of guilt. "Yeah. I would have been here if I could have." *And if I'd known her name.*

David patted him on the back. "I know, Will. I

179

wasn't trying to make you feel bad. What happened with you and Izzy was unfortunate."

"It sucked."

"Yes, it did. But you're here now and that's what matters." He paused while they both watched Janey proudly present her gift to Seamus.

"My daddy helped me pick it out. Happy birthday, Uncle Seamus." She handed him the present and sat on his lap while he opened it. Seamus seemed to get a kick out of the action figure and told Janey he'd set it on his fireplace mantle as soon as he got home. Mac noticed Seamus's girlfriend, Sloane, didn't seemed thrilled by the idea. He knew neither Izzy nor Janey cared much for the woman and he had to agree with them. She was beautiful—model level gorgeous—but positively oozed control issues. Mac had tangled with women like her before and could see the signs. If Seamus was smart, he would run far and fast in the opposite direction.

***

On Monday morning, right after he arranged for his dad to meet him and Darius for lunch, Chris called.

"Lyon is out on bail." She didn't waste any words on a greeting.

"Son of a bitch," Mac muttered.

"Sorry, Mac. The judge wouldn't hold him without a strong link to the hit-and-run. We've come up empty, for the most part, on evidence he's done anything more than make extremely generous donations to the Southwest Anti-Poverty League. His lawyer claims Lyon had no idea they were in any way connected to domestic terrorism."

He scrubbed his hand over his face as he listened. "This is a fucking nightmare. Okay, I'll see if I can get the evidence bumped to a higher priority on our end. Shit."

"I know. Listen, what I *can* do is put a tail on him for a couple days." She was silent for a moment. "I'm worried about Izzy too."

"I know, Chris. Thanks. Can we meet later to go over the interview transcripts?" He needed to see them for himself.

"Sure. Meanwhile, he won't be able to take a shit without us knowing about it. Try not to worry."

Easier said than done. He spent most of the afternoon sweet-talking the guys in the evidence room to fast-track the analysis of the copies of the files they'd received from the state police. In the end, it cost him the two box seats to the University of New Mexico Lobos' final basketball game of the season he'd been hoping to share with his dad, but it was a price he was willing to pay. He probably would have had a rough time dragging his father away from Janey for an entire evening, anyway.

Once he'd managed to light a fire under the forensic team, he headed to the state police precinct to read Lyon's interview transcripts. Chris wasn't there, but Finn set him up in a small room with the transcripts and videos from the interviews. He even unbent enough to offer Mac a soda from the break room, which gave him some hope for their future relationship.

Lyon didn't say much in the four hours of interview Mac searched. The lawyer seemed to do nearly all the talking, stating repeatedly that George Lyon was an honest business owner and philanthropist. Lyon Architectural Millwork was a family business and his father had instilled in him the need to give back to the community that supported his family for so many years. As far as he knew, the Southwest Anti-Poverty League was a charitable organization devoted to education and the relief of poverty for low-income residents of New Mexico, Arizona, and West Texas. He had no knowledge, and was appalled, that it was connected to domestic terrorism.

After nearly two hours, Mac could find nothing incriminating in anything Lyon or his attorney said. He clicked the monitor off and stuffed the pages into the file folder. *What an epic waste of time!* The guy seemed to be clean and Mac had no idea what he was supposed to do next. *What I do know is the woman I love was nearly run down and there's no way it was an accident.* He drove back to his office and was soon engrossed in some mindless paperwork while the Lyon Millwork case ran through his mind. He suddenly remembered the photos he'd taken of some of the evidence before it was returned to George Lyon. He sent the pictures to his desktop so he could get a better look at them and began to search for anything interesting. It occurred to him that Lyon could easily have cleaned up the records between the time Izzy sent them back and Homeland Security had taken control of them. The only problem was he didn't know what to look for. He decided to send the photos to the guys in forensics so they could compare them to the records they already had. As he was attaching the last photo to the email, he noticed something he hadn't caught before: in the upper corner of the photograph was a small slip of paper attached to the main document he'd photographed. He zoomed in on it and saw a handwritten memo:

AMCI: March.

Izzy had insisted she'd seen it and there it was. He saved the close-up and sent it with the email. Then he spent forty-five minutes trying to find any reference to the letters *AMCI* without success. It was a conundrum, but at least he could tell Izzy she was right. He made a few notes about things he wanted to look into the next day, then turned off his computer and headed out to pick up Janey from daycare.

He shared what he'd learned with Izzy as they prepared dinner that evening. David was entertaining Janey in the living room while they worked to get dinner on the table and Mac found he enjoyed working alongside her, watching her slim figure flit around the kitchen. He stepped behind her as she stirred ground beef in a skillet, sliding his arms around her waist as he pushed her dark hair aside to kiss her neck. "This is one of my absolute favorite places to kiss," he murmured.

"Mmm. Mine too. What's one of your other favorite places?"

He whispered his answer in her ear and enjoyed

the flush that crept up her neck and cheeks.

"You're so naughty, Mac." She stirred the meat then turned in his arms. "I love it." She gave as good as she got, whispering sexy suggestions of her own.

"You think Janey or my dad would notice if we just slipped off to your bedroom for a while?"

She laughed and kissed him before turning back to the stove. "I think they might. So, back to the investigation. You didn't find anything about what *AMCI* stands for?"

"Not a thing." He reached for plates and began setting the table. "Have you thought any more about the car that hit you? You said a few days ago it might have been a woman who was driving the car instead of a man. I was just wondering if there was some reason you said it. What did you see, Izzy?"

She shook her head as she added marinara sauce to the ground beef. "Nothing, really. It was just an impression, I guess. I remember thinking about a ponytail while I was in the hospital, but I'm not sure why." She set the lid on the pan and turned the heat down to low. "Ugh! It's so frustrating, Mac!"

"Hey." He pulled her to him and wrapped her in his arms. "It's okay, sweetheart." It wasn't—not really—but it served no purpose to freak her out. "Listen, hon. Would you be willing to talk to someone about that night?"

She stared into his face, a frown between her brows. "A shrink? You want me to talk to a psychiatrist? Am I not getting better?"

"No, no sweetheart! That's not it, I promise! I was thinking about a hypnotherapist, actually. You

184

might remember more about that night if you underwent hypnosis. The FBI has some great people we've worked with in the past when a witness can't remember important details."

"I don't know, Mac. It sounds pretty far out there."

Mac chuckled and stroked her face. "It's not. I've seen it done. I've even been under myself a few times. It's not a big deal and it might help you remember."

She sighed and leaned her head on his shoulder. "Will you be with me? The whole time?"

"Of course. I'll stay with you the entire time, angel." He stroked his hands up and down her back.

"Okay. Fine. Can we do it tomorrow? I don't want to think about it for too long." She chuckled ruefully. "I'm a big chicken."

He pulled her head up and framed her face in his hands. "No, you're not. You're the bravest woman I've ever known, Izzy, and I love you more than I can say." He kissed her tenderly, trying to show her what he couldn't begin to put into words.

Chapter Ten

Izzy

Mac parked his SUV in front of the low adobe building and killed the engine. He wore his khaki and denim uniform and carried his badge and gun since he planned to go in to work after her appointment. "Izzy, love." He reached for her hand. "You don't have to do this. We can go home."

She'd been staring out the passenger window, chewing on a fingernail and dreading what she was about to do. Now she turned to him with a crooked smile. "Really? You'd let me forget about all this? You'd take me home if I asked?"

"Of course." He took his hand from hers and reached for the ignition switch.

She watched as he prepared to restart the vehicle, realizing she was witnessing evidence of his love for her: she knew how much he wanted her to undergo hypnosis so he could get the information he needed to solve the case, but he was willing to take her home because she was afraid. Deep shame washed over her. "No." She touched his arm. "Let's go in."

He stared at her, searching her face. "Are you sure, sweetheart?"

She smiled and nodded. "Yes, I'm sure, Mac." She wasn't. The idea of undergoing hypnosis freaked her out. She'd tossed and turned for hours the night before, finally getting up and moving into the living room so Mac could get some undisturbed rest. She'd read until 3 a.m. and was tired and grainy-eyed this morning. She shook her head and released her seatbelt.

Mac met her around her side of the SUV and pulled her into his arms. "There's nothing to this, hon, and I'll be right beside you the whole time. I promise."

She kissed him softly and pulled back to look into his handsome face. "I'll be fine. I don't know why I'm being such a baby about it." She chuckled ruefully. "The thought of someone messing around in my mind totally wigs me out."

"It's not like that. You'll just talk to the therapist and you'll be really relaxed." He took her hand and pulled her gently toward the entrance.

Once inside, they found the suite marked **'Southwest Counseling Professionals'** and Mac held the door for her. He checked them in, then joined her in the small reception area. They weren't kept waiting long. A sharply dressed, slim, middle-aged woman entered the waiting room from the hallway behind the reception desk and approached them. She had short, stylish salt-and-pepper hair and wore black-framed glasses. Izzy hoped she aged

187

as gracefully as this woman obviously had.

"Isabelle? I'm Renee Madrid," she said, shaking hands with both of them. "And you must be William. Come on back." She led them to her office, a surprisingly spacious room painted a muted gray with dusky purple couches piled with inviting throw pillows. The paintings on the walls were abstract, with large swaths and swirls of colors that made Izzy think of frosting. The lighting was dim and soft music played, obviously meant to promote relaxation, although it failed where Izzy was concerned. She tried to swallow her nerves as Mac ushered her toward the largest sofa.

"Should I lie down?" Izzy asked as she sat.

"If you like, but it's not necessary."

Izzy decided to sit and gave Mac a look that made it clear she expected him to sit next to her. "I want Mac to stay while you hypnotize me." She knew she probably sounded borderline bitchy, but she couldn't seem to help herself.

"Of course." Renee's voice was quiet and soothing, without even a hint of amusement. "I know you're nervous, Isabelle, but I want to assure you this will be very easy. You don't even have to close your eyes. You'll be aware of everything that goes on and you'll remember everything."

Izzy listened to her soft, even voice and felt herself relaxing a bit.

"You won't do or say anything embarrassing. I will not implant any sort of post-hypnotic suggestion or anything else you may have heard about or seen on television."

Izzy nodded and wiped her sweaty palms on her

slacks. "Okay."

"Good. Let's begin."

Izzy reached for Mac's hand again and took a deep breath. "Ready."

"Let's start with breathing. I want you to breathe in through your nose and out through your mouth. That's it. Keep it easy and rhythmic. Concentrate on your breath." She demonstrated and then breathed along with Izzy for several long moments. "Good. Keep it going. Now let's focus on relaxing your muscles. Soften your face and neck. Feel the tension slip away."

Izzy consciously relaxed her facial muscles and shrugged her shoulders a few times, trying to get her neck to loosen up.

"Don't fight it, Isabelle. Just let it happen. Let the tension seep out of your body."

As Izzy listened to Renee, she felt herself relaxing bit by bit. The therapist continued speaking, gradually lulling Izzy into a state of utter relaxation, something she would never have believed possible. Her eyelids drifted shut as she melted into the sofa, her head resting against the back.

"How are you feeling, Isabelle?"

"Hmm. Good. Calm." She tried to pry her eyes open, but it was too difficult. She felt like she was floating and it was wonderful.

"Excellent. Let's go back to the night of the accident, okay?"

"Okay."

"Let's go back to that night. I want you to picture yourself there. Where are you?"

"I'm with Cara. She's my sister. We're at a new sushi place on Central she wanted to try. It's really good and we're having fun." She smiled and laughed softly. "She wants to hear all about how things are going with Mac. She's so nosy."

"Most sisters are. What are you eating?"

"I'm having the spicy tuna roll. Cara's eating the caterpillar roll and we're sharing."

"Good. Tell me what happens when you leave the restaurant."

"I'm in front of Cara. She's wearing these ridiculous heels she paid way too much for and she's fussed with them all night. They're supposed to be Jimmy Choo, but I think she bought fakes. She has to stop yet again to fix the damned strap as we're leaving and I'm sick of it. Yeah, they make her legs look great, but it's the middle of winter, for heaven's sake! I tell her she can catch up with me and I start to cross the street." She frowned as the rest of the memory flooded into her mind.

"Isabelle? What's happening?"

"There's a car. It came out of nowhere! God, it's going so fast!" She whimpered and felt Mac squeeze her hand. Her heart pounded as she gasped for air.

"Breathe, Isabelle. Concentrate on your rhythm. Good. Now, tell me what happens after you saw the car."

"I can't move. I freeze. The car is coming right at me! I'm going to die." She drew in a ragged breath and felt Mac's arm slip around her and pull her close.

"Slow down, Isabelle, and tell me what you see.

You're safe here. Nothing can harm you. What does the car look like?"

"Black. It's big and black. It's shiny."

"Can you see the driver?"

"No. It's...I can't. The woman's head is in the way. Her ponytail..."

"There's a passenger? Tell me about her."

"I don't...she has a long, dark ponytail, but I can't see her face. I'm trying to move. I jump but the car gets my leg. Ugh! It hurts! Oh, God, it hurts!" She could feel the sharp pain rip through her calf again. "I'm falling! My head–"

"Okay, Isabelle. Breathe. That's good. Let's come back now. You're here in my office. William is with you."

"Mac?" She couldn't feel his hand any longer as her leg and head continued to throb.

"I'm here, love." He grabbed her hand again and squeezed gently.

"Open your eyes now, Isabelle."

She obeyed without thought and lifted her lids slowly. She was still in the therapist's office, sitting on the purple sofa next to Mac. "Wow. It was like I was there again! I remembered. There was a woman in the car that night. She had a long ponytail." She reached down to rub her calf, which still throbbed a bit.

"Did you see her face, Izzy?" Mac asked.

She frowned and shook her head. "I don't think so. I'm sorry. This wasn't very helpful."

"Izzy, hon." He turned her to face him. "It helped a lot." He lifted her chin and smiled at her.

"Really?"

"Absolutely." He reached to pull her leg into his lap and gently massaged around the nearly healed stitches. "We know there was someone in the car with Maldonado. We'll go back and examine the security videos again. How's your leg?"

She stilled his hands. "It's fine. It's kind of crazy how a memory could make it ache again, huh?"

"It's a fairly common phenomenon for patients under hypnosis. I'm sorry you had to feel that pain again, Isabelle." Renee stood, signaling the session was at an end.

Izzy smiled crookedly. "Well, it wasn't super fun, but I'm okay with it if it ends up helping the investigation."

"Take it easy for the rest of the day, if possible. Call me if you have any problems." The therapist held the door for them and followed them to the front desk.

Mac took her hand as they walked to his car. "I'm really proud of you, *Isabelle.*" He smiled crookedly, teasing her.

"Why thank you, *William.* I'm kind of proud of myself. A little bit." She held her thumb and forefinger closely together in front of her face.

He brought the hand he was holding up and set it next to her other. Then he spread them far apart. "How about this proud?" He leaned in to kiss her quickly. "Are you still planning to go into work today?"

"Yeah, of course."

"I wish I could convince you to take one more day off."

"That's not necessary. I'm fine and I have to run

payroll today. You need to stop worrying, Mac."

He pulled her close and draped his arm over her shoulders. "Not even remotely possible, love. If I can't talk you into going home, can I at least take you to lunch?"

"Sure. I was too nervous to eat breakfast, but I'm starving now. Can we do Mexican?"

He grinned and kissed her temple before reaching to open the passenger door for her. "I'm always up for Mexican."

She directed him to Monroe's, one of her favorite restaurants, which he said he hadn't tried yet. "They have the best salsa in town." They chose their seats and placed drink orders. "I need to run to the bathroom. Excuse me." Izzy stood and pushed her chair in.

She was washing her hands at the sink when the bathroom door swung open. She glanced up at the mirror and saw the reflection of a woman with long brown hair enter. The counter was directly in front of the stalls and it was a tight fit, so Izzy straightened and slid as close to the sink as possible to allow the woman to pass. She was annoyed when the woman crowded against her anyway and started to give her a dirty look.

The woman stepped even closer and grabbed Izzy's hair, pulling her back against her tall body. "Hello, Izzy. Remember me?" she growled in her ear.

Izzy began to scream, but the woman slapped her hand over her mouth.

"None of that. I promise you'll regret it."

Izzy felt something sharp prod at her back below

her ribs. Her scream turned into whimper.

"Wise decision. My first attempt to shut you up didn't go quite as I planned, so I decided to go for a more direct approach."

Izzy felt the knife push harder against her, breaking the skin and sinking in painfully a few centimeters. She felt the warm, wet flow of blood seep into the waistband of her slacks. Abject terror flooded her as she realized she was completely at the mercy of this unknown woman.

"Oh, I'm not going to kill you. At least, not right now. I'm simply here to let you know what a terrible idea it would be to tell anyone about what you saw in the financial records from Lyon Millwork. We'll consider this a little warning, a reminder to keep your goddamned mouth shut." The knife pushed a bit deeper, causing the blood to flow again. Then the knife was removed and the woman swiftly exited the bathroom.

Izzy reached a trembling hand to her side and felt the warm, sticky blood soaking through her shirt. She didn't think it was terribly deep or serious, but she felt woozy nonetheless, most likely from the shock of having a knife pulled on her. She'd stupidly left her purse and cell phone at the table with Mac, so she knew she had to get herself out of the bathroom. She stumbled to the door and made her way to the edge of the dining room. She could see Mac at their table across the room, his back to her as he sat facing the door, like cops tended to insist upon. She hated to cause a scene, so she clasped her arms against her side to hide the worst of the blood and walked shakily to Mac.

***

Mac

She sure is taking a long time in the bathroom. He grabbed another tortilla chip and scooped it into the salsa bowl. He shoved the entire thing in his mouth, savoring the blend of tomatoes, jalapeño, onion, and green chile with just the right amount of cilantro. Izzy appeared and slowly slid into her seat. "You were right about this salsa, hon. It's the best I've ever—what's wrong?" He frowned as he noticed how pale she was and how she was clutching her side.

She peeled her hand away from her body and he saw it was covered with blood, as was her blouse.

"Shit!" He leapt out of his seat and knelt beside her. "What the hell happened?" He gently lifted her blouse and saw a small cut just above the waistband of her slacks. It looked fairly deep.

"Please, Mac. Can we go? People are starting to look over here."

He didn't give a flying fuck if everyone in the restaurant was watching, but he knew Izzy would be embarrassed. It couldn't be helped, however. He turned to wave down the waitress. "I need a first aid kit!" He turned back to Izzy. "What happened?"

"A woman." She hissed as he touched the skin near the wound. "In the bathroom. She slammed me up against the sink and stuck a knife in my back."

"You were mugged in the bathroom? Is she still here?" He swept his gaze wildly around the restaurant. "What did she look like?"

195

"I don't think she's here. It wasn't a mugging. She was the one who tried to run me over, the one in the car." Izzy was valiantly trying to hold back her tears. "She warned me not to talk about what I found in the Lyon files."

The waitress returned with a first aid kit and the manager. Izzy appeared mortified to see all the people around their table craning their necks to check out what was going on. "What happened?" the manager asked. "Should I call an ambulance or the paramedics?"

"No!" Izzy exclaimed. "Please, no. I'll be all right."

Mac ignored her. "Call the police. She was attacked in the bathroom." He flashed his badge and explained he was with Homeland Security, which seemed to propel the manager to action. "Izzy, what did she look like?"

Izzy described the woman—long brown hair, tall—and Mac stood to look around the restaurant.

"I saw her," the waitress said. "She left in a hurry a couple minutes ago."

Mac cursed under his breath and knelt again beside Izzy to examine the wound. "All right. This looks pretty deep. I think you may need a couple stitches, so I'll take you to the emergency room after we talk to the police."

"Fine." She looked exhausted suddenly and he wanted nothing more than to wrap her in his arms. The police showed up within minutes—a violent attack in a restaurant apparently rated higher than a traffic accident—and Izzy repeated her story several times. They asked her to stop by the downtown police headquarters later that day so she could sit with a police sketch artist.

Mac drove her to the emergency room as soon as the police released them and the emergency room doctor cleaned her wound and applied liquid stitches. It wasn't serious, but it also wasn't simply a scratch. She insisted they go home so she could change clothes before they went to the police station, saying she had some hope of soaking her slacks in cold water before the blood completely dried. The blouse was a complete loss and he winced as she threw it in the trash.

"I am officially over this whole thing, Mac! I never wanted to be part of a police investigation!" She slammed the lid of the trash can and marched to her closet to find another.

"Hey." He rose from the bed and walked to stand behind her. He placed his hands gently on her shoulders and watched her face in the mirror on the closet door. "I know, sweetheart. This sucks, but we're going to find her. I won't let this happen again. I'll keep you safe from now on." The guilt burned through his gut; he'd been right there, only a dozen or so feet away while some bitch shoved a knife in Izzy's back!

Izzy turned in his arms and began to cry softly. "I was so scared, Mac. She could have killed me."

He let her cry it out while he stroked his hands over her back, careful to stay away from the bandage. He was scared too. He couldn't be with her every second of the day and night. And what about Janey? If they could find Izzy while she was at lunch, they certainly knew about her daughter.

"Why don't you get a new shirt on and we'll head to the police station." The sooner they got a sketch of the unsub, the sooner he'd be able to sleep at night.

While she was in with the police sketch artist, he spoke to the captain on duty and arranged for a protective detail for Izzy and Janey. Once that was taken care of, he knew he needed to notify her family. He sighed and realized the best one to call was Finn; he'd be pissed to hear it from someone else, and he'd be able to rally the others quickly. Plus, as a police officer, he'd understand what was happening better than any of her other siblings. *Shit. I am not looking forward to this conversation.*

Finn answered on the first ring. "This is DeLuca."

"Finn, it's Mac." He told him, as succinctly as possible, what had happened to Izzy. "We're at the downtown police station now. She's still in with the sketch artist, but we should be finished soon."

"Are you heading back to Izzy's house? Chris and I will meet you there. I'll handle telling the rest of the family. Goddamn it, Mac! What about Janey? Who's picking her up?"

"Shit. I haven't gotten that far." He scrubbed his hand over his face as he realized all the details he hadn't thought of. "We'll pick her up on the way home. I've already arranged for protective details for both Izzy and Janey, but I'm sure they're not at the daycare yet." His blood ran cold at the thought of anyone hurting his daughter.

"Chris and I can head over right now and pick her up. I'm on the approved list, so it shouldn't be a problem. Can you give them a quick call and tell them we're on our way and let them know to be extra vigilant about Janey for the time being?"

"I'll do it as soon as I hang up with you." He speared his hand through his hair, causing it to stand on end. "Thanks, Finn. We'll meet you back at Izzy's place as soon as we're finished here." He pushed the end button and shoved the phone in his pocket before joining Izzy in the small room with the sketch artist.

"Can you make the jaw a bit more angular?" Izzy asked as she peered over the woman's shoulder. "And maybe arch her eyebrows a little more?"

The artist made the changes requested and presented the sketch for Izzy's approval.

"Well, it's the best I remember. It's not exactly like the woman who attacked me, but I can't think of anything else to change." She shrugged and handed it to Mac.

He frowned as he stared at the drawing; it reminded him of someone, but he couldn't think who. He handed it back to the artist. "Is she finished?"

The woman nodded and left, taking the drawing with her.

He explained about the protective detail as he drove them back to Izzy's house.

"I just want to lock Janey and myself inside the house until they catch that woman. I don't suppose that's very practical though, is it? Aren't we going to pick Janey up?" She turned to him, frowning, as he drove past the freeway exit that would take them to the preschool.

"Finn and Chris are getting her. They'll meet us at the house."

She sighed and reached for his hand. "Along with the rest of my family, I suppose. Well, it's for the best. They'd all throw a fit if they found out later. Who did you call?"

"Just Finn. He said he and Chris would take care of calling everyone else." He rubbed his thumb across her soft fingers as they drove.

The driveway and curb in front of her house was packed with cars when they pulled up ten minutes later, including a police car.

"Looks like your protective detail is here."

Inside, the house smelled like coffee and was buzzing with conversation. Janey ran to meet them at the door and Izzy knelt on the floor to hug her tightly.

"Momma, why is everyone here? There's a policeman too! Grammy is making him coffee in the kitchen." Janey pulled away from her mother and frowned.

"Hey, Princess." Mac scooped her into his arms. "Your mom's had a rough day. Let's go sit on the couch and I'll tell you what's going on." He told her as succinctly and calmly as possible about how Izzy was attacked and injured in the bathroom while they were at lunch. He didn't go into great detail, but he had promised never to lie to her again and figured she deserved to know why she would be watched extra close in the next few days. He prayed it would only be a few days before they caught the woman.

"Did Momma ever get to eat lunch?" Janey asked, her green eyes wide.

Mac stared at her, dumfounded for a moment. "Uh, no. I guess neither of us did."

"I'll tell Grammy." She hopped from his lap. "She'll make you something." She skipped into the kitchen, leaving Mac to marvel at her sweetness and practicality. He'd told her about some pretty scary stuff and she took it all in stride, choosing instead to focus on more practical matters. He stood and went to find Izzy.

She was talking to her older brother, who had apparently decided to take the blame for the entire situation. "Knock it off, Hugh. It's certainly not your fault and no one blames you."

"I'm the one who asked you to look through those goddamned files in the first place!" He spit the words out and Mac could see his jaw pulsing.

"That's just business, Hugh. You had no idea Lyon Millwork was anything except a legitimate option for our finish carpentry contract. Please don't waste time beating yourself up about this, okay?" She hugged him quickly and turned to Chris. "A little help here?"

Chris calmly sipped the coffee she'd brought from the kitchen. "Oh, I've already told him the exact same thing at least a dozen times. He's too stubborn to listen to anyone and prefers to obsess over it and take all the blame. It's a common trait amongst DeLuca males, or so I've heard."

"Hey!" Finn approached holding two beers. He handed one to Hugh. "So she's on to us already, huh?"

"I'm sure she figured it out about thirty seconds after she was assigned to be your partner," Mel said as she slipped her arm around Finn's waist. She was sipping a cup of tea, chamomile, by the smell of it. Finn draped his arm over her shoulder and kissed the top of her head.

Mac watched the two married couples as jealousy—sharp and cutting—stabbed through his gut. The intimacy between a loving, married couple was different than that between a girlfriend and boyfriend. He glanced at Izzy and saw her watching Finn and his wife, a soft, somewhat sad expression on her face. He sighed and reached for her hand. "I think your mom has some food for us in the kitchen, love."

"What?" She looked up at him blankly.

He leaned down and kissed her softly. "You haven't eaten all day. You were too nervous to have breakfast and lunch was interrupted. Janey is worried."

She smiled and nodded. "Yeah. I could eat."

***

It was past midnight when they were finally able to seek their bed. They'd had to repeat the story of the events of the day again and again to her various family members and finally to his dad, whom he'd called after they'd eaten the small meal Moira prepared; David had hurried to Izzy's house to be with the rest of the family. He'd been great, keeping Janey occupied while the rest of the adults discussed the attack on Izzy and what the police were doing to find the woman. Moira and Hugh had both volunteered to keep Janey for the night, but

Mac and Izzy refused, saying they needed their daughter at home. There would be no protective detail while Mac was with them, but it would pick up in the morning when Izzy was at work and Janey at daycare.

"It's been a hell of a day," she murmured against his chest.

He chuckled and caressed her bare shoulder. "God, I'm glad it's finally over. I'm exhausted, but I doubt I'll be able to fall asleep. How's your back?"

"It's okay. I took an ibuprofen a little while ago." She was silent for a time. "Mac, I feel so helpless and I hate it. Twice now someone has almost killed me. Isn't there anything I can do to protect myself? Can you teach me how to shoot a gun or wield a knife or something? Please?"

"I don't think carrying a weapon is a good idea, love."

"I don't love the idea, either, but I have to do something! It's so frustrating!" She made to roll over, away from him.

"Hey, come here." He pulled her back to his side. "I didn't say I wouldn't help. How about I teach you some self-defense moves? It would make you feel a little bit more empowered, at least."

"Really? That would be great, Mac! Can we start tomorrow?"

"I promise we'll start as soon as your wound is healed. You need to take it easy for a week or so."

"I'm getting pretty sick of being injured." She ran her fingers through his chest hair, tracing his tattoo. "Since you can't sleep, I can think of something to pass the time."

He stilled her fingers, bringing her hand to his lips. "Not tonight, sweetheart. You need to rest." He rolled to his side, turning her and spooning against her warm body. "Go to sleep, Izzy. I love you."

She sighed, but snuggled into him. "Love you too, Mac. I'm so glad you're here."

"Always, love." He listened to her breathing, waiting for it to even out as she slipped into sleep. She had to be utterly exhausted. He knew how draining a large hit of adrenaline, like she'd experienced during her attack, was on a body. She was sound asleep within five minutes, her soft snores causing him to smile. He slipped out from under the covers, pulled on a pair of sweatpants, and treaded softly from the room and across the hall to check on Janey. She'd thrown off her covers and her little feet were icy. He warmed them in his large palms for a moment before tucking her under her thick pink comforter. He kissed her forehead before doing yet another sweep of the house, triple checking all the windows and doors to make sure they were securely shut and locked. He finally slipped back into bed beside Izzy, vowing nothing and no one would ever harm them again.

Chapter Eleven

Izzy

This protective detail is going to drive me insane! She shut her office door behind her, leaving the uniformed police officer—it was Kelly today— to cool her heels in the reception area with Malva. There was no other way into her office except through the waiting room, so the officers assigned to watch her all day, every day, were willing to let her have a bit of solitude and privacy while at work. She turned on her Keurig and sat at her desk while she waited for the coffee to brew. She set her elbows on her desk top, steepling her fingers under her chin. *How much longer can this possibly go on? I need my life back!* There was an officer waiting to take her to work every morning while another waited at the preschool when Mac dropped Janey off. This had to cost some city or state agency a freaking fortune, and she wondered how much longer it could possibly continue. Judging by the frown lines that had taken up permanent residence between Mac's eyes, not too much longer. The coffee finished brewing and she stood to retrieve it from the machine. She stopped in front of her window, sipping the strong, dark brew while she stared outside. She knew she should be grateful for the protection—and she was—but it was beginning to wear on her, causing her to be short-tempered and snappish. Mac was moody and withdrawn, and Izzy didn't know how to reassure him. Janey was the only one in the household happy with the new state of affairs. She seemed to love the extra attention and had made friends with all the officers assigned to watch her, choosing small toys and books from her collection to take for them every day.

"But, Momma," she'd said as she kissed her mother goodbye earlier that morning. "I have to take them for my policeman! I don't want him to get bored while he watches me. He has to stand in the hallway all day! And when we go to the playground, he doesn't get to play with anything!" Janey held a bulging tote bag in her hands, stuffed to the brim with the little girl's daily offering for her assigned officer.

The worst part was how distant and preoccupied Mac had become since Izzy had been attacked at the restaurant. He'd turned her down the first night when she'd suggested they make love, which was understandable considering her injury, but he'd refused her every night since, saying he needed to be alert. He stayed up late, finally crawling into bed next to her well after midnight, and got up before her alarm went off. She didn't know what to do or say to get through to him, and was afraid about what it meant for their future. Was this his way of starting to distance himself from her? She knew he loved Janey and would always want to be part of her life, but what if he was already tired of being in a romantic relationship? Her stomach hurt to think about not having him in her life. Why was love so hard? Wasn't it supposed to be all sunshine and rainbows...at least for a while? They'd barely had any time before life became so difficult. A soft knock sounded on her door, so she plastered a smile she wasn't feeling on her face and turned. "Come in."

Hugh entered, a thick ivory-colored envelope in his hand. "Hey, Iz. Listen, I've messed up and I need you to bail me out."

She chuckled. "What have you done?"

He folded his long frame into one of the pretty accent chairs and sighed. "I RSVP'd for this fancy pants lunch the mayor's giving next Friday, but I can't make it. I need you to go in my place. Pretty please with sugar on top?" He flashed her a pleading glance from his bright blue eyes.

"Why can't you go?" She plucked the invitation from his hand and sat on the sofa to read it.

"Because Chrissy has the day off and I promised her we'd ride the train to Santa Fe and stay the weekend at the La Fonda. You wouldn't want me to disappoint my wife, would you? She's been working too hard lately and we desperately need a romantic getaway. Come on, Iz. Be a pal?"

"I hate this kind of stuff, Hugh." She read through the invitation—a $100 per person plated lunch at the downtown Hyatt Regency—and sighed. "But fine. I'll do it for Chris. You are *so* going to owe me, big brother." She folded the invitation and stuffed it back inside the envelope. "The La Fonda, huh? I've heard it's really nice. You'll have to let me know. Maybe I could convince Mac to go some weekend. We could use some time away."

"Yeah, I'll let you know. Has he had any luck finding the woman who attacked you?"

She shrugged and stood to retrieve her coffee. "Not yet. It's really starting to get to both of us."

He stood and flung an arm around her shoulder, hugging her to his side. "They'll figure it out. Mac and Chrissy and Finn won't stop until they find out who is trying to hurt you." He let her go and crossed the room to make himself a cup of coffee. "I wasn't sure about Mac at first, but it's become pretty clear he loves you and Janey more than life itself. He's a good man, Izzy. Sorry I was such an ass at first."

"At least you didn't try to punch him."

He laughed. "I won't say I wasn't tempted, but I'm glad I resisted. It was a lot more entertaining to watch him take down Tony like that than it would have been to be the one taken down. And I've no doubt Mac could take any one of us, even Finn with all his cop training. Your boyfriend is a little bit scary."

"No, he's not. He's gentle and kind, and the best thing that's ever happened to me." She ended in a rush, horrified to realize she was crying. She started to leave the office, but Hugh lunged to his feet and pulled her into his arms.

"Hey, shh." He patted her back. "I know it's

rough right now, but it'll be over soon."

"What if it's not? What if they don't catch her? Mac is barely talking to me anymore, and he doesn't even come to bed until early morning. I hate this, Hugh!"

"Okay, I know." He continued to attempt to soothe her. "Listen. You can't do anything about the investigation, but why don't you take the afternoon off and see if Mac can take a couple of hours too? Maybe a little uninterrupted time together—without Janey—would be good for you."

"I don't know if he'll agree. He'll probably say he can't afford to take the time away."

"Well, you'll never know unless you try." He stepped away and picked up his mug. "You know, I didn't think you, of all people, would give up so easily on something so important. Huh." He shrugged as he sipped his coffee.

She frowned, then squared her jaw and pushed back her shoulders. "Fine. I know what you're doing, but you have a point. Now, if you'll excuse me, I have a date to arrange." She raised her eyebrows at him and tilted her head toward the door.

Hugh grinned and left, taking his coffee with him.

Izzy sat at her desk, wracking her brains over how to implement what Hugh had suggested. How in the world could she get Mac to agree to take an afternoon off? She knew she'd never get him to agree to take time off during this investigation, but maybe she could finagle a couple of hours alone with him this evening if she was especially clever and canny. A quick phone call to Chris secured the first and most difficult part of her plan, then another to her Uncle Teddy smoothed the way further. One more phone call, and she was good to go. She finished up a few tasks that couldn't wait until tomorrow, then cleaned off her desk and locked her office.

"Malva, I'm taking off early. I'll see you tomorrow. Have a good evening."

"You too, Izzy. Oh, I hope they find that awful woman soon. You give Janey and that hunky boyfriend of yours my love, all right?" The receptionist bustled out from her desk and hugged Izzy.

Izzy hugged her back, smiling at the concern the older woman always showed. She'd been with DeLuca Construction for many years—since long before Izzy's time—and had known all the DeLuca children since they were in diapers. Malva's change of heart where Mac was concerned also amused Izzy. Once she'd learned he was Janey's father and why he'd been absent since her birth, she had accepted him wholeheartedly.

Kelly, her assigned police officer, opened the door for her and then led the way to the police cruiser. Izzy told Kelly where they were headed, then sent a quick text to Mac to let him know she would pick Janey up from preschool so he could come straight home. It was a small fib—for the greater good, she hoped.

Kelly pulled the police cruiser into the parking lot of the day spa, then waited patiently while Izzy enjoyed several hours of luxurious pampering. By the time she walked back to the car with the police officer, she'd had a facial, deep tissue massage, mani/pedi, and Brazilian wax. She was ready for a romantic evening with the man she loved. They stopped by Bella Marcone to pick up the food Izzy had ordered—a perfect evening didn't include slaving over a hot stove—and finally headed home. She fixed tea for Kelly and herself after she put the main dish in the oven on warm.

"Big night, huh?" Kelly asked as she sipped her tea.

"I hope. It's been tough lately, you know? Mac's really stressed." She refused to meet the other woman's eyes, choosing to stare into her herbal tea.

"Hey, I understand. My husband is a firefighter and our schedules can be crazy. He knows your brother, Seamus. They used to be at the same station. Anyway, when we get a night off together, we try to make it special too."

"Do you have kids?"

Kelly shook her head. "Not yet. We're saving for a house first. I'll get out of your hair as soon as Mac gets home. I'm sure you don't want a third wheel hanging around."

Izzy excused herself and moved a small table into her bedroom and covered it with a deep blue tablecloth, then set it with two place settings of her good dishes. She fashioned a centerpiece from a few candles and crystal dishes, realizing it wouldn't do much for Mac, but she was compelled to create a pretty table nonetheless. She glanced at the clock and grimaced; he'd be home in less than half an hour. She rifled through her closet until she found a slinky black dress that clung to her slim figure and was low cut, then dug through her lingerie drawer until she found the lacy black thong she'd bought on a whim on a shopping trip with Cara and had never had the guts or occasion to wear. Mac was going to have to do some fancy talking if he wanted to get out of taking her to bed tonight! She shivered as she thought of his hands removing the dress and skimming over her body. *You'd better hurry home, mister!* She spritzed some perfume Mac said he liked, making sure to get it in a few interesting places, and went back to the kitchen to check on the manicotti.

Kelly looked up as she entered, choked on her tea, and coughed. "Wow. You look amazing, Ms. DeLuca. I guess you weren't kidding when you said you had a special night planned."

"I'm not messing around, that's for sure. I just hope Mac goes along with it." She bit her lip as she worried.

"Well, he's crazy if he doesn't." Kelly stood and crossed the room to put her mug in the sink. "I'll wait in my patrol car until he gets home. He should be here within a few minutes. I think I better plan a similar evening for my husband soon. It seems like it might be just what we need."

She was tossing the salad when she heard the key in the lock. She set the salad aside and went to greet him.

"Hey, hon, where's Janey? I figured—" He froze as he caught sight of her coming out of the kitchen. "Oh, my God. You look amazing, Izzy. Are we going somewhere? Did I forget something? I'd rather stay home in the evening until we find the woman who attacked you."

She shook her head and smiled, trying to quell the nervousness in her stomach. "We're staying in tonight. Janey is with Chris and Hugh."

"But her protective detail stops at five o'clock. She should be here with me." His words lacked the conviction they might have held if Izzy had been wearing more clothes. And if she hadn't stepped as close to Mac as humanly possible and wound her arms around his neck.

"Do I need to remind you that Chris is a police officer? And Hugh would die before he let anything happen to Janey." She angled her head to run her lips along his scratchy jaw. "We need some time alone, Mac. Please. This whole investigation and protective detail thing is making us both crazy. I miss you. I miss us."

He drew back and stared into her face, his bright green eyes concerned. "Ah, God, Izzy. I'm sorry. I've been preoccupied by this whole thing, haven't I? The truth is, I'm scared shitless by the thought of anyone hurting you or Janey. I'm not sure I can keep you safe. It's all I can think about."

She smiled softly and leaned in to kiss him, putting her whole heart and soul into it. She molded her lips to his, letting her tongue slip between to tangle with his briefly before pulling away. "I absolutely believe in you, Mac. But tonight, for one night, let's forget about it and focus on each other." She kissed him again, begging him with her mouth, her lips, to see things her way.

He resisted for a long moment and she knew he

was thinking of all the reasons he should say no and continue his obsessive patrolling and checking of the house. She slid one hand from his neck and covered his heart, feeling how it pounded. He brought his own hand up to cover it as he surrendered to her. His lips took over the kiss, his tongue demanding, taking, as his hand slid from atop hers and curved around her waist and down to her bottom, pulling her hard against him. She felt his desire for her, hard against her stomach, and exulted in it. With his other hand he slipped the spaghetti strap from her shoulder and let his lips wander from her mouth, down her neck, and onto the smooth stretch of skin he'd bared.

"You smell divine, love." His hand slid up to cup her breast through the soft fabric.

"Oh, God, Mac. That feels so good. Please don't stop."

He lifted his head and grinned at her, before sliding the fabric away and replacing his hand with his lips.

She let her head fall back as she reveled in his love making. "I had planned for us to have dinner first," she managed to whisper.

He grunted and managed to pry his lips away from her briefly. "Later." Then he stood, scooped her into his arms, and carried her to the sofa. "I'm going to make love to you right here. And I'm not going to be quiet about it."

He certainly wasn't. He'd definitely been holding back on account of their daughter sleeping across the hall. He pulled her onto his lap, sliding the dress down to her waist, and filled his hands with her bared breasts.

An hour later, she lay drowsing against his chest and wondered when he'd covered them with the blanket. "Mac," she breathed.

"Izzy. Love." His voice was gravelly with the aftermath of their loving and his exhaustion.

"I think we should have dinner now."

He chuckled wearily and brushed her hair away from her face. "Give me a minute, okay? I think you might have killed me. I'm not as young as I used to be."

She pushed herself up and smiled into his handsome face. "You did pretty well for an old man."

"Pretty well?"

"Don't worry. I'll give you another chance later. Maybe you can make it to 'really well.'"

He swatted her bare bottom and swung her off the sofa. "Watch it, brat." He pulled on his boxer shorts as he spoke.

She laughed as she searched around the sofa. "Where are my underwear?"

"I'm not sure this tiny scrap of cloth qualifies as underwear." He held her black thong dangling from one finger.

She smirked and took it from him, slipping the lacy fabric over her hips. "You don't like it?"

He pulled her into his arms and slid his hands down to run over the thong and all the skin it bared. "On the contrary, I adore it. I think I'll have it framed and hang it on my cubicle wall. It will remind me of this night."

She laughed and danced out of his arms. "Not on

your life! Can I wear your shirt?"

He tossed it to her and groaned in appreciation as she slipped her arms into the sleeves, which hung far below her wrists. He stepped close and rolled them up. When she reached to fasten the buttons, he stilled her hands. "Don't." He slid his hands inside to cup her breasts. "This is more fun."

"Agreed." She let him fondle her for several moments, then took his hand and led him to the kitchen. "Time for food. I'm starving."

***

Mac

"Here." Mac set the green and white paper cup on Darius' desk. "I want to see the security feed again from the night Izzy got hit by the car."

Darius glanced at his watch and frowned. "Thanks. Everything okay at home? I was starting to get worried."

Mac felt the heat creep up his neck. "Sorry I'm late. Everything's fine. I just…I mean we…I guess I forgot to set my alarm."

Darius narrowed his eyes at his partner. "Hmm. I've known you for over a decade and never once have you forgotten to set your alarm." He raised his eyebrows in appreciation. "I see." He chuckled and punched Mac lightly on the arm.

Mac coughed and busied himself sorting papers on his desk. "I think I've mentioned before that mine and Izzy's sex life is off limits. Can you do something useful and get a copy of the security video?"

Darius laughed and picked up his phone. "Fine. Spoilsport." He spoke for a few minutes, then grabbed his coffee and left.

Mac shook his head and rolled his eyes. He *had* forgotten to set his alarm; Izzy had seduced him so completely he hadn't remembered. Not that he was complaining, of course. He probably should have had a clue something was up when she texted to tell him she'd pick up Janey, but he hadn't suspected a thing. He'd been so preoccupied lately with the safety arrangements he hadn't had much of anything left at the end of the day for Izzy. His mistake had been in assuming she was okay with that. She clearly wasn't and he felt like the world's biggest asshole for making her feel rejected. God, as if he'd *ever* not want her! He'd thought he was doing the right thing, but he apparently had a lot to learn about Isabelle DeLuca. He'd nearly swallowed his tongue when she walked out of the kitchen wearing that dress. It hugged every curve and pushed her creamy breasts up and nearly out. He loved how it left very little to the imagination, but doubted if he'd ever let her out of the house in it. His big brain had quickly taken a well-deserved vacation and his insistent little brain had taken over. He'd slipped that amazing dress off her, tasting each square inch of warm skin as he bared it. The surprises continued when the dress was puddled on the floor and he caught sight of the lacy black scrap she wore as panties. Good God! Hell yeah! She always wore pretty underthings, but nothing like that thong! Just thinking about it was making him heated and uncomfortable. He'd completely lost his head and taken her on the couch, for chrissake! They'd finally eaten the delicious manicotti while standing at the kitchen counter, digging their forks into the foil dish from her uncle's restaurant. He'd barely tasted the food, completely distracted by the glimpses of her small, taut breasts between the front panels of his shirt, which she'd donned after they made love. They shared a bottle of dark red wine; he savored the taste of it on her lips as he backed her against the counter and slid the shirt off her shoulders. Making love in the kitchen was a bit of an adventure, but they'd managed well enough. He'd certainly never look at the kitchen table the same way again. They'd shared the cheesecake she'd bought for dessert while sitting cross-legged on her bed, naked. He couldn't recall exactly how many times they'd made love, but he couldn't resist one more time when he woke up this morning, the sun just beginning to peek through the shades. They'd fallen asleep afterward, neither waking for hours. All in all, it was one of the best nights of his life. They were both late for work, but it was completely worth it and he was determined to secure more nights like it by making Izzy his wife. He thought about the diamond and sapphire ring he had tucked away in the back of the drawer of the nightstand by his side of the bed; he wanted to propose, but he thought she deserved something better than some sort of post-coital, off-hand proposal. She deserved a fancy restaurant or some special place, bended knee—the works. If he could figure out who was trying to hurt her and put them away, he would plan a special evening for them and he'd pop the question.

He forced himself to focus on work and unlocked his desk drawer, shuffling through the files until he found the one he'd started for the investigation into Izzy's stalker, or whatever she was. He re-read the transcript from the interview with George Lyon three times, looking for any clue he'd missed, but it was over fifty pages and he couldn't find anything useful. He flipped the booklet over and found himself staring at a copy of the police sketch of the woman. *Where have I seen her before?* It was maddening, but he couldn't quite place the face. Almost, but it was still out of reach. He ran his hands through his hair as he sat back in his chair and growled in frustration. Darius came in a few minutes later.

"I got it." He sat in front of his computer and plugged in the flash drive. He clicked on the icon on the desktop and the security feed video began playing. They watched it through, then Mac backed it up and zoomed in the car.

"I think I can see the ponytail Izzy talked about. There." He pointed to the screen.

Darius leaned closer, squinting. "If you say so." He continued to look for a moment then sat back. "Did you look over the rest of the evidence?"

"Yeah, but there's sure not much. The interview with Lyon was a bust and I've been staring at that damn sketch every day trying to figure out where I've seen her. It's driving me nuts!"

"Let me see it again." Darius held out his hand for the picture. "Hmm. You know, this kind of reminds me of Lyon's receptionist. What was her name?"

Mac snatched the sketch from Darius and swore. "Shit! You're a genius, Dar. That's why she looked so familiar! This is Gina! Come on! We need to get over to Lyon Millwork now!"

"Whoa, slow down, Mac." He handed the sketch back to him. "It may be the receptionist, but we can't just go rushing over there to confront Lyon." He held up his hand to forestall the objection Mac started to launch into. "We're out of our jurisdiction with that part of the investigation and you know it!"

Mac grumbled but reached for his phone. "Fine. I'll call Finn and see if we can tag along when they go."

The two detectives were happy to have their Homeland Security colleagues accompany them, so Mac and Darius met them an hour later outside Lyon Millwork.

"Okay, Mac," Chris spoke as she studied the copy of the police sketch she held in her hands. "You're sure about this? I didn't get a good look at Lyon's receptionist when we arrested him."

"Yeah, I'm sure. She's the same woman who's been after Izzy. She walked out that day and told us she quit, but we can get her full name from Lyon."

"Well, let's do this. Finn is going to do the talking today; ol' George took a disliking to me when we had him in custody." She shrugged and slipped the drawing in the folder she carried.

Mac resisted—barely—the temptation to check his watch and urge them to hurry. This was the strongest lead—and pretty much the only one—

they'd had so far, and he was eager to verify his conclusions. He clamped his lips together and waited while the others checked their weapons and attended to various other useless details. Finally, Finn led the way into the building that housed the finish carpentry shop.

The men running the noisy machinery looked up curiously as their entourage passed through on the way to the stairwell leading to the upstairs offices. A new receptionist was seated at the desk, this one a middle-aged woman with short, blonde hair.

"How may I help you?" If she was startled to see four law enforcement officers, two with visible sidearms, she covered it well.

Finn flashed his badge as he spoke. "We need a few moments of Mr. Lyon's time."

She simply nodded and picked up the phone. "You can go straight back."

George Lyon glanced up from his desktop computer, grimacing, as they entered his office. "Again? Do I need to call my lawyer?"

"I don't think that will be necessary, Mr. Lyon," Finn said. "We have a few questions for you. It will take just a couple minutes of your time."

"Fine, but if I don't like where this is going, I'm calling my attorney."

"Of course," Finn agreed amiably. Mac had to admire his people skills. "We would like to know more about your previous receptionist, Gina."

"That bitch? Why do you want to know about her?" Lyon stood, agitated, fishing in his shirt pocket for a pack of cigarettes. He lit one, daring the detectives with a glance to naysay him. "She walked out the day you all barged in here to arrest me. She didn't even call my lawyer."

"We need her full name and any contact information you have for her." Finn smiled calmly. "How long did she work for you?"

"Nearly five years." Lyon frowned but picked up his phone. "Grace, get me the personnel file on Gina Rodale."

No one spoke while they waited for the file to arrive. When the receptionist appeared with the file, Lyon took it, opened it, and pulled out a single sheet, which he handed back to the woman. "Make a copy of this and bring it back."

The copy was delivered in under a minute.

"Here." Lyon handed it to Finn. "Anything else? I do have a business to run, you know."

"Of course, but I wonder if we might also ask about your accounting department?"

"Department?" Lyon laughed. "We've never had more than a bookkeeper. I had the same one for years, but he left about four years ago. I haven't much luck finding a good one since then."

"Thank you for your time, Mr. Lyon. We can see ourselves out." Finn ushered the other three toward the door.

As soon as they reached the parking lot, Mac rounded on him, hand outstretched for the paper. He scanned the contents quickly. "She lives in an apartment not too far from here."

"Let's go see if the lovely Gina is home," Chris said. "I doubt we could get a warrant for her arrest right now, but let's see what she has to say."

She was, and answered their knock with a smile.

"Well, if it isn't the delicious Detective DeLuca and your Homeland Security friends. Do come in." She completely ignored Chris as she held the door open wide for them. "What can I do for you?"

"Ms. Rodale," Chris began, "You were working for George Lyon until a few weeks ago. Is that correct?"

"Yes. I walked out the day the old man got arrested. I don't need that kind of drama in my life." She sat in a side chair, crossing her legs, causing her short skirt to ride far up her thighs. She was an attractive woman and obviously used her wiles working on the men in her vicinity.

"And have you found another job yet?" Finn asked.

Gina turned a dazzling smile on him. "No. It seems no one's hiring."

"Ms. Rodale, where were you last Thursday at approximately 12:30 p.m.?" Chris asked.

"Hmm, let me think." She tapped a long, coral-colored fingernail against her teeth. "You know, I don't remember. I was probably right here." She spread her arms and gestured around the tidy apartment.

"Chris, can I talk to you for a minute?" Mac motioned for her to join him by the front door. He turned his back to the rest of the group and spoke quietly. "Can we get her in a line up? Izzy might be able to identify her and the waitress at the restaurant got a good look at her. We're not going to get anything useful from talking to her." He jerked his head toward Gina.

Chris narrowed her eyes at him for a moment.

"We can take her in for questioning and hold her for 24 hours. That should be long enough to arrange a line up." She turned toward the others. "Ms. Rodale, we're going to need you to come with us for more questioning."

"Are you arresting me? On what charge?"

"No, not at this time. But I am requesting that you accompany us to our precinct for questioning." Chris's voice was firm, brooking no refusal.

Gina glared at her and stood. "Fine. Let me get my purse."

Mac noticed the others all reach to rest their hands on their sidearms as Gina fetched her handbag from the hall closet. He'd done the same thing, of course. You could never be sure when a suspect might be reaching for a gun.

It took nearly four hours, but they were finally able to track down the waitress who'd witnessed the woman leave the restaurant after Izzy was attacked. Mac had driven to Izzy's office to pick her up, and now held her hand as she stepped close to the viewing window.

"Number four. That's the woman who attacked me." Izzy's voice was strong, but Mac detected a slight quaver. He squeezed her hand.

"Are you sure, Izzy?" Finn asked.

"Yes," she said with a nod. "I saw her face in the mirror as she stood behind me. That's her."

Chris nodded. "The waitress also gave a positive I.D. You did great, Izzy."

"Are you going to arrest her?" Izzy asked.

Chris nodded. "Yeah. You've been really brave through all this, hon. It's over. We've got her. I've got to question her now. You'll make sure she gets home?" Chris raised her eyebrows at Mac.

"Of course. What about the protective detail?"

"I imagine it will end tonight, once they bring Janey home. If she somehow gets out on bail, I'll make sure it gets reactivated, I promise. I don't think she will, though."

Once in the cab of Mac's SUV, Izzy turned to him, wariness in her eyes. "Is it over, Mac? Really?"

"I don't know, hon. I think so."

She launched herself into his arms and held him, her hands fisting the back of his shirt. "I need it to be over."

He felt the same way, but worried there was more to come.

Chapter Twelve

Izzy

She slid the stuffed pork roast in the oven and turned her attention to the wild rice pilaf she planned as an accompaniment, reveling in the freedom of having her kitchen to herself—no police officer in sight. They'd all been friendly and understanding, but she much preferred this return to normal. Janey was in the family room with Mac's father, watching a movie and coloring. David was leaving the following day, returning to his home in Cleveland, and everyone was going to miss him— especially Janey. Izzy was putting extra effort into the meal, hoping to make it a special farewell dinner. She'd grown to love David over the past few weeks and was sad to see him leave. She knew Mac wished he didn't have to leave, either. He'd been so busy with the investigation—as well as his regular workload—since his dad arrived, he felt like he hadn't spent enough time with him. Izzy was determined to create a warm, loving, and delicious celebration for David's last night with them.

At least Mac was in a better mood since they'd arrested that woman, Gina Rodale. He'd reluctantly accepted the end of the protective detail—he hadn't had a choice, of course—and seemed to finally sleep soundly the night before. Izzy suppressed a shudder as she thought of the woman who'd tried to run her over and had stabbed a knife in her back. *Enough! Don't think about it tonight. She's in jail and my daughter and I are safe.* The future was definitely looking bright and Izzy was ready to embrace it.

The pork roast was nearly done and filling the house with a delectable aroma when Mac got home, a brown bakery box in his arms. "I picked up that cake Janey likes, that berry and cream thing." He set the box on the counter and pulled Izzy into his arms for a long kiss. "Mmm. You taste good."

She grinned and pulled his head down for another kiss. "You too," she murmured against his lips. "Dinner will be ready in about ten minutes. Your dad is in the family room with Janey."

"You need any help in here, love?"

"No. It's all nearly done. Go wash up."

"Yes, ma'am," he said with a half-grin and a salute.

She narrowed her eyes. "Are you implying I'm bossy?"

He laughed, but didn't answer as he exited the kitchen.

"And make sure Janey washes her hands too," she called after him.

***

"Izzy, this is the best meal I've had since the last time I was here." David pushed his plate away and sighed with satisfaction. "I couldn't eat another bite."

"Thanks, David. You are a wonderful dinner guest, the kind it's fun to cook for." Izzy had always enjoyed cooking for an appreciative audience. Janey didn't qualify, as she could exist on quesadillas and macaroni and cheese, and Mac would eat anything, no doubt a product of his many years in the military.

"Grandpa Dave, did you save room for cake?" Janey slid from her chair and moved to sit on her grandfather's lap.

"Well, I don't know." He curled an arm around the little girl while he patted his stomach. "I'm pretty full, but maybe I can manage a small piece."

"We can share a piece, Grandpa!"

Izzy caught David's amused glance, but he readily agreed to share cake with Janey. As she watched her daughter fork a mouthful of creamy frosted cake in her grandfather's mouth, Izzy realized it was one of the precious moments she would keep close to her heart for years to come. She looked over at Mac to see if he had noticed; judging by the misty look in his eyes, he was well aware.

"Dad, are you sure you have to go back to Cleveland? I really like having you here with us."

David swallowed the bite Janey had just fed him, then cleared his throat. "Well, son, I'm glad to hear you say that, because I'm seriously considering relocating here permanently. Everything I care about is in Albuquerque." He paused to kiss the top of Janey's head. "I'm retired and can travel wherever I need for my contract work. I was thinking of going back to finish up the contract I've already promised and see about putting the house on the market."

Mac relaxed visibly. "Ah, Dad. That would be great. We can help you look for a new place, maybe nearby, when you get back."

David coughed slightly. "Um, I was actually thinking maybe I could rent your town house. It's kind of perfect and I seriously need to downsize. I'd be interested in buying it from you if you decide to make this arrangement," he gestured between Mac and Izzy, "more permanent."

Izzy froze with her fork halfway to her mouth. She darted her eyes sideways to see Mac's reaction. Rather than shock, he was smiling crookedly at his father, shaking his head slightly, as if to say, 'well played.' David looked amused and raised his eyebrows at his son questioningly.

"We haven't really had a chance to talk about it yet, Dad. It's been kind of busy and stressful around here lately." Mac calmly forked another bite of cake into his mouth.

"Oh, of course. I thought I'd mention it, nevertheless." He sipped his coffee, a small smile hovering on his lips.

Izzy set her fork on her plate, the bite of cake uneaten and unwanted. *What in the world? This dinner couldn't get more awkward!*

"Can I have a baby brother?" Janey asked.

Well, I guess I was wrong. It can get a whole lot more awkward. Mac dropped his fork with a clatter, David choked on his coffee, and Izzy screeched, "What? Why would you ask that, Janey?"

The little girl appeared completely unfazed by the adults' dramatic reactions. "'Cuz Auntie Mel is having a baby and Uncle Hugh said I'll probably have lots of cousins because he has so many brothers and sisters. I want brothers and sisters too, but I want a baby brother first." She licked the last of the frosting from her fork and smiled up at her grandfather.

"Janey, sweetheart, I, well, we…" Izzy looked helplessly at Mac, begging for help.

Mac laughed ruefully and scrubbed his hands over his face. "Listen, Princess, all I can say is I promise you'll be the first to know if we decide to have a baby, okay?"

"Okay." She seemed satisfied by her father's answer and slipped off David's lap. "I'm going to get my jammies on."

Izzy watched her daughter skip out of the dining room and wished she could escape too. What must Mac be thinking? Poor guy, to be put on the spot like this! She had no idea what to say, so she simply began clearing the table. David, with an apologetic glance, stood to help her.

"I'll go check on Janey," Mac said and escaped.

David told her he'd clear the table while she stacked the dirty dishes in the dishwasher. When she finished, she turned to find him seated at the kitchen table. "I'm sorry, Izzy. I shouldn't have said anything."

She chuckled softly and sat across from him. "It's all right. I think you took us by surprise, that's all. And Janey's question came out of the blue."

"Oh, I don't think Mac was terribly surprised...by *my* question, at least. I'll concede Janey's question was a shock to everyone."

She didn't know what to say, so she fell back on hospitality. "Can I make you some tea, David?"

"No, thank you. I need to get going. My flight leaves early tomorrow."

Mac and Janey reappeared in time to send David off with hugs and kisses and the promise of his quick return.

Once he'd left, Mac scooped a tearful Janey over his shoulder and carried her to bed. Izzy poured them each a glass of Malbec and sat on the sofa, wondering how awkward it would be between them.

Mac came in and flopped next to her. She handed him the wine and wondered what to say, if anything.

"So, that was an interesting dinner," he said and tossed back half the wine in his glass.

"A slight understatement, but yes." She sipped from her own glass, watching him over the rim. "Are you glad your dad wants to move here?"

He smiled and set his glass on the table. "Yeah, for sure. He's the only family I have."

"Hey." She reached for his hand. "You have Janey and me."

He raised her hand to his lips. "You're right. I meant my extended family. I don't have any grandparents left and my dad was an only, like me."

"What about your mother? Was she an only

child?"

He shook his head. "She had a brother, but they weren't close. I haven't seen my Uncle Darren for over twenty years."

"That's kind of sad. My mother's parents live overseas, so I understand. Well, except for the large quantity of siblings I have."

"Yeah, there is that."

They sat quietly for several moments until Izzy couldn't stand it. "Mac, how do you feel about marriage?" At his shocked look, she rushed to continue. "I mean in general, you know? Are you opposed to it?"

"No. Not at all."

"Oh. Good. I mean, well, I wondered if maybe, sometime in the future, of course, if maybe you might want to..." She allowed the words to fade, horrified by what she'd been about to ask. She grabbed her wine and chugged the remainder.

"If I might want to what?" He looked decidedly amused now.

She stood, flustered and embarrassed. "Nothing. I should check on Janey."

He grabbed her hand and pulled her back down beside him. "She's fine. If I might want to what?"

She gulped, took a huge breath and blurted, "Marry me?"

He grinned. "Why, Izzy, are you proposing?"

She wondered if her face was as red as she thought it might be. Sweat beaded on her forehead and upper lip as she looked anywhere but at him. "No, of course not. I mean, if you...well, not that you...shit."

He grinned again and leaned in to kiss her quickly. "You are adorable. Hold that thought, love. I'll be right back." He disappeared down the hall and jogged back less than a minute later. He tugged her to her feet and into the center of the room. Then to her amazement, he knelt on the carpet in front of her, a small blue velvet box in his outstretched hand. He opened it to reveal a gorgeous diamond and sapphire ring, sparkling at her as it caught the light from the table lamp. "Isabelle DeLuca, I love you more than life itself. Would you do me the honor of becoming my wife?"

She let out a soft cry and placed a trembling hand over her lips. "Yes. Yes, I will." She felt tears leak from her eyes and slip down her cheeks as he wrestled the ring from its moorings and slipped it on her finger. It fit perfectly, and she thought he must have snuck a ring from her jewelry box for size comparison. "Mac, it's beautiful. I love you." She stroked his wonderful face, biting her lip, unable to believe this was happening. It was as if she wished it into being.

He stood and pulled her into his arms. "I was planning to wait until I could plan a really special evening, but, well…" He shrugged and smiled crookedly.

"No. This is perfect." She stared at the ring, laughter bubbling from deep inside. "I'm so happy."

"Me too." He kissed her, long and deep. "Are you mad I didn't let you finish proposing to me?"

She hid her face against his shoulder. "Not at all. Oh my God, I did, didn't I?" She felt his body shake with laughter.

"You did, and don't think I'll ever let you forget it. It's going to make a great story to tell our grandchildren." He pulled back and tilted her chin up. "Thank you, Izzy. You've made me so incredibly happy."

"This hardly seems real, Mac. We're engaged." She stared at the ring, loving the way it looked on her finger. "You're going to be my husband."

"And you're going to be my wife." He tugged her hand as he returned to the couch and pulled her onto his lap. "I want you to have the wedding of your dreams, Iz, but please don't make me wait too long. I'm ready to be a family."

"We already are a family." She kissed him and was distracted by his wonderfully scratchy jaw, as she ran her lips across his warm skin. "But we don't have to wait. I don't want a big wedding. I'd like to have my family there, but I've never wanted all the pomp and circumstance."

"Are you sure? I don't want you to feel like you're missing out."

"I'm sure. How about a month? We can surely put something nice together by then."

"I can wait a month. I'd like to make sure my dad can be there." He groaned as she caught his earlobe between her teeth.

"Of course. Mac, I can hardly wait to tell everyone, but tomorrow. Right now I need you." She kissed him, then rested her forehead against his. "Please."

He said nothing, but gently pushed her off his lap as he stood and took her hand to lead her to their bedroom.

***

Mac

He woke minutes before his alarm and reached to turn it off so it wouldn't wake Izzy. He turned to look at his fiancée and saw that Janey had crawled into bed beside her mother sometime during the night. Izzy's arm was around the small girl and both were still asleep. He smiled at the sight and eased out of the bed, hoping to not disturb them. He pulled the comforter up to cover Izzy's arm and found a pair of sweatpants and a hoodie before he went to the kitchen to make coffee. It was chilly in the house and he wasn't surprised to feel a bitter wind when he went outside to fetch the newspaper. Albuquerque winters were nothing compared to the Midwest, but when the wind blew hard through the canyon, it was miserable. He shut the door against the icy blast and turned the heat up a couple degrees. He wanted Janey to be warm when she got up. He was pouring his first cup of coffee when he felt slim arms curl around him from behind. He thrilled at the sight of the sparkling diamond ring he'd placed on her finger the night before. He reached for another mug and poured her a cup before turning in her embrace.

"Did Janey have a nightmare?"

"Mmm-hmm." She sipped the coffee and nodded. "She came in about three a.m."

"I didn't even hear her."

She smiled and kissed him softly. "Neither did I. She was really quiet."

"I think we should tell her first. She should be the first one to know about our engagement."

"Yeah. Then you should call your dad. I hope you can get hold of him before his plane leaves."

"Me too. How do you want to tell your family? All together? One at a time?" He set his coffee down and looped his arms around her waist. He brushed her dark hair, messy from sleep, behind her ear and drank in the beauty of her face. She had beautiful skin, creamy and free of makeup, with the slightest hint of freckles across her nose.

"Hmm, I'm not sure. Let me think about it today. It would be more expedient to tell them all together, but I'm not sure I'll be able to keep it to myself very long. Hugh and Chris are out of town until Sunday, but they'll be back in time for dinner at my parents' house. Maybe that would be the best time to make our announcement."

"Okay, sounds like a plan. What's on your schedule today?"

She grimaced. "I've got a luncheon downtown for the mayor. I'm filling in for Hugh and he owes me big."

He chuckled. "Not your kind of thing, huh?"

"Nope. Pretentious people, rubbery chicken, and boring speeches isn't my idea of a fun afternoon. How about you? Anything interesting on your agenda?"

"Nah. We have a corporate training and then a whole afternoon of paperwork. Not very glamorous, huh?"

"I have a feeling it's a lot more glamorous than my job. I sit in front a computer and run spreadsheets all day." She turned as she heard Janey's slippered feet padding down the hallway. "Good morning, sweetie."

Janey mumbled something unintelligible and sat at the kitchen table, Sophie cuddled in her arms. Her brown hair was a rat's nest of tangles and her eyes drooped sleepily.

"Hey, munchkin." Mac knelt in front of her. "You had a bad dream last night?"

She nodded sleepily.

"You want to tell me about it?"

She shook her head. "I don't 'member."

Izzy set a glass of orange juice in front of her and kissed the top of her head.

"Did Grandpa Dave go on the airplane yet?" Her lip trembled as she spoke and Mac realized how much his daughter would miss her grandfather.

"I'm not sure. You want to call him and say goodbye?"

Janey's eyes lit up as she nodded. "Can we?"

"Of course, but your mom and I have something to tell you first, okay?"

She looked between the two adults warily. "What?"

He couldn't keep a grin at bay as he stood and reached his hand toward Izzy. "Well, last night after you went to bed, your mom asked me to marry her. Ow!" He rubbed his arm where Izzy had planted her fist.

"She did? Did you say yes?" Janey's eyes were wide as she stared from her mother to Mac.

"Absolutely." He grinned and put his arm around Izzy. "I gave her this ring." He took Izzy's hand and displayed the engagement ring to Janey.

"Wow, it's so pretty! So, now can I have a little brother?"

Mac laughed and glanced at Izzy, who was rolling her eyes. "Slow down, Princess. Your mom and I just got engaged. We need a little time before we start talking about babies. But I promise we'll talk about it, okay?"

"Okay. Will you make pancakes?"

Mac shook his head in wonder at the way his daughter could change subjects so quickly. "Sure. Pancakes it is."

***

Darius shuffled into their cubicle and stopped short at the sight of the paper bag on his desk. "Einstein's Bagels? Sweet!" He dug into the bag, pulling out a green chile cheese bagel and taking a huge bite. "What's the occasion?" His words were muffled by the food in his mouth.

"Bagels need no occasion, but I figured they'd be nice on a Friday morning." He waited for Darius to take another gigantic bite. "Oh, and I got engaged last night."

Darius' jaw dropped, a disgusting mass of half-chewed bagel in his gaping mouth. "No shit?"

"No shit." He wondered if his grin was as goofy as he feared. He'd called his dad right after they'd told Janey and had to listen to his insufferable gloating. He'd been happy to hand the phone off to Janey once he'd assured David they would let him know the date as soon as it was official.

Darius swallowed and wiped his hands on a paper napkin. "Congrats, man! That's awesome! When's the big day? I assume I'm invited?"

"You're my best man, so you better be there. We're thinking sometime next month."

Darius grinned. "You're not wasting any time, huh? What, are you afraid she'll change her mind if you give her too long?"

"Something like that. Eat up. We need to head out for the training."

"Yeah, yeah. Give me a minute."

Their active shooter training at the community college went well, mainly because Cara had helped them revise their presentation to make it more engaging—or at least not as deadly dull. They'd made their PowerPoint much more interactive and even gave out small candy prizes for correct answers. Mac saw only two people on their phones, and no one fell asleep, which was a new record for them. Both were in an upbeat mood as they packed their equipment.

"Let's stop at Mario's for lunch," Darius said as he slid the projector into the black case. "I'm starving."

"No arguments from me. Hang on." He fished his cell phone out of his pocket. "This is MacNeil."

"Mac, it's Finn. Can you and Darius get down here to our precinct?"

"Uh, sure. We're on our way to lunch right now, but we can swing by on our way back to the office."

"You can eat later. Come now. Gina finally broke and it's urgent. How long will it take you to get here?"

"Ten minutes." He clicked off and shoved his phone back in his pocket. "That was Finn. He needs us at the precinct now."

"But…shit. Fine." He sighed deeply. "I had my heart set on a calzone."

"Don't be a baby, Dar. We can eat later." He shouldered his computer bag and grabbed one of the boxes. "Let's go."

***

Finn was waiting impatiently at his desk. Mac remembered Izzy telling him Chris was in Santa Fe with Hugh for the weekend. "We finally got some intel from Gina." He directed their attention to his computer screen and clicked the 'play' icon. "I've cued it to the relevant part." He stood back to let them watch.

They saw Gina and Finn in an interrogation room, Gina's attorney at her side. The man spoke, reading from a prepared statement. He made it clear that Gina was willing to trade information about upcoming threats from the Southwest Anti-Poverty League in exchange for the charges of attempted murder being dropped. Finn said he could make no promises, but would see what he could do if the information was good. Mac clenched his fists when he thought about the woman who had hurt Izzy getting off with a lighter sentence, but he knew it was how the game was played.

"What have you got, Gina?" Finn asked. "You dragged us all down here, so spill."

"So impatient, Detective." Gina made a clucking sound and examined her fingernails. "I could sure use a cup of coffee."

Finn stared at the woman for a moment, a slight smile hovering on his lips, but said nothing as he stood and left the room. He returned a few moments later with a steaming Styrofoam cup and set it in front of Gina, along with a handful of sweetener and creamer packets and a stirrer stick.

Gina meticulously prepared her coffee, stirring it far longer than was necessary. She finally took a sip, grimaced, and set it down.

Finn sat back in his chair and crossed his arms. "I have a lot of other work to do, Gina. I don't think you have anything new." He stood. "I'll have you taken back to your cell."

"Wait." Gina glared at her lawyer, then turned back to Finn. "I know what the next target is."

Finn returned to his seat. "Okay. I'm waiting."

"It's the governor. She's the target."

"When? Is there a specific event?" Finn pulled a small notebook from his shirt pocket.

"Maybe."

Finn smiled tightly and glanced up from his notebook. "I'm running out of patience, Gina."

Gina took another sip of her coffee. "That's unfortunate."

Finn slammed the notebook shut and stood, striding to the door. "Forget it." He opened the door and called to the guard standing outside.

"It's a ribbon-cutting ceremony for the new gymnasium at a school," Gina called.

"What school?"

"The Santa Fe School for the Blind."

Finn grabbed his cell phone and talked quietly for several moments before cursing and swinging back to the two people seated at the table. "Goddammit, Gina! That ribbon-cutting ceremony is today!"

"Is it really? Huh." She sipped her coffee, unconcerned.

Finn stopped the video and addressed Mac. "I called you right afterward. I alerted our office in Santa Fe and the governor's office, but I knew you'd want to know."

"Thanks," Darius pulled out his phone and walked away. He returned a moment later. "We have a helicopter waiting on the helipad."

"Let's go. We'll keep you informed." Mac led the way out of the office.

Twenty minutes later they were en route to Santa Fe, onboard a Homeland Security helicopter. Within twenty-five minutes they were landing in a field adjacent to the School for the Blind. They flashed their identification and joined the ground team gathered near the entrance.

"The governor is set to arrive in ten minutes. She refused to cancel the event." The speaker was a state police captain who was clearly in charge. "We've set up a perimeter and have a team sweeping the school right now." He continued to talk about the details, unrolling a set of building plans as he spoke.

Mac and Darius had come solely to lend their support and provide backup if necessary, so they stood at the back of the group and listened. When the captain finished, Mac spoke up. "Captain, my partner and I did the initial threat assessment for the governor. Nothing about the Southwest Anti-Poverty League turned up. We're here to help."

"Thanks. I'll have you talk to the governor and her staff when they arrive. If you can get them to call it off at the last minute, it would be helpful."

"We'll do our best." He and Darius turned and jogged to the area set aside for the governor's motorcade. Mac could feel his phone buzzing in his pocket, but declined the call when he saw it was Izzy. He knew she'd understand when he told her what he was in the middle of. Early on in their relationship he'd let her know he might occasionally have to ignore her calls if he was knee-deep in a case or situation. The governor's black SUV turned in at that moment. His phone buzzed three more times as they greeted the governor's team and he felt the first twinges of alarm. It wasn't like her to keep calling. They weren't successful in convincing the governor to cancel the event and had to settle for briefing her on the possible danger she faced during the ceremony. It was nearly fifteen minutes later when he was finally able to look at his phone again. The banner on his home screen indicated he had a voicemail. His gut clenched as he listened. He tapped the screen to call her back; no answer. *Fuck.* "Dar! We gotta go now! Izzy's in trouble!" He didn't wait for his partner as he ran full speed back to the helicopter.

Chapter Thirteen

Izzy

She checked her watch as she hit 'save' on the spreadsheet. "Damn," she muttered and grabbed her purse out of the bottom drawer. "Malva, I've got to run or I'm going to be late." She pulled on her coat, trying to shut her office door at the same time.

Malva moved to help her. "Let me hold that." She took Izzy's purse and closed the door for her.

"Thanks. I lost track of time. I hope I can find a parking space. I hate driving downtown!" She took her purse from Malva and began the search for her keys, which always managed to sink to the very blackest corner of her bag. "I should be back in a few hours."

"No worries." Malva held the front door for her. "Try to have a good time."

Not likely. She took liberties with the speed limit on the freeway as she drove to the Hyatt, trying to remember which of the various one-way streets the parking garage could be accessed from. By the time she found a parking space and walked as quickly as she could without running, she had only five minutes to spare. Of course the luncheon was being held in the ballroom farthest from the entrance; by the time she found it, nearly everyone in the large crowd was seated. She showed her invitation to the woman manning the table by the door, picked up her name tag, and went inside to find a seat at one of the tables toward the back. She found one of the last remaining seats and draped her coat over the back of the chair before sitting and introducing herself to the people nearby. A salad was waiting on the table and the woman seated next to her passed the bread basket.

Izzy thanked her and took a rock-hard roll, barely resisting the urge to tap it on the edge of her salad plate. *Hugh is gonna owe me!* He usually handled events like this, as he was so much better at chatting people up and networking. He could bat those gorgeous blue eyes and flash his self-deprecating smile and have any woman in the vicinity eating out of his hand. The irritating part was he didn't even realize how handsome and charming he was. Finn was known as the good-looking one of her brothers, but it was only in comparison; all her brothers were extremely handsome. Well, she could be chatty and charming when she tried, so she dug deep, turned to her neighbor, and struck up a conversation. Most of the people at her table were local business owners, from businesses as varied as a tech start-up company to a Nob Hill jewelry store Izzy thought she would need to visit soon. Maybe she could find something fun for the wedding. The entrees arrived and Izzy was pleased to note the Chicken Cordon Bleu was decent. By the time their plates were cleared and small pieces of dense chocolate cake were placed in front of them, the entire table was chatting happily and exchanging business cards. Izzy ate a few bites of her cake, but found it too rich for her taste and pushed it aside in favor of the coffee waiters were circulating the room with. As she moved the dessert plate, she uncovered the folded paper program, which had been hiding underneath. The first speaker stepped to the podium and began welcoming everyone, so Izzy took the opportunity to glance at the program, hoping it wouldn't be too long. She had high hopes of getting back to the office in time to finish the account she'd been working on. It didn't look too hopeful, however: there were two speakers scheduled after the mayor took the podium to talk about—what was the theme of this luncheon, anyway? She closed the program and studied the front: ***Albuquerque Multi-Cultural Initiative, March 4, 2017.*** The words were fashioned into a logo of sorts, with the first letters of each word bold and stylized. Izzy frowned as mental bells began to go off; what was it? There was something there, in the back of her—oh, God! She stared hard at the program cover, everything blurring except the letters *AMCI March.* Her hand trembled as she set the program on the table and reached for her phone. *This is it. This is the event the note in Lyon's file referred to and now the mayor and all these people are in danger!* She wanted to scream at everyone to take cover or yell at the mayor to get off the raised dais at the front of the room where he was a perfect target, but she knew it would only cause a panic and/or get her arrested.

She forced herself to walk calmly to the hallway outside the ballroom before punching the button on her phone to call Mac. It rang three times before going to voicemail, a sure sign he had rejected her call because he was in the middle of something. *Sorry, Mac. This can't wait.* She dialed again; still no answer. Cursing, she called Finn and was also sent straight to voicemail. "Goddammit! Answer your phone once in a while!" She paced, wondering what to do now. Should she call 911? Would they believe her? She heard the mayor being announced and realized there was no time for anything else. If there was a danger here to the mayor, she was the only one who knew and was in the position to help. She quickly dialed Mac again and left a brief message. "Mac. AMCI March is this luncheon I'm at. It's the Mayor! Something's going to happen to the mayor! Hurry!" She jogged back to the ballroom, cursing her decision to wear high heels today. She stopped to kick them off, slipping them into a potted plant and hoping she'd see them again.

"Ladies and gentlemen, I believe Albuquerque is the finest city in the southwest, and I'm proud to be your mayor." He paused for the obligatory applause. "As business owners, I don't have to tell you that it's also a challenging city. Being a majority-minority community is wonderful, but it brings with it a unique set of circumstances—"

Izzy tuned him out as she slipped into the room and stood in the back beside a stand with a large

247

tray to hold dirty dishes. Waiters and waitresses were weaving in and out of the tables, clearing plates and refilling coffee cups. She craned her neck, straining to see everything going on in the large ballroom, hoping to spy something unusual. Nothing. Everything seemed absolutely normal and boring. Was she wrong? Maybe the letters *AMCI* and the word *March* were simply a coincidence, brought on by her obsession with this stupid case she'd never asked to be involved in. *What have I done? Are Mac and Finn going to show up, guns blazing with all sorts of officers for nothing? Oh my God, what have I done?* She reached for her phone, intent on calling them back and telling them she'd been wrong. *Maybe they haven't left yet.* As she was about to punch the speed dial for Mac, she caught a movement out of the corner of her eye. She jerked her head up and stared. *What did I see? Something that doesn't fit.* She walked toward the east side of the ballroom, her phone forgotten for the moment. There! The velvet drapes at the far side of the room, probably blocking unsightly kitchens from view, were disturbed. Something—or someone—was behind them, moving steadily toward the stage. Izzy's heart pounded nearly out of her chest as she headed in that direction. *Am I really going to do this? Am I really going behind that curtain? I don't do things like this! What about Janey? If something happens to me, what will happen to her?* But even as she had the thought, she was already slipping behind the curtain. *There's no one else. I have to do something! I couldn't live with the guilt if I stood by and let it happen.*

The audience broke into loud clapping at that moment, startling her so she dropped her phone. Hoping the unseen figure ahead of her hadn't heard, she left her phone on the floor and sped toward the stage where the mayor continued to speak. She had no idea what she would do when she caught up; she was making this up as she went. She fought her way through the heavy velvet drapes for another twenty feet, then sensed the person in front of her had stopped. Izzy slowed, flattening herself against the wall, glad she'd ditched her shoes. As she slid around a corner, she saw someone kneeling a few feet in front of her. Izzy slipped back quickly and peeked around the corner. A man, dressed as a waiter, knelt in front of a black duffle bag, rifling through its contents. *Okay, it could be totally innocent. He could be changing his shirt. Maybe he spilled something—nope. That's definitely a gun.* The man pulled a lethal-looking black handgun from the bag, followed by an ammunition clip, which he snapped into the butt of the gun, then screwed what she thought must be a silencer on the barrel.

Izzy's heart pounded even harder; she could hear it in her ears, drowning out the sounds from beyond the curtain. She prayed for the disruption of police and/or Homeland Security bursting into the room, but as the man raised the gun to eye level, there was no such reprieve. *Oh God! It's now or never. You can either do something to stop this or you can stand here like a damned statue!* She took a deep breath and charged, tackling the man from behind.

He was a lot bigger and stronger than she'd

expected. She didn't knock him to the ground like she'd hoped; in fact, she mostly rolled right over the top of him. Her shoulder hit the floor hard and she cried out in pain. But she'd distracted him, causing him to lose his balance. She heard him curse as she regained her feet and charged him again. This time she hit him full-on and took him down. Her shoulder screamed in pain—or was the scream ripped from her throat? She had no time to think about it before she found herself on her back, the heavy body pinning her to the ground. By now they'd rolled out from under the curtains into the room. People at the tables nearby screamed and shoved to their feet, causing chairs to fly in all directions.

"Gun! There's a gun!"

This pronouncement caused a general panic in the ballroom as luncheon attendees pushed and shoved to escape. The man pinning her to the floor cursed and tried to pull away. Izzy knew she couldn't let him escape while he still had the gun. She grabbed it, attempting to wrestle it from him. She was ridiculously out-matched, but she hung on, panting with the effort. He reared back and punched her on the side of her head. She saw stars and felt her grip on the gun loosen.

"No!" she screamed and lunged toward him again. Her fingers scrabbled for purchase, fumbling with his.

The explosion as the gun went off deafened her; then came the pain.

***

Mac

The helicopter ride was endless. He spent the time trying repeatedly to call or text Izzy, but she simply didn't answer. It scared him to death to not know what was happening. He took her voice mail seriously, realizing the information Gina had passed on earlier that morning had been nothing but a clever diversion. He finally got through to Finn as the helicopter approached Albuquerque.

"Have you talked to Izzy?" He didn't bother with a greeting.

"I got a voice mail. I'm guessing you did too. She's not answering her phone." Finn's voice was clipped and official; it was clear he was on speaker phone in his car. "I've got units and a S.W.A.T. team on the way to the Hyatt. My E.T.A. is three minutes."

"Homeland should be there around the same time. We're still about ten minutes out." Mac paused as he heard Finn's police radio.

Finn cursed. "We've got 911 calls coming in from the Hyatt saying there've been shots fired in the ballroom."

Mac's stomach dropped. *Izzy. Please, God. Please keep her safe.* He'd never been much for prayer, even when he was shot in Iraq, but he prayed constantly for the remainder of the trip, until they landed on the helipad on the roof of the hotel. He leapt from the helicopter, not waiting for Darius, and ran for the roof access door.

"Mac! Wait for me, man! Do not run in there without your partner!"

Shit. He's right. "Then hurry up! Izzy is down there!" *I can't lose her, I can't lose her.* The words ran through his head like a mantra.

Darius didn't respond, but he ran faster. Mac wrenched the door open while his partner pulled his phone out and checked in with the Homeland presence below stairs. He talked briefly, then shoved his phone in his pocket. "Okay. The situation is contained. We can take the elevator."

"Izzy?"

Darius shook his head. "No info. Sorry."

They were silent as they rode the elevator to the second floor. When the doors opened, their captain lowered the radio he'd been speaking into. "S.W.A.T. has it under control. We've got a shooter injured, possibly deceased, and another female victim." The large area outside the ballroom was crowded with law enforcement officers and civilians, many with shocked, vacant expressions.

He knew. In the depths of his soul he knew it was Izzy. "Can I go in?"

The captain nodded.

He stalked into the ballroom, his head buzzing. He vaguely heard Darius speaking behind him, but he had no idea what he was saying. He looked around furiously for any sign of Izzy, craning his neck left and right. Paramedics were working on someone near the stage; with a hollow feeling in his gut he threaded his way through the crowd to get a closer look. At first all he could see was the blood, but a closer look showed it was a man. The paramedics were using paddles on him, but Mac could see it was a lost cause; the man was almost certainly dead. He turned away, ramming his hands through his hair in frustration. *Where the hell is she?* He was about to resort to shouting her name at the top of his lungs when Darius grabbed his arm and pointed across the room.

"That's Finn. I'm sure Izzy is with him."

Mac sped toward him. Finn was crouched in front of someone; as Mac got closer he saw it was Izzy. A paramedic was attending her, asking questions and touching her shoulder, but all Mac could see was the blood covering her torso. She glanced up at that moment and saw him.

"Mac! Oh, God, Mac!" She stood and lunged toward him, stopping at the last moment as she saw his face. "It's not my blood. You shouldn't hug me though because you'll—"

He didn't wait to hear the rest. He pulled her into his arms and held her tightly. They stood, holding each other for several long minutes, then he pulled away and ran his hands up and down her arms. "Where are you hurt? What happened?"

She shook her head. "I'm not." At a cough from Finn she shrugged. "My ear. I can't hear very well out of my right ear because the gun went off right next to it. And my shoulder hurts a little."

Mac's knees buckled as it all began to sink in. Darius stepped up to catch him, supporting him while Finn grabbed a chair and pushed him into it. Someone shoved his head between his knees and told him to breathe. He waited until the haze in front of his eyes cleared, then sat up and looked at his fiancée. "What the hell happened?"

"I saw the program." She knelt in front of him

and covered his cold hands with hers. He needed her warmth and turned his palms up to clasp her fingers. "I didn't see it until dessert and it was almost too late, but the logo made me think of the note I found in the file from Lyon. *AMCI: March.* I tried to call you and Finn but I couldn't get through. When I came back into the ballroom, I saw someone behind those curtains." She pointed to the velvet drapes on the east side of the ballroom.

"So you decided to chase after the unsub on your own?" Finn broke in. "Goddammit, Izzy! You could have been killed!"

"Hey!" Mac stood, a bit wobbly still, and put his arm around her before turning to glare at her brother. "Ease up." He was thinking the same thing, of course, but she didn't need anyone yelling at her.

But Izzy shrugged his arm away and advanced on Finn, her finger jabbing at his chest. "What the fuck was I supposed to do, Finn? Stand back and watch the mayor get shot? I couldn't live with myself if he was killed right before my eyes while I stood and watched!"

"You were supposed to wait for law enforcement! I don't care who's about to get shot! I don't want my sister playing superhero and trying to save the day!" He stared back at her, his face furious. Then he pulled her into his arms. "You scared the shit out of me. Don't ever do that again."

She didn't answer; she had started to sob into her brother's chest.

"Okay. Shh. I'm sorry I yelled at you." He shot an imploring look at Mac.

"Come here, love." Mac pulled her back into his

arms. He held her while she cried, running his hand over her hair and soothing her with soft, nonsense murmurs. He sat in the chair, pulling her onto his lap.

"We're going to need to get your statement, Iz," Finn said.

"Give us a few minutes, okay, Finn?" Mac knew she was in no shape to talk right now; she'd obviously held it together as long as possible, and needed the release of a good cry. Finn nodded and turned to speak to the various police officers who were waiting to take her statement.

Nearly ten minutes later, when her sobs had quieted and she had stopped shaking, she spoke quietly. "I was so scared, Mac."

"Me too." He kissed her hair. "I think I aged about ten years on the helicopter ride here."

"Helicopter? Where were you?" She raised her head to look at him. Her face was ravaged, mascara running down her cheeks, eyes red, and nose running.

God, she's beautiful. He turned to Darius. "Get me a paper towel or something, man." He waited until his partner returned with a cloth napkin. He handed it to Izzy and watched while she mopped her face. "We were in Santa Fe. Gina told us there was an attack planned against the governor today. It was obviously a ploy to distract law enforcement and it worked beautifully. We went for it hook, line, and sinker."

"I really, really hate that woman."

"Yeah, I get that." He saw Finn approaching again. "Do you think you could answer a few questions? The police aren't going to leave you alone until you do."

She nodded and reached up to smooth her hair. "Do I look okay?"

Really? Her eyes were red and swollen, her hair looked like she'd slept on it, and her blouse was covered with blood. He brushed her hair behind her ear and kissed her forehead. "Yeah, you look fine. Come on." He stood with her and led her to the group of officers.

They asked her to go over her story from the beginning, which he'd heard, but he listened carefully as she told how she'd slipped behind the curtain and followed the man dressed as a waiter through the curtained corridor toward the stage. She'd dropped her phone halfway through, which explained why no one could get in touch with her. He cringed when she explained how she had leapt on the man as he aimed a weapon at the stage. They'd wrestled for the gun for several seconds until it went off next to her ear, but luckily pointed at the suspect's chest. Mac needed to sit again as her realized just how close she'd come to dying.

"What about him? He was shot at really close range. Is he alive?" She craned her neck to look around the room.

"We don't have that information."

Mac could tell the man was lying and figured Izzy could too. "Guys, she needs to get her shoulder looked at. Could we finish this tomorrow? I'll make sure she gets to the station."

They nodded and handed him a business card with phone numbers and an address.

She was silent as they walked away, her arms wrapped tightly around her waist. "He's dead, isn't he?"

He sighed and reached for her hand. "I think so. Please don't tell me you feel responsible in any way for that man's death. He was an assassin and a domestic terrorist."

She pulled her hand away and crossed her arms, anger apparent in every line of her body. "I don't know how I feel, Mac."

He'd known her long enough to realize she needed to say her piece. "But?"

She glared at him, her jaw tight and her chin thrust forward. "But they're *my* feelings! If I want to feel guilty about shooting someone, I will!"

Jesus Christ. "Izzy, love, you didn't shoot him—"

"I think I did. I think I pulled the trigger. We were fighting and I got my hands on the gun and I felt the trigger and I think I squeezed it." She rambled for another moment, making less and less sense as she talked.

"Come here." He opened his arms.

She glared at him again, then finally broke and launched into his embrace. "Please get me out of here."

"You got it." He steered her through the crowd to the ballroom doors. "Where's your purse?" He remembered at the last minute that he hadn't driven to the hotel.

She looked around helplessly. "I don't know. I think I lost my phone too."

He found a chair for her and told her to wait

while he jogged back to the tables and began scouring them for any sign of her handbag. He finally found it under one of the tables in the back, then headed to the curtain to see if he could locate her phone. It lay discarded on the floor, right where she'd said she dropped it. As they exited the ballroom, she grabbed her shoes, which were stashed in a potted plant. Against her loud protestations, he drove her to the emergency room and sat with her while they examined and x-rayed her shoulder. It was badly bruised, but nothing was dislocated or broken, so the doctor taped it up and put her arm in a sling, instructing her to alternate ice and heat, along with Tylenol and rest. Her eardrum was ruptured and would take up to six weeks to fully heal.

She called her mother to pick Janey up after daycare, then acquiesced to being taken home and tucked into bed for a well-deserved nap after she changed into sweats. "Do you have to go back to work?"

He shook his head. He had no intention of leaving her alone after what she'd been through. "I'll be here when you wake up, love."

She reached her good arm toward him. "Would you lie here with me for a little while? Please?"

He melted at the vulnerable look in her eyes. "Sure. Scoot over." He lay on top of the comforter and spooned around her body. He'd intended to put her filthy clothes in the wash, but it could wait. She needed him right now. In his opinion, it was good riddance to the shooter, but he'd been trained to kill in battle—and he definitely considered what Izzy had been through a battle—and she hadn't. He knew she would have a tough time in the days and weeks to come; he would strongly encourage her to get some counseling as soon as possible.

"Mac?" Her voice was a soft whisper.

"Yeah, love?"

"Is it over? I need it to be over. I don't know how you and Finn and Chris do it every day, but I want to go back to crunching numbers and running payroll. I can't handle any more shootings or stabbings."

He pulled her closer. "It's over for you, hon. I promise. But for the record, I think you can handle anything life gives you. You're the strongest, bravest woman I've ever known. I can't even begin to express how proud I am."

"I don't feel brave or strong. I'm so tired." The last words were stifled by a yawn.

He smiled and kissed her hair. "Sleep, sweetheart. Janey and I will be here when you wake up."

Epilogue

Mac

He woke to the sound of retching coming from the bathroom. He flung the covers off and rushed to find Izzy hunched over the toilet. He wet a washcloth and handed it to her as she nodded her thanks, then crumpled against the side of the tub, pale and shaky.

"Nerves, huh? Is the thought of marrying me today so awful? You wouldn't fake an illness to try and get out of it, would you?" He crouched beside her and brushed her messy hair behind her ear.

She gave a weak half-smile and shook her head. "Did that," she pointed to the toilet, "sound fake to you? God, I hate throwing up. No, I'm not trying to get out of it."

The smell was enough to tell him it wasn't fake, but he declined to mention it. "Good. Are you going to be okay? Are you nervous, sweetheart?"

"Nope." She stood and crossed to the sink to rinse out her mouth and quickly brush her teeth.

"I'm pregnant."

He stared at her blankly as his brain tried to process what she'd said. "Oh, my God."

"Yeah, it's a real kick in the pants, huh?"

The impact of what she'd said finally registered; a slow grin spread across his face, and he pulled her into his arms and swung her around. "Oh, my God!" He kissed her and then laughed. "We really suck at the whole birth control thing, huh?"

She laughed with him. "Yeah. We might want to figure that out before we end up with six kids."

"Hey, it worked for your parents. Janey is going to be so excited!"

"She will be beside herself. Sorry to spring it on you the morning of our wedding."

"I can't think of a more perfect time to tell me. How long have you known?" He led her to the bedroom and pulled her into his lap in the large chair in the corner.

"I've suspected for about a week, but I bought a pregnancy test yesterday. I was trying to keep it a surprise for after the wedding, but it's hard to keep morning sickness to yourself. I've made a doctor's appointment for next week when we get back from our honeymoon." They were taking a cruise to the Bahamas, something neither of them had ever done. "This could be a Christmas baby."

"Best Christmas ever."

She sat up and stared at him, a frown between her brows. "You're not upset by this, are you?"

"Of course not. Why should I be? We're going to be married in," he stopped to look at his watch, "three hours. You are about to be my wife, and this time I get to be here for your pregnancy. I want to go to all your doctor appointments."

She leaned in to kiss him softly, reverently. "You are the most amazing man in the entire world, and I love you more than I can ever express."

He pulled her back for a longer, deeper kiss. "Mmm. The feeling is quite mutual. Although I would love to continue this, we have a wedding to get ready for."

She kissed him again before slipping from his lap. "Do you mind getting Janey up and feeding her breakfast? I desperately need a shower."

"Will do. Do you want some toast or something to settle your stomach?"

"Maybe after my shower. Do you mind if we wait to tell my family until after we get back from the honeymoon?"

He put his arm up to block her from entering the bathroom. "Izzy. I don't mind, but can I ask why?"

She shrugged, but refused to meet his eyes.

He sighed and pulled her into his arms. "I can't pretend to understand what you went through with Janey, being pregnant and single, but I'm here this time. You don't have to do this alone. I kinda want to shout it from the rooftop, you know. I'm inordinately proud that I've managed to knock you up." He attempted to coax a smile from her.

"You're crazy. Let me think about it, okay? It's just...I don't know. I'm happy, but I wish I could have done it right this time."

"What's right, Izzy? We love each other and we're getting married today. We have a beautiful daughter and we're having a baby. Life is pretty wonderful for us."

She reached up to stroked his cheek. "You do have a way of putting things into perspective, Mr. MacNeil."

"You better believe it, Ms. DeLuca." He grinned and kissed her. "Soon to be Mrs. MacNeil."

***

Izzy

"Are you sure you want this, Isabelle? If you're not, I will walk out there and tell everyone to go home. You won't have to see anyone." They stood together at the door of the bride's room. Cara and Janey, her attendants, had just left to precede them up the aisle.

She smiled up at her father and fussed with his tie before smoothing his lapels. "I'm sure, Daddy. I love Mac and want to spend my life with him."

"Well, he's a good man. I couldn't stand to let you go if he wasn't."

She bit her lip and refrained from pointing out that she hadn't lived at home for more than a decade. "He is a good man." She paused, then asked. "Did you give Cara the same option when she married Aidan?"

He cleared his throat and nodded. "I truly wish she would have taken me up on the offer. It would have saved us all a lot of heartache."

Izzy smiled sadly. "She loved him. I think she still does. Nobody could foresee what happened."

"I know, but it doesn't make it any easier. She's

my little girl and I hate that she had to go through that. Just like I hate that you had to go through your pregnancy all by yourself."

She hugged him and reached up on tiptoe to kiss his cheek. "I wasn't by myself. I had my family. And this time I'll have Mac."

"This time?"

She smiled up at him and rubbed her hand over the silk covering her stomach. "Yep. I'm pregnant. At least I'll be married in a few minutes."

He laughed and hugged her again. "Does your young man know?"

"He does. He's ridiculously happy." She shook her head and laughed. "He isn't bothered at all by the timing."

"He's a good man," he said again. "Are you ready, my little Izzy-belle?"

She teared up at his childhood endearment. "I am."

As they approached the doors of the sanctuary, the wedding coordinator signaled for them to pause. She cracked one of the doors and waved to the organist. She pulled open the double doors as the "Wedding March" began. Izzy found herself inexplicably nervous as she saw all the congregants turn to stare. They rose as she and her father began to proceed up the aisle. She gulped and forced one foot in front of the other. When she glanced up and saw Mac beaming at her from the front of the church, she breathed a sigh of relief. It was all going to be okay. All she had to do was walk to him.

The ceremony passed in a blur as she focused on Mac's face and the feel of her hands in his. She hoped she said the right words; no one laughed or gasped, so she'd apparently done all right. Before she knew it, the priest was leading the Lord's Prayer and reciting the blessing. Then Mac swept her into a magnificent kiss that had the congregation applauding.

They'd decided to have the reception at a winery in the North valley. She'd toured it when Mel was looking for a wedding venue and had fallen in love with it. She was secretly glad Mel had decided to have her wedding and reception in the backyard of her parents' house and left the winery for Izzy and Mac. They hadn't gone all out on a totally formal wedding; Izzy wore a simple ankle-length ivory dress and Mac wore a regular suit and tie. With only a month to plan, there had been no time to order a wedding dress and Izzy hadn't wanted one. Mac had been agreeable as long as the wedding was soon. When they sat down to dinner, she noticed he joined her in filling his wine glass with sparkling water.

"Just exhibiting my solidarity," he said when she raised her eyebrows at him.

"You are a very sweet man." She pulled his face down for a kiss. The room filled with the sound of clinking as everyone laughed and wolf-whistled while banging their knives against their glasses.

"Let's give 'em something to talk about." And so saying, he stood, pulling her up with him, and bent her over his arm in a dip. Then he kissed her, full and deep.

"Show offs," Cara muttered as Izzy regained her seat a few moments later.

Mac simply grinned at her and took a sip of his water.

Cara looked pointedly at the water in his glass, in Izzy's glass, then at Izzy's stomach, and then at Izzy. "Really?"

Izzy grinned even as she felt herself flush. "Yeah."

Cara stood and pulled Izzy into a huge hug. "Oh my God! Congrats, you little sex maniac! Remind me to tell you about the pill someday."

"Apparently I need a refresher." She laughed and hugged her sister back.

"I wish you could see your face right now. I've never seen you look so happy."

"I am. I love him so much." She turned to watch her husband accepting congratulations and back slaps from his new brothers-in-law.

He saw her glance and winked at her.

"You two are so perfect together." Cara sounded wistful.

Izzy slipped her arm around her sister's waist, realizing weddings must kind of suck for her. "We are. It will happen for you too, Cara. I know it will."

Cara laughed unconvincingly. "Sure. But this is your day, Iz, and since you can't drink and Mac won't, I better take up the slack. Challenge accepted." She refilled her glass from the nearby bottle of wine.

Mac came to claim her at that moment; she gave Cara's hand a quick, sympathetic squeeze and went with him to greet their guests.

"Everything okay with your sister?"

She shrugged. "I think weddings are a bit tough

for her. She'll be fine."

He nodded and walked her through one of the open French doors. "Come here, Mrs. MacNeil. I need a moment alone with my wife."

She grinned. "I really like the sound of that. And I think I need a moment alone with my husband."

"You can have all my moments, Izzy." He laughed self-consciously. "That was pretty sappy, huh?"

She brushed her thumb over his lips. "Sappy works today. I love you, Mac."

"And I love you, Izzy."

She pulled his head down and kissed him, sealing their love and commitment in the cool night air. "Mmm. What if we slipped away right now? We could get a lovely head start on our wedding night."

"Don't tempt me, girl." He put his hand on the small of her back and guided her to the open doors. "We have all sorts of wedding stuff to do still. And I plan to take your garter off with my teeth."

She laughed, but allowed him to usher her back to the party. "If you think I'm going to object, you can think again. My dad, maybe, but not me."

"Yeah, well, your dad can just...never mind. I guess I won't use my teeth, at least not here at our reception. Later though."

"Definitely later." She smirked at him, then they returned to their reception.

The End

Acknowledgments

I wrote the first draft of this book during November 2016, and many of you know what that means: NaNoWriMo. I want to express my thanks and appreciation to this amazing organization for all they do to encourage writers.

I want to send out a special thanks to my editor, Toni Rakestraw. She does such an amazing job and is so patient and helpful. I really love working with you. Toni!

Extra-special thanks to proofreader extraordinaire, Lacey Reece, who nitpicks beautifully. Love you, Lacey!

Thanks always to my wonderful husband, Lyle, who supports, encourages, and loves me through all the writing chaos.

About the Author

Amy Reece lives in New Mexico with her incredible husband and two ridiculous mutts, Greta and Sodapop. When she's not writing, she's teaching high school English and social studies or maybe wandering through a thrift store in search of the next lucky teapot for her vast collection. She is an unrepentant bookaholic and has overflowing bookshelves in nearly every room of her house. Her favorite authors include J.R.R. Tolkien, J.K. Rowling, and C.S. Lewis–must have something to do with initials! She loves to travel and is hoping to need many research trips for future writing projects.

Did you enjoy this book? If so, please, please, please leave a short, but stellar review on amazon and/or GoodReads. I would really appreciate it!

If you want to cyber-stalk me, here are some helpful links:

Good Reads:
https://www.goodreads.com/author/show/13884337
.Amy_Reece

Amazon author page:
https://www.amazon.com/Amy-
Reece/e/B00WDG12RO

Facebook Fan Page:
https://www.facebook.com/areeceauthor

Twitter Fan Page:
https://twitter.com/AReeceAuthor

Website:
https://www.amyreeceauthor.com/

Blog:
https://amyreece.wordpress.com/

www.ingramcontent.com/pod-product-compliance
Lightning Source LLC
Chambersburg PA
CBHW030326200626
46816CB00006BA/1942